Dead
on
Account

Also by this author

Dead Ringer

Death Duties

Death Benefit

Salvation Hall

Dead
on
Account

A Rose Bennett Mystery

MARIAH KINGDOM

~ Perceda Press ~

First published in digital form 2015 by WL Fowler

Previously published in digital form under the title Collusion 2015

Copyright © Mariah Kingdom 2020

This paperback edition Perceda Press 2020

Mariah Kingdom asserts the moral right to be identified as the author of this work.

A catalogue record for this publication is available from the British Library

ISBN 978-1-8380834-0-3

Cover design by www.ebooklaunch.com

To Pablo, for putting up with All This

·

1

'Tommy! Stop it! You'll cause an accident!' The girl shot an anxious glance at the kerb-crawling car beside her. The driver's lips moved in reply but the music pounding through her headphones drowned out his words. Still running, she slipped a hand into the black runner's pouch at her waist to pause the pink iPod hidden there.

'Come on Pandora, come for a drink. It's too warm to run.' Tommy's tousled head leaned out of the open car window and his tone was soft, cajoling. 'I'll take you to The Boar. We can sit in the garden, chill out for a bit.'

Keeping her eyes fixed on the road ahead she tugged at her sweat-soaked singlet, pulling the damp fabric away from taut flesh and small firm breasts. 'Dressed like this?'

'I'll take you home to shower and change.'

She forced a smile in his direction and shook her head, swishing a long blonde ponytail. 'I can't. I'm meeting Craig in The Feathers tonight.'

Tommy's own smile faded. 'He's a prat. You're too good for him.'

She turned her face back to the road and quickened her pace. 'Maybe.'

'What's he got that I haven't got?'

She didn't answer.

'What is it, Pan? Money, is that it? His daddy's richer than my daddy?'

'Now you're just being stupid.'

'Am I?' Tommy pressed in the clutch and shoved the gear stick down into second, revving the engine. 'It's your last chance. I'm not going to keep asking.'

'You said that last week. And the week before.' She threw a worried glance behind her. 'Please just go away, Tommy. There are more cars coming up the hill. If they try to overtake you they might hit me.' She turned back to look at Tommy but he was gone, his blue Golf now a distant image turning left at the roundabout at the top of the hill.

The approaching cars sped past her, one after another, a green saloon she didn't recognize, a black people-carrier, an aging silver Volvo convertible with the top down. The driver of the Volvo waved and sounded her horn in recognition, and Pandora lifted a hand in response. She glanced at her watch as she lowered her hand. It was ten to seven.

She was beginning to tire now. Her calf muscles ached and her legs felt heavy. It was warmer than she'd realized and the run up the hill had been a challenge, not least because of Tommy's interference. She was glad he'd gone. She tried to be pleasant to him but he was becoming a nuisance, his persistent interest in her ever more difficult to laugh off, even at work.

Especially at work.

Work.

She'd been trying to forget about work and Tommy, who sat beside her at the counter in the banking hall day in and day out, had brought it back to mind. Her train of thought drifted away from him and back to the day's events. Had she done the right thing?

The branch manager clearly hadn't thought so. What had she said? 'I think, Pandora, that if you take a little time to think about it you'll see that you're mistaken. We all make mistakes from time to time, so it's not the end of the world is it? Nothing to be embarrassed about.'

Patronizing cow. Patronizing, condescending, stupid bloody cow.

She was at the top of the hill now. The road had

inclined steeply before leveling out at the top, and the ache in her calf muscles was getting worse. She took a swig of lukewarm water from the bottle she always carried then bent over, hands on knees for support, breathing deeply. Gradually she straightened, shook the long blonde ponytail and stretched her neck, rolling her head from side to side. Below her the small town of Market Melbourne lay bathed in evening sunlight, its small red-brick Georgian centre clearly visible within a rash of new-build housing, its artery routes radiating out from the centre like wheel-spokes, their paths marked by the slate roofs of the Edwardian and Victorian villas that lined them.

She glanced again at her watch. It was five past seven. If she took the shorter, faster route back down the hill the way she had come she could be home in twenty minutes. If she branched off at the roundabout and took the slower road it would take at least half an hour. Either way she would be back in plenty of time to shower and change and meet Craig at eight. Larch Road was a slow run but it was quiet, undulating and gently curving through cornfields and farm cottages, past the retirement home and other assorted Victorian villas down into the heart of the old town. Of the two routes it was the most likely to clear her mind of Tommy, Janis and work. She switched the iPod back on, adjusted the volume and started to jog towards it.

Craig Bradman had been waiting in The Feathers for over forty minutes. He'd tried her mobile a dozen times at least since eight o'clock, and every time his call had transferred to her answer service. His first message had been brief and teasing. 'Pan, it's ten past eight babe, where the hell are you? Stop soaking in the bath and get over here, your wine's getting warm.'

After more calls and several texts, none of which received a response, his tone was more urgent. 'Babe I'm getting worried … call me … please.' He disconnected the call and stared at the phone's display, willing it to register an incoming call or text.

Suddenly aware of being watched, he looked up towards the bar. Leaning on the counter, pint in hand, Tommy Fletcher was watching him intently. Craig scowled, but Tommy met his gaze with a smirk and raised his pint in a mock toast. 'Alright Craig mate? Has she stood you up, then? Finally come to her senses?' His flat vowels echoed across the bar, and a room full of evening diners turned their heads to stare at Craig.

Craig's freckled cheeks flushed. 'You wish. She's just been held up, that's all. She was out for a training run tonight.'

Tommy leered at him. 'Tell me about it. She looks something in them little green shorts, don't she? They don't leave much to the imagination, especially when she's all warm and sweaty, if you know what I mean.'

Craig felt the colour in his cheeks spread onto his throat in angry blotches of emotion, but he said nothing.

Tommy's smirk deepened. 'You are sure she's gonna turn up, then? She didn't sound that sure when I saw her. She said something about a long bath and an early night.'

Craig swigged the dregs of his pint and swallowed, then stood up and took his empty glass and Pandora's lukewarm wine back to the bar. He placed the glasses gently on the counter and turned to Tommy, considering his response.

'Now then lads, alright here? Can I get you another?' The pub's landlord, his nose sensing the faint smell of trouble, had materialized silently from the other end of the bar in little more than the time it had taken Craig to put down the glasses.

Craig heeded the warning and grunted. 'No thanks, George, not for me. Billy no-mates here might want one, though.' He gestured towards Tommy. 'He doesn't mind drinking alone. I've heard he's had plenty of practice at it.'

Outside in the street the evening sun was still warm.

Craig pulled his mobile phone out of his pocket and tried Pandora's number one more time. No answer. He flicked at the keypad with stubby impatient fingers and dialed another number. It answered immediately. 'Hi Danny, it's Craig. Is Pan there?'

Pandora sprawled in the chair. Her body was still wet with perspiration from her run, and her green singlet and shorts clung to her body, outlining her youthful curves. The blonde ponytail, once tied tightly at the back of her head, had started to come loose and lay draped over her left shoulder, its damp ends starting to curl. Her head had fallen sideways and slightly forwards, and a small trickle of saliva had escaped from her parted lips and was making its way down her chin. The blue eyes were still open, bulging and bloodshot now from the force of the ligature around her neck. Death had crept up behind her unexpectedly, and the end had been quick. Mercifully quick.

A shaking hand reached out and hovered tentatively in front of her face, the fingers flexing and twitching at the thought of touching the corpse. A nervous flick of the hand and the right eyelid closed. Another flick, nothing. Again, flick. Again. Again. Nothing. Fear was taking hold, the flicking fingers not venturing close enough to the eyelid to touch it. The hand steadied for a moment then reached out more purposefully and slowly, gently rolled the eyelid down.

She looked peaceful now, a sleeping angel. The hand reached out again and stroked a stray blonde hair away from her face, caressing her cheek as it went.

Oh Pandora, you silly girl … look what you've made me do now.

2

Rose Bennett was happy to be outdoors. She took a seat at the small wooden patio table outside the kitchen door, kicked off her sandals, and stretched out long, thin white legs to put up her feet on a second chair opposite. She wrapped an equally thin white arm around her head to shield her eyes from the late evening sun, and settled back in the chair to enjoy the view down the garden, a long narrow vista across a jumble of unrestrained planting. Beneath a stone bench at the end of a long narrow York stone path, a bedraggled one-eyed terrier twitched and trotted in its sleep. She gave an almost inaudible sigh of contentment. The drive up from Hertfordshire had been long and tiring, but at least a trip to Market Melbourne meant the comfort of Lu's cottage rather than the cold loneliness of a hotel room.

Inside the cottage Lu Aylesbury, her mother's younger sister, was rattling kettle and crockery. Rose had grown up in Market Melbourne, but neither she nor her brother returned to their home town after university, and her parents had long since retired to Cornwall. Only Lu remained, retired now from a chaotic career in journalism. Funny, she mused, to think of Lu the Livewire choosing to be buried here in this little market town while all the rest of the family had bailed out in search of a wider world.

'Making yourself comfy?' Lu clattered a tea-tray down on the small wooden table, and set about pouring cups for them both.

'Mm. I'm just glad to be out of the car, really. The A1

was a pig tonight. A three-car shunt at Biggleswade, and two jack-knifed caravans between Grantham and Doncaster.'

'You should have taken the train. I would have picked you up from the station.' Lu poured a third cup of tea, stirred in milk and half a spoonful of sugar, and then emptied the contents into a chipped saucer. 'Wake up Mac, it's tea time.' The terrier, already awakened by the chink of teaspoon against china cup, ambled up the path and started to lap happily from the saucer under the table.

Rose screwed up her nose. 'You spoil that dog.'

'Of course I do. Isn't that what dogs are for?' Lu settled into her seat. 'And nieces? I spoil you, but I don't hear you complaining.'

Rose laughed. 'And you never will. Just keep it coming.'

The two women fell silent. A casual observer would not have placed them in the same family. Lu, her white hair carefully waved to show her fine cheekbones to their best advantage, was as tanned and toned has her niece was pale and ethereal. Beside her Rose looked gauche, her unruly mop of red curls frizzing in the damp August heat, and her thin limbs pale and slightly flaccid from too many desk-bound hours. But they had the same eyes, and the same sense of humour, and according to Rose's father the same streak of bloody-minded stubbornness.

It was Rose who broke the silence. 'I was sorry to hear about Frank.' She glanced over into the adjoining garden, almost expecting to see Lu's elderly neighbour still pottering about in his vegetable patch. 'Was it just old age?'

'Old age, whisky and too many cigs.' Lu sipped on her tea. 'God knows how I'm going to get the stink out of the walls. The whole place reeks of Woodbines.'

'You're definitely buying his cottage, then?'

'Oh yes, it's all going through. He left the place to his sister, and she doesn't want it, so we've agreed a fair price. We should complete by the end of next week, and then the builders can get started. I'm going to have some doorways knocked through to begin with, just to give me access, and take the dividing fences down in the front and back gardens. I just want to live with the extra space for a while, and get used to it, then I'll think about a full remodelling. I'm not in any rush.' Lu sighed. 'Of course, the building work is only part of it. He wasn't exactly house-proud. And his sister has left all his stuff in the cottage. We agreed I'd clear the place out as part of the deal, because she didn't want to be bothered.'

'I can give you a hand in the evenings, if you want? I might as well do something useful while I'm here.'

'That would be a huge help. It won't seem so bad if there are two of us tackling it.' Lu put her empty cup down on the table and turned to face her niece. 'So tell me more about why you've trekked all the way up to Market Melbourne? You said on the phone that it was something to do with work.'

'Yes, it is.' Rose slipped her legs off the chair and turned to face her aunt. 'Do you remember Clive Barden?'

'Clive Barden?' Lu frowned and thought for a moment. 'Yes, of course. He was that banking bore that Janis married on the rebound after she was jilted.' She sucked in her cheeks in contemplation. 'Average height, average build, average intelligence. And prematurely bald, if I remember rightly? Or was it just prematurely middle-aged?'

Rose laughed. 'I suppose that's a fair assessment. He's Head of Risk now, at the East and Northern Bank.'

'My, that must be a fun job.' Lu arched an eyebrow. 'Head of Risk at the country's most risk-averse provincial bank? I bet that keeps him awake at night. Did you know that Janis is a branch manager at the ENB now, here in Market Melbourne?'

'Yes, I did. That's why I'm here. It's not my usual line of work but Clive has some concerns about the account opening process at the branch. He thinks they're getting a bit careless, and he's asked me to come up and take a look. I'm to spend a couple of days helping them improve things. It's just a case of reviewing what they do, and maybe running a training session or two if I think they need it.'

Lu leaned back in her seat and eyed Rose with incredulous amusement. 'And you expect me to believe that? He could deal with that internally, he doesn't need an external consultant to do it for him, especially one with your background.' She frowned and pursed glossed lips in contemplation. 'Unless there is some possibility of wrong-doing, of course.' She paused, and gave the idea momentary consideration. 'Yes, that would be uncomfortable for him, wouldn't it? A suggestion of something improper in his own beloved bank? Breach of regulations, maybe? Fraud, financial crime, mis-selling, exposure of his inadequacy at managing risk, and even worse the offences committed at the branch managed by his ex-wife?' Pleased with her assessment of the situation, Lu topped up her empty teacup from the pot and smirked. 'Am I getting warm?'

Rose wrinkled a pale nose. 'Do all retired journalists still think in gutter press clichés? What if I tell you that you're completely wrong, and that I really am here just to help them iron out some glitches in the process? Will you tell me that you don't believe me, and that I'm just keeping client confidentiality?'

'I don't believe you, you're just keeping client confidentiality.'

Rose gave a non-committal smile. 'Clive thought it prudent to ask for an external review, given that his ex-wife is involved. You know how transparent banks have to be about everything these days. Anyway, it gives me a chance to spend a few days with my favourite aunt.'

'I know how transparent they are *meant* to be. And I'm your only aunt.'

'It's really no big deal.' Rose shook her head. 'Look,

bad news stories about banks sell newspapers these days. Staff at the branch have made a few mistakes lately, and Clive is embarrassed because Janis is involved. It's all very close to home, so he's just trying to be discrete and diminish the risk of any bad publicity for the bank.'

'But why you? Why not deal with it internally?'

'Like I said, to protect himself with an independent view. He's asked me to help out as a favour because Janis and I used to be friends, and he knows I'll be discrete. To be honest, I haven't seen or spoken to Janis for years, so I have no idea whether she will welcome my involvement or resent it.'

'If I remember Janis rightly, she'll welcome you with open arms. You were always her favourite slave at school.' Lu's tone was tart enough to convey her equally tart opinion of Janis. 'Still, I suppose I should be grateful if it means we get to spend some time together. You'll be here for the rest of the week?'

Rose smiled at the thought. 'Yes, is that OK?'

'Of course it is. You'll be going back to Hertfordshire for the weekend, though?'

A mask of inscrutability settled on Rose's face and she turned away from her aunt's expectant gaze. 'No. I thought I might stay here, if you don't mind. It's the last week of the school holidays and the kids have come to stay with Mike. They're not going back until Sunday tea-time. I thought I'd give them some space to do whatever it is that families do.'

Lu absorbed the words, and then nodded in understanding. Always sensitive to the forbidden areas in her niece's life, she'd long since learned it was best not to pry.

PC Dave Gilling slowed the patrol car to a halt at the top of Market Melbourne hill and switched on the hazard warning lights. He had been cruising the back roads around the town for almost two hours now, with no result. He switched on the cabin light and used the car radio to call back to the station.

'Bob, are you there?'

Bob Shepherd grunted a response. 'Found anything yet?'

'What do *you* think? It's like looking for the proverbial needle. I've tried the petrol station, the supermarket and all seven pubs. No one's seen her. I've driven up and down every artery road from the town for about five miles. Nothing.' He sighed. 'Any news from the family?'

Bob grunted again. 'Her mother rang twenty minutes ago. Her father's still out driving the lanes looking for her, the boyfriend's with him, the mother's staying at home in case she contacts them.' He sniffed. 'Your missus has been on the phone again. I've told her you're cruising the streets looking for a tasty blonde.'

'Funny guy.' Gilling tapped his fingers rhythmically on the dashboard. 'I think we ought to assess this as a medium risk, Bob. The family are convinced that she's hurt herself running off road, twisted her ankle or knocked herself out. I can't tell if that's what they really think, or whether they're just trying to keep optimistic. I'm not so sure myself.'

'Something suspicious at the house?'

'Not that I can tell. They seem genuinely worried, answered all my questions, let me take a look around. But she's a bonny lass, they showed me a photo.'

'A looker?'

'Every weirdo's dream, Bob. Five foot four of curves, long blonde hair, pout. If she was my lass, and she'd gone missing wearing a vest and a pair of skimpy shorts, I'd be crawling the walls in panic.' He tapped on the dashboard again. 'There's not much else I can do tonight. I'm coming back to the station to do the paperwork.'

'OK. I'll make us a brew.'

Gilling switched off the radio and put the car into gear,

muttering to himself. 'Might as well take one more look on the way back.' He navigated slowly round the roundabout at the top of the hill, switched the headlights to full beam, and started to cruise back down Larch Road towards the centre of town.

The dream was clear, clearer than any dream had a right to be after twenty years and more.

Danny Mitchell, tall and blond and casual in faded jeans and denim shirt, was standing at the altar of St Benedict's next to his cousin Callum. Callum was smiling his big Highland smile, his stubbled face bristling with good humour. By contrast, Danny's handsome face was blank, expressionless as Janis, radiant in white summer cotton, practiced her walk up the aisle to stand next to him. Rose, trailing behind Janis in green dungarees and plastic flip-flops, dragged a recalcitrant flower girl behind her.

Just as they reached their spot behind the bride and groom, the child shrieked and kicked at Rose's ankle. 'Stoppit,' she spat. 'I don't want to do this. Don't want to. Don't want to. You can't make me.' She struggled to break free of Rose's grip and stumbled, falling to the cold floor of the church, bruising her knee on the smooth, unyielding stone.

Her patience tried to the limit, Rose yanked the girl up by her thin wrist. 'Get up Sadie, and stop making an exhibition of yourself.' She looked down at the child to remonstrate further, but the face looking up at her was Danny's. Danny was kneeling on the floor in front of her, shrieking. 'I don't want to do this. Don't want to. Don't want to. You can't make me.'

Rose screamed and dropped the child's arm, and turned to look at Janis. Janis's face was melting with tears, her wide mouth working in silent cries of anguish. They were outside the church now, peering through the railings at the wedding scene, the happy congregation gathering for photographs. Danny, resplendent in morning suit and top hat, held his arm tightly around the waist of his lovely bride Selina. Selina. Not Janis. Selina. Rose turned again to Janis, but there was no one there. Janis was gone. Gone into the churchyard. 'No Janis, come back. Come back, Janis. For God's sake come back.'

It was too late. Janis was there, in amongst the congregation, clawing and spitting and punching. She knocked little Sadie to the ground, pushed the bride against the wall of the church and slapped her, punched and kicked at Danny until Callum's big Highland hands got a firm grip of her arms and lifted her, wailing, into the church.

Rose stared wide-eyed at the aftermath. Blood from Sadie's nose was splattered down the front of Selina's wedding dress. Selina's tears drenched Danny's jacket as she sobbed into his shoulder. Wedding guests ran back and forth in chaos, noiselessly mouthing their outrage in Rose's silent dream. And Danny … Danny's face was white with restrained fury. He stared at Rose through the church railings and mouthed 'this is all your fault'.

Rose tried to speak, but no words would come. She shook her head violently. 'Not my fault, not my fault, I tried to stop her. I couldn't help it. I couldn't hold her.' The words finally escaped. 'Not my fault, it wasn't my fault.' Her face and hands were heavy with perspiration and guilty tears.

'Of course it wasn't your fault. Rose. Rose. Stop it.' Lu had hold of her arm now, and was shaking her awake. 'It's OK. It's a dream. Only a dream. You fell asleep in the chair.' She knelt down beside her niece. 'Whatever were you dreaming about?'

'Janis. What Janis did at Danny Mitchell's wedding.' Rose rubbed her eyes with her fists and turned to Lu. 'It was all so clear, so real.' She shivered. 'Not something I ever wanted to remember.'

'No, well, it's hardly surprising if it comes back to

haunt you now and again. Not everyone gets to see their best friend run amok at her ex-fiancé's wedding.'

Rose closed her eyes and shook her head. 'She was ill. She had a breakdown.'

'So everyone said. Frankly, I always thought that was an excuse. As far as I could see, the only thing wrong with Janis was that Janis wasn't getting her own way.

3

'It's nice to see you again after all this time, Janis. Sorry it's professional and not personal.' The lie tripped effortlessly off Rose's tongue but she was under no illusion that Janis would be taken in by it. The ability to bend the truth convincingly had become an integral part of her skill set now, but it had not escaped her that this job was going to be more challenging. Gaining the confidence of strangers was a lot easier than re-gaining the confidence of an old friend, and a distrustful old friend at that.

Janis forced an unconvincing smile. 'It's nice to see you, too. How long has it been?'

Long enough, Rose thought, to forget we were once inseparable. 'Nearly twenty years, I should have thought.' Nearly twenty years since I stopped you from wrecking Danny's wedding, nineteen since you married Clive on the rebound, probably nearer eighteen since you decided to cut me out of your life altogether. 'I don't know where the time goes. Still, at least we know each other. That should make things a bit easier.'

'Easier?' Janis latched on to the word and her eyes narrowed a little. 'I'm not sure what we can do to help you, but we'll do our best. Clive didn't give us a lot of notice that you were coming, so I'm afraid I haven't had time to brief the team. It's the account opening process that you're interested in, is it?'

She was going to be difficult, then. There was to be no "old pals act", no reminiscing, no opportunity to pretend that they were on the same side. What else could I expect,

Rose thought. She offered a friendly smile. 'Yes, it's account opening. Clive wants to get a company-wide view of how well the processes are being adhered to, and the internal compliance team are up to their eyes in other regulatory work, so he asked me if I could help out. He knows that the Bank has been a bit lax in auditing lately, so he's asked me to visit three or four branches at random.' More lies. 'I suppose it was a bit cheeky of me to pick Market Melbourne, but I thought I could combine it with a visit to Lu. She still lives here, you know.'

It was a fresh invitation to put the conversation on a more personal footing, but Janis chose not to accept. 'We know Lu well, she's a customer here.' She paused, and then said 'I don't know how much assistance we can give you, Rose. We're a small branch and I don't have many staff. Just five, as it happens, and one of those is on maternity leave, so you can appreciate how busy we are.'

Rose turned and glanced through the glass wall of the meeting room, out into the banking hall. Save for two bored-looking tellers in unflattering polyester uniforms it was completely empty. She turned back to Janis. 'That's another reason why I chose this branch. I have to be balanced in the review – two small market town branches, and two large city branches. The city branches have big sales targets, and Clive feels they're more likely to take risks with the process in order to secure new business. The small ones have lower sales targets, know most of their customers personally, and are less likely to take risks. I don't want to pre-empt the results of my work, but I fully expect your branch to be squeaky clean and the city branches to need a lot of work.' She paused and gave Janis time to digest this thought. 'All I need is an hour or so with maybe two or three members of staff, to talk through the process with them. If there are any issues, I will discuss them with you before I report back to Clive, and we can work together on how to resolve them. That way we can tell him that there are effectively no problems, because we've already put the corrective action in place. Is that fair?'

She waited for a response, but none came. Janis's face had taken on an odd, blank appearance. Her features were motionless, frozen, her eyes slightly glazed and distant. Rose recognised the expression from her school days and suppressed the desire to smile. She may not have seen Janis for the best part of twenty years, but she could still recognise the expression her old friend adopted when the cards appeared to be stacked against her.

Outside in the banking hall, the two bored-looking tellers were having their own dialogue about the purpose of Rose Bennett's visit.

'She's come from Head Office.' Marge Baker frowned and put a chubby hand up to brush a strand of greying hair away from an equally chubby face. 'And Hazel, how many times do I have to ask you not to bring your coffee into the banking hall?'

Hazel, a neat pixie in the shadow of Marge's ample curves, screwed up her nose. 'Oh chill, Marge. There are no customers in. Anyway, I didn't have time for breakfast this morning, and I've got Mrs Henderson coming in at nine thirty. I can't face that on an empty stomach. God, that woman just doesn't know when to shut up. She's been in four times in the past ten days to talk about applying for a personal loan. I wouldn't care if she could afford it.' She sipped on the illicit coffee. 'So, this woman in with Janis ... her name's Rose Bennett and she's come from Head Office. Come to do what? Are we all for the chop?'

'I shouldn't think so. That sort of thing would come from HR, wouldn't it?'

They both turned and furtively glanced through the glass wall of the bank's interview room. Rose and Janis were deep in conversation, and Janis was nodding and smiling, and just being Janis. They both knew their branch manager well enough to know that Janis smiling and nodding was no indication of what Janis was actually thinking.

'Does she work for the bank?' Hazel asked.

'No, she doesn't. I called Pam at the Kirkby branch to see if she'd heard of her. Apparently she's someone Clive brings in when he wants an independent person to look at branch processes. She's been to Kirkby before.' Although no one else was in earshot, Marge leaned towards Hazel and lowered her voice. 'They said she was just looking into the process for selling mortgages, to see if any improvements could be made, and that the Kirkby branch had been chosen at random to help her.' Marge lowered her voice still further. 'Dan Hickey ended up on disciplinary a week later.' Her voice became a hoarse whisper. 'Accused of mis-selling mortgage products, if you please.'

'Nasty.' Hazel sniffed and sipped again on her coffee. 'Have we been doing anything we shouldn't have?' The question was purely rhetorical, and they both knew it.

Marge shook her head. 'Not that I'm aware of.' She crumpled the chubby face and her smile was bordering mischief. 'Let's face it, I would know. If the good ship Branch has to sail a bit close to the wind these days, one of us has to keep a weathered eye out to make sure we don't get caught in a storm.' She sighed. 'Despite all our best efforts I suppose our sales figures will be below target again this quarter, but we won't be the only branch with that predicament. They're not likely to send this Rose Bennett in for that.' She thought for a moment. 'Which is why we need to re-think Mrs Henderson. Are you sure she isn't good for something? What have you tried?'

'She wanted six thousand for a kitchen. The computer said no, so we tried lower amounts down to two thousand, and it still said no'. Hazel sucked in her cheeks. 'It might be worth forgetting the loan and trying another tack. I haven't tried selling her buildings and contents insurance yet. What about that?'

Marge opened her mouth to reply but a pinging doorbell at the front of the banking hall pronounced the arrival of Mrs Henderson, a haze of wet umbrella and dripping supermarket carrier bags. Hazel rolled her eyes and brought them to rest in a pleading gaze at the older woman's face. 'You can have the commission points … '

'You're on.' Marge nodded and stepped forward to greet the woman, leaving Hazel to silently drift away past the end of the counter and into the open doorway of Janis's office.

Lu was half way to Kirkby when the local radio station announced details of Pandora's disappearance and appealed for information or sightings of the girl. She pulled the Volvo into the next lay-by, and called Market Melbourne police station from her mobile phone. Dave Gilling answered, and she told him everything she could remember from the previous evening.

'I can't tell you the exact time, I think it was about a quarter to seven. I turned up Market Melbourne hill from the by-pass, and she was running on the other side of the road. Yes, going up the hill. She was talking to somebody in a blue Golf. The Golf was cruising alongside her, and then it sped off up the hill. No, I can't remember which way it turned off, sorry. I sounded my horn as I passed her. I know her from the bank. She waved to me. No, she didn't seem to be in difficulty. No, I'm afraid I didn't see which way she went at the top of the roundabout. I was on my way to The Larches to visit a friend, so I turned off down Larch Road before Pandora reached the top of the hill. Have you any idea what might have happened to her?'

Dave Gilling answered in the negative. Everyone was hoping, he said, that she had had a minor accident while she was out running. 'With a bit of luck we'll find her this morning and she'll need nothing more than a good breakfast, a hot bath and a bit of TLC'.

From her vantage point in the doorway of Janis's office, Hazel was getting a better view of Rose Bennett. She looked younger than Janis, comfortably dressed in a well-cut linen trouser suit, her mane of red curls pinned back from a pale face that was punctuated only by mascara and a subtle lipstick. Beside her Janis looked rather cheap in her regulation polyester uniform, her poker-straight bleached hair growing out beyond tell-tale dark roots, her wide mouth a gash of ill-chosen crimson lip-gloss. It just goes to show, Hazel thought, that good taste has nothing to do with money. Because let's face it, Janis isn't short of a bob or two.

She tried for a moment to mentally calculate Janis's monthly income based on her branch manager's salary and bonuses, her husband's income and the hefty child maintenance payments she was bound to receive from her ex-husband Clive, and came up with an estimate of roughly treble her own monthly pay. It was alright for some. Abandoned last year by her own husband, Hazel had been left with two unruly toddlers, an empty bank account and no forwarding address for the solicitor's letters. She was still musing on the unfairness of life when Janis opened the door of the interview room and called her in. 'Hazel, can we borrow you just for a minute please?'

Delighted to get closer to the mystery, Hazel nodded in agreement and trotted into the interview room. She greeted Rose with her best professional smile, the one she saved for those special customers who had clean credit files and could afford to take on additional mortgage borrowing.

Rose held out a hand. 'Nice to meet you, Hazel. I'm Rose.'

'Nice to meet you, Rose.'

Janis pointed to a vacant chair. 'Take a seat, Hazel. I'm going to leave you to have a chat with Rose for a few minutes.' She paused, considering her words carefully. 'Rose is going to be spending a few days with us to look at our account opening process. She's preparing some documents for Head Office, and our branch was chosen at random to assist by sharing our working practices with her. I know you're an expert when it comes to account opening, so I'd like you to give her the benefit of your experience.'

Out in the banking hall Tommy slid silently onto his seat behind the counter and unlocked the cash drawer. He pretended to check that everything was in order, counting silently to himself, and waited for the inevitable reprimand.

To his left, Marge was passing a paying-in book back to a customer. 'All done, Mr Steel. See you again in the morning.' She waited until the man was out of earshot, and then swivelled on her chair. 'Second time this week, Tommy. You're over an hour late.' Her tone was reproachful.

He slammed the cash drawer shut and started clicking away at the keyboard in front of him, his eyes fixed firmly on the computer screen at the side of his desk. 'Sorry Marge, problems with the car again.' He knew she wouldn't believe him, but he didn't really care. 'I sent you a text, it's not like you didn't know I was going to be late.'

'That's not the point. It's the second time this week, and it's only Wednesday.' She pursed her lips. 'It's not as if we don't know *why* you're coming in late.' She waited for a response, but none came. 'Those morning huddles are important, Tommy. We don't have them for fun, you know. Janis is livid with you. You can't keep avoiding them like this.'

Tommy winced, but didn't look at her. Those morning huddles were his worst nightmare. Fifteen excruciating minutes every morning before the branch opened, during which Janis quizzed each of them in turn about their sales prospects for the day, and how close they were to meeting their monthly targets. It wasn't his fault he was useless at selling. He didn't sign up for this when he joined the bank, he just wanted to serve customers, not harass them into buying products they didn't need. He used to be happy working here, but not now. Not now there were sales targets to meet, and ritual humiliation from Janis to be endured when he missed them. 'Are you and Hazel on target then, Marge?' He wasn't sure why he asked the question, the answer was always "yes". Even when it wasn't true.

Marge frowned and thought for a moment. 'Yes. I think so.' She paused. 'Well I know I am, and I think Hazel is close enough.'

Close enough? Tommy bit his lip. Why did she have to lie about it? Why did missing the total branch target always have to be his fault?

He glanced around the branch, looking for a distraction, an excuse to change the subject. 'Where's Pandora?'

Marge eyed him for a moment. 'We don't know.' She leaned towards him and lowered her voice. 'I don't suppose you have any idea where she is?'

His spirits lifted for a moment and he turned to her with a grin, his eyes wide. 'You think she's been with me this morning?'

'Hasn't she?'

He shook his head. 'I wish. She's still playing hard to get. She must be with that tosser Bradman.'

Marge rapped him sharply on the arm. 'Language, Tommy. This is a bank, not an ale-house.'

He grinned again, the tension between them easing. 'Sorry Marge.' He stopped clicking at the keyboard and turned to face her. 'Hasn't she rung in?'

'No.' Marge was thoughtful. 'It's not like her, is it?

She's not answering her mobile, and I've twice tried calling her at home but the number was engaged both times. I'd better try again now.' She sighed. 'It's organised chaos in here this morning. You late, Pandora absent, and Janis in a state over our Head Office visitor.' She nudged him, and pointed towards the glass wall of the meeting room. 'That person with Hazel is Rose Bennett. She's been sent by Clive to look into the account opening process for the next few days, and we're all to spend some time with her.'

Tommy's eyes narrowed. 'Head Office spy?'

'We think so. Clive's calling it an informal audit, to see whether or not we need to tighten things up across the bank.' Marge dimpled her plump face and nudged him again. 'In other words they want to check up on us, and make sure we're doing things by the book when we write new business.'

He frowned. 'What if we're doing it wrong? Will we get into trouble?'

'I don't know, Tommy. I shouldn't think so. I wouldn't worry too much. I'm not worried, am I?' She leaned back in her chair and gave him a mischievous smile. 'Mind you, I've been opening accounts at the ENB for nearly forty years. It'll be a bit of an embarrassment for them if I've been doing it wrong all this time.'

'I'm still not really sure why you think I need to speak to a solicitor?' Craig Bradman had given in to his father's request to meet him at Henry Campling's office, but was still waiting for an explanation. 'I've been up all night driving around with Danny, I need a shower and a shave, and a couple of hours sleep. Is this really necessary?'

'It was Henry's idea, son.' Benny Bradman laid an outsized hand on his son's arm. 'I told him about Pandora disappearin', and he thought we ought to have a chat to see if there's anythin' we can do to help. Ain't that right, Henry?'

'Absolutely, Bradman. Absolutely.' Henry Campling smiled condescendingly at Craig from behind his antique mahogany desk. 'Is there any news of the young lady yet?'

Craig shook his head. 'No, nothing. We searched all the local roads last night, and the family are walking all her off-road running routes this morning. The police have been out looking as well, but we're still waiting to hear if there will be a full-blown police search. They'll need extra men for that.'

Campling nodded in understanding. 'And you yourself have absolutely no idea whatsoever of the young lady's whereabouts?'

'No, I …' Craig paused. It took a moment for the question to sink in. He turned again to his father. 'What is this?'

Bradman held up the outsized hand. 'Now don't fly off the handle, Craig. We're thinkin' of you. Henry thinks it would be a good idea to make a statement, just in case the police start to get ideas. No-one likes to think of anythin' bad happenin' to Pandora, but if she don't turn up today people's imaginations are goin' to start workin' overtime. And we don't want them imaginin' that you had anythin' to do with it.' He laid the hand on Craig's arm again. 'Why don't you just listen to what Henry has to say? Eh? For me?' He nodded at Henry Campling. 'Go on Henry, tell him what you told me. About missin' people.'

Campling cleared his throat. 'Yes, well … in the case of a missing person the police have an obligation to consider all possibilities. You will no doubt have thought last night, when the local police were speaking to you about Pandora's disappearance, that they were just being sympathetic and helpful. That, of course, is only part of the picture. I'm sure you realise that a report of a missing person may very often be the first indication of something more serious, and the police will bear this in mind at all times. They may be wondering, for example, whether Pandora had an argument with her family, or perhaps with yourself.'

'Are you suggesting that I had something to do with Pandora's disappearance?' Craig's voice was low, incredulous. He turned to his father. 'Have you lost the plot completely?'

Campling persisted with his train of thought. 'Your father, far from losing the plot as you put it, is being remarkably circumspect. What I am trying to make clear to you, Craig, is that you are in a position of risk until Pandora Mitchell turns up. The police will be keeping a very close eye on you, and on her family and other friends.'

'I don't have to listen to this.' Craig pushed back his chair and started to get to his feet.

'Is it true that you had a public argument about Pandora Mitchell last night?'

Craig paused, half standing. 'What did you say?'

'Did you get into an argument yesterday evening, in The Feathers public house? Did you argue with another young man about Pandora Mitchell, and whether or not she had ... I believe the phrase is "stood you up"?'

The young man sat down again and looked first at Campling, and then at his father. Bradman stared directly into his son's eyes. 'I heard you had another ruck with that lad who works in the bank. Is that true? Well?' Craig didn't respond. 'I'll take your silence as confirmation of the affirmative, then, shall I?'

The colour rose in Craig's face, up through the roots of his tightly cropped dark curls and then down his throat, depositing angry red blotches across his white skin. 'How did you hear about that?'

Campling leaned across the desk. 'How we heard about it is far less important than the fact that we heard about it at all. People gossip, Craig. They love to gossip. If we have heard about it, then so have others. If we can take a snippet of gossip and put two and two together, then so can others. Including the police. I would strongly suggest, for your own safety, that you recount to me now your last communications with Pandora Mitchell, and any other relevant facts.' He watched the heightened colour drain from Craig's face and throat. 'I appreciate that the thought may cause you some distress, but we must be practical. The girl has been missing for fourteen hours now, and the circumstances are not propitious. There are several obvious and unpleasant reasons why an attractive young woman might go missing. The likelihood of her safe return diminishes as time passes. As your father's solicitor I consider it my duty to ensure that you are protected. Now I'll ask you again, when did you last see her, and what were the circumstances of your meeting?'

Craig put a hand up to his head and rubbed at his brow. The air in the room was stale despite an open window, its natural odour of tobacco smoke and ancient leather and fusty yellowing paper even more nauseating than usual in the in the humid August atmosphere. 'I met her for lunch yesterday. That was the last time I saw her.'

Benny Bradman stifled a smile as his son left the room. 'Wait outside for me Craig, I'll only be a minute.' He shook his head. 'Sorry if he was a bit sharp with you, Henry. He's a bit hot headed these days. Kids, eh? I always knew I'd be sorry payin' for all that education.'

Campling scowled. 'Nothing to do with education, Bradman. I would say he's just a chip off the old block, wouldn't you?'

If the remark was meant to offend it fell short of the mark. Bradman chuckled and leaned over the desk. 'Look, he's all fired up 'cos his bit of comfort's disappeared. I appreciate you're tryin' to help Henry, but he's twenty two years of age. What am I supposed to do? Put him over my knee and give him a spankin' because he was rude to you? Anyway, if he does know more than he's lettin' on, and gets himself into more bother, you'll only charge me double for gettin' him out of it again, so you ain't gonna lose out either way, are you?'

The solicitor shrugged. 'As you wish. It's fortunate that

he has an alibi for the approximate time of her disappearance. The police of course may wish to challenge your contribution to that alibi, given your close relationship, if the need arises. We'll cross that bridge if and when we come to it.'

Bradman's face clouded. 'I hope you're not suggestin' that I'm being economical with the truth, Henry.'

'Perish the thought, Bradman. Perish the thought.' Campling smarmed a greasy smile. 'Meanwhile, I strongly recommend that you continue to question him at home. Perhaps when he's calmed down he may feel inclined to be a little more open with you.' He pulled a piece of paper from the in-tray on his desk and passed it to Bradman. 'On another matter completely, while you're here you may wish to take a look at this. I have drafted another letter to Lucinda Aylesbury, increasing our offer on her property.'

Bradman took the paper and glanced at it, his dark eyes taking in all the salient points. 'She's turned us down four times. This ain't about money.'

'Oh, I think everyone has a price. It's just a question of how high. Are you happy to meet your share of the increased offer?'

'I suppose so. But I don't think it'll work. What if ...' The thought was interrupted by the ring of his mobile phone, and he snatched it up from the desk and snapped into it. 'Bradman.' A pause. 'Oh, hiya Sal.' Another pause. 'Oh for fuck's sake, can't you just deal with him? Alright, alright, keep yer dolly in the pram will yer? I'm on me way.' Irritated, he shoved the phone into his trouser pocket. 'Sorry Henry, I'll have to go. Sal's havin' trouble with a punter in the shop.' He tossed the paper onto the desk. 'Let me know how you get on with old Lucinda. If she turns you down this time, we'll have to be a bit more creative.'

Campling nodded and relaxed back into his chair. 'Agreed.' He picked up his fountain pen and twizzled it between nicotine-stained fingers. 'And don't forget,

Bradman, talk to the boy again … do what you can to get him to tell you the truth.'

4

Janis tapped on the glass door of the meeting room and walked straight in. Rose and Hazel both looked up at her. She looked tense and irritated, her red glossy lips pursed in annoyance before parting to speak. 'I've just had the police on the phone. They want to know if anyone has seen Pandora. She seems to have gone missing.'

Hazel rolled her eyes and turned back to Rose. 'Pandora is our fast-track trainee.' She turned back to Janis. 'What do they mean by "missing"? Has she been out all night?' She smirked at the thought. 'Tarty little madam.'

Janis sat down at the table beside her. 'She certainly hasn't been seen since last night, but I don't think it's what you're hinting at. She went out for a training run just after six and didn't come back. They're searching for her now. The police want to come here and speak to us. All of us.'

'Like we'd know what's happened to Princess Pandora.' Hazel snorted and turned again to Rose. 'She's a nice enough girl but a bit high maintenance, if you know what I mean. Her dad runs that big car dealership, Mitchells, on the by-pass.' She cast a sly glance at Janis. 'We could never understand why she wanted to come and work for the bank. She got good enough A-levels to go to university, but Daddy persuaded one of his golfing pals to get her a fast-track traineeship with the ENB. I just think she was too lazy to leave home. She didn't want to leave Mummy and Daddy and all the home comforts. Some kids are like that. Janis was hoping she'd move on to Head Office in Kirkby, weren't you Janis?'

For a moment Rose thought she had misheard or at least misunderstood. 'Danny's daughter?' She mumbled the words under her breath. 'Danny Mitchell's daughter?' The question was directed at Janis now and Janis, who looked suddenly pale and vulnerable, answered by turning her face away. Rose felt an unexpected surge of sympathy for her, and momentarily forgot that they weren't alone. 'Couldn't you have done something about that? Tell the Bank about …'

'I tried.' Janis checked herself, uneasily aware that Hazel was still in the room. 'Hazel, could you go and help Marge and Tommy in the banking hall, please? With Pandora out we're short-staffed.'

For a moment it looked as though Hazel might resist the suggestion. Thoroughly engrossed in the unfolding drama, she looked hopefully at Rose, but sensing no encouragement to stay rose reluctantly to her feet. 'I'll go and see how Tommy is. He'll be worried about Pandora.'

As Hazel closed the door of the meeting room behind her, Janis pulled a cotton handkerchief from the pocket of her jacket and sniffed into it. 'I tried to have Pandora placed somewhere else, but Danny knows too many people at the bank. You must know what the ENB is like. It's always who you know, not what you know.' She gave another sniff for effect. 'I asked Clive to sort it. I thought at least he would understand, but he just said I'd have to rise above it, otherwise people would think I still had feelings for Danny.' She twisted the handkerchief round a finger. 'Funny, isn't it, how all this has blown up today, when you're here?'

Funny? Not the word I would have used, Rose thought. But certainly interesting how suddenly you've decided I'm a friend to confide in when less than an hour ago you were keeping me at arm's length. She sat back in her chair and considered Janis closely. 'I know it's been a long time, but do you still have feelings for Danny?'

'No, of course not. I've been married twice since then,

I've had three children. I'm not the same person. All that happened to a different Janis.' The words sounded convincing, but there had been an almost imperceptible pause before she spoke them, and Rose knew that they were only words. 'Of course I was hugely embarrassed by it. Especially as it looked as though Danny Mitchell had more control over bank affairs than I did, and he doesn't even work for the bloody bank.' She sniffed again into the handkerchief. 'The stupid thing is, Pandora's a nice kid. She can be a bit precious at times, but she's likeable. The first day she was here she asked to speak to me in private. She told me that she knew I'd once been engaged to her father. She said she was sorry if her being here upset me, but she just wanted a good job close to home. She said "after today, let's never mention it again. I'm just Pandora, who works for you at the bank."'

As Janis rambled on, Rose observed her old friend with interest. She may claim to be a different Janis, Rose thought, but she's just like the one I remember. A young girl has gone missing, anything might have happened to her, and yet here we are again on "Planet Janis". And worst of all, she thought, I nearly fell for it again. I felt sorry for her. Me, who knows how easy it is to be taken in by her.

She waited until Janis stopped speaking and then reached down under the table and grasped for the soft leather briefcase at her feet. 'I think under the circumstances it might be best if I got out of your way for a while. You'll have enough on your plate talking to the police. I've had a brief chat with Hazel, and she's going to give me an hour of her time later this morning. I'll have a word with Tommy on the way out, and see what I can arrange with him. I'll pop back about eleven thirty.'

Janis stopped snuffling for a moment and looked up from her handkerchief, bemused. 'Pop back? You're not still thinking of doing the review? Surely that will be cancelled now, won't it?'

'Cancelled? Why?'

'Because of Pandora. You can't expect me to deal with Pandora's disappearance, and the review as well?'

Rose shrugged. 'To be honest Janis, I can't really see that Pandora's disappearance prevents me from doing my job. But then it's not up to me. My directions from Clive were to do the review this week. I guess we could check with him.' She pulled a mobile phone from her pocket and offered it to Janis. 'Do you want to give him a call, or shall I?'

Rose's call to Clive Barden was a fairly brief one, and his directions were clear. 'Yes, HR has told me about Pandora Mitchell's disappearance. It's very inconvenient, but it's nothing to do with the bank. Janis doesn't particularly care for the girl – you'll know why, of course – so she shouldn't be personally affected by her disappearance. I'll speak to Operations and ask them to arrange for a temp to cover Pandora's work. That should remove the need for any excuses about staff being too busy to speak to you.'

'Janis won't like this much.'

'No, she won't. But for one reason or another, Rose, you and I have both had experience of dealing with Janis when she doesn't like things much. Why do you think I chose you for the job?' He paused, and then said 'it is possible that Pandora's disappearance will cause us some operational risk – press interest, speculation about her relationship with her colleagues, and so on. I'd better have a think about that.'

'What about the police? If I'm here when they arrive do I need to tell them what I'm doing at the bank? That there have been process problems, I mean?'

'Absolutely not.' Clive's tone was suddenly sharp. 'Pandora's disappearance is a domestic affair, nothing to do with the bank. Bank affairs are confidential. I rely on your absolute discretion, Rose.'

'But if they ask me ...'

'If they ask you anything about the bank, refer them to me.'

There was something just a little too brusque in Clive Barden's manner, something which sparked Rose's interest. 'Don't you think it seems a little odd, Clive, that a member of staff disappears just as I turn up to investigate irregularities at the branch? Are you sure you've told me everything I need to know about this job?'

'Rose, you have all the relevant facts available to you. This review has to go ahead, and as soon as possible. The sooner your work is done, the sooner any of this ceases to be your concern.'

Benny Bradman slipped a chubby finger under the edge of the blind, and teased it gently away from the glass. Below the window, out in the street, his son strode purposefully towards a blue BMW. Benny watched as Craig flicked the key fob in the car's direction, pulled open the door, threw his jacket on to the passenger seat, slipped into the driver's seat, closed the door behind him. The car pulled away, but Benny continued to stare at the space it had occupied for some minutes, until it was filled by the local butcher's van. The delivery boy jumped out of the van, and Benny pulled back from the window and leaned against the wall, closing his eyes.

Losing his only son to another kind of life, another social class, he had got used to that. He had become accustomed to staying in the background, absent from parent days at school, hiding behind a screen of fictitious business commitments so that his own ignorance and lack of finesse wouldn't embarrass Craig in front of his peers and their families. He'd wanted Craig to never have to say 'Dad, this is Jeremy's dad Montague, he's an investment banker. Montague, this is my dad Benny, he's a bookie.' But losing him over a girl, a dim bit of skirt in a rural backwater, where had that come from? He hadn't seen that coming. He snorted, a half-laugh of self-derision. He should have known that no amount of fancy schooling would disconnect the lad's brains from his most basic desires.

In a way it hurt him that his son had chosen such a girl. Craig had never complained too much that Benny stayed in the background, conscious of the social chasm between his home life and his school life. Benny had hoped that if he stayed out of the way then Craig would find himself an educated girl, an ambitious girl, a challenge worthy of his own sacrifices, not some blonde dimwit whose only ambition in life was to run twenty six consecutive miles without needing a pee.

He went back to his desk, picked up the phone, and jabbed the chubby finger at the keypad. 'Sal, is Spivey down there? Send him up, will you?' He sat down and reached into the desk for a packet of chewing gum. The office door opened, and he glanced up. 'Bloody knock, why don't you?'

'Sorry Benny.' Michael Spivey, greasier than usual, closed the door behind him. 'Did you want something?'

'Just the pleasure of your company.' Benny shook his head and muttered under his breath. 'Of course I bloody want somethin'. Sit down.' He pointed at the chair opposite, and Spivey sank silently into it. 'I've just had a barney with our Craig. He's determined to do this bloody appeal thing with Mitchell on the telly tonight. I'm not happy about it.' He yanked a piece of gum out of its silver paper, and set about chewing it. 'I've told him he's better off keepin' his head down until she shows up, but he won't listen. He's gone off to Mitchell's place now, and he reckons he's going to be stayin' there for dinner. I want you to follow him. Use your own car. He won't recognise it.' He opened another drawer and took out a couple of twenty pound notes, placing them in front of Spivey on the desk. 'Keep an eye on him, and report back to me every couple of hours. I want to know that he's definitely with Mitchell, and if not I want to know where he goes, and who he talks to. There'll be no peace until she shows up.'

Spivey smiled, revealing an uneven row of nicotine-stained teeth. 'She's done a runner with another bloke, that's all.'

'Don't be ridiculous, she's Mitchell's precious princess, ain't she? She's not likely to run off without Daddy's blessin' and a fistful of his cash. Mitchell's just been on the local radio news, offerin' a reward for information.'

'Could be a double bluff. Golden-bollocks Mitchell isn't going to want to admit his girl's a bit of a slapper, is he?'

Benny leaned across the desk and stared into Spivey's oily face. 'He's lost his girl, Spivey. Show some respect. I don't like Mitchell, and I don't much like his girl, but I wouldn't want to be in his shoes right now.'

Spivey grunted and picked up the twenty pound notes, folding them roughly and shoving them into his trouser pocket. 'I don't see what good it'll do, me following some lovesick lad around. We'll be busy this afternoon, you know there are three big meetings on today.'

Benny shook his head. 'I pay you to do as you're told. So piss off and do as you're told.'

Thwarted, Spivey got up and made for the door. 'What am I supposed to do if she turns up today?'

'Come back and tell me.'

'Dead or alive?'

Benny stiffened, and when he spoke his voice was low. 'Do you know somethin', Michael?'

'No, just asking.' He smirked. 'If I knew anything, I'd be telling it to Danny Mitchell and pocketing the reward money, wouldn't I?'

5

'Janis is in a foul mood. Really put her nose out of joint, you have.' Hazel beamed at Rose with mischievous pleasure. 'She's been in a right old paddy since you were in earlier on.'

Rose smiled as she pulled a large spiral-bound notebook from her briefcase, placing it on the meeting room table along with a sheaf of printed papers. 'It'll wear off. When we were kids she was always threatening that she'd never speak to me again. Nine times out of ten she'd just forget that she was meant to be ignoring me. Anyway, I can't take all the credit. She's probably just a bit wound up about the review, and this thing with Pandora won't have helped.'

'So you knew each other as kids, then?'

'We were at school together. I grew up in Market Melbourne.'

Hazel's eyes widened slightly in anticipation. 'You must know Pandora's dad, as well, then?'

'More of the past tense, Hazel. I haven't spoken to him for years. But that's not what we're here to talk about today, is it?' Rose good-humouredly rebuffed Hazel's attempts to gossip, but dangled a juicy carrot just in case. 'Of course, if I were to have a coffee later …'

Across the table, Hazel was beginning to relax. 'I'll look forward to that.' She leaned her elbows on the table and rested her chin in her hands. 'What exactly is it you want to talk about, then?'

Rose opened her notebook at a blank double page, and

scribbled the date and Hazel's name on the top line. 'I want to talk about the process for opening a new current account for a customer who doesn't have any existing business with the bank. In particular, I'd like to talk about the steps you have to take to verify a customer's identity.' She glanced up at Hazel. 'So, for example, what ID documents do you ask for, and what do you do to make sure that they are correct.' She studied Hazel's face as she spoke, and saw an unmistakable flicker of interest. 'We'll do that tomorrow, though. Janis has agreed that I can spend an hour with you today, and an hour tomorrow, so today I'd like to get some background on the branch, so that I can put everything into context. Is that OK with you?'

Hazel shrugged. 'I don't see why not. There's not much to tell about the branch. There are six of us working here – you know Janis, there's me, Marge, Tommy, Pandora and Melanie. Melanie's on maternity leave, her baby's due next week.' She paused, giving Rose time to write down her words. 'Marge is the assistant manager, Melanie only does branch administration, Pandora's the trainee, and me and Tommy do all the donkey work.'

Rose glanced up from her note-taking. 'Who opens new current accounts, then?'

'Theoretically we all do. Before they introduced the new commission structures, we used to divide the sales up between us depending on who was most experienced in a particular product. Marge used to do the mortgage and investment sales, and business banking. I used to do loans and insurance, and Tommy and I shared the savings and current account sales.' She frowned. 'Mind you, Tommy was never one for selling, so I did most of it.'

'That's changed now, has it? Since the sales performance targets were introduced?'

'I'll say it has. Marge still does mortgages and investments and the small bit of business stuff we deal with, and Tommy's trained now in selling loans and insurance products as well as current accounts. But you can't always make your target by sticking to the products you're used to selling.' She sighed. 'They don't all carry the same commission points, you see?'

Rose did see, but she feigned ignorance. 'So you make more commission for selling some products than others?'

'Mm. You get fifteen hundred points for a new mortgage advance, but only three hundred for a new current account. That means you'd have to sell five current accounts to make the same number of points as one mortgage. So for me and Tommy, it means a lot more sales prospecting to try to meet our targets.'

'That sounds like a challenge. Are the targets achievable?'

Hazel snorted. 'Of course not. I'm supposed to hit twenty eight thousand points every quarter. That's like …' She gazed up at the ceiling, lips moving silently as she tried to calculate. 'That's like ninety-odd current accounts. Thirty-odd a month. I mean, how can I possible sell thirty-odd current accounts a month in a backwater like this?'

Rose hoped the question was rhetorical, because she didn't have the answer. 'Forgive my asking, Hazel, but has this changed the way you get on as a team? I mean, you're all in competition now, aren't you? How do you decide who is going to sell to a customer? Is it just the luck of the draw who happens to be serving the customer when they make an enquiry?'

'We have to "prospect".' Hazel sucked in her cheeks. 'Every customer that comes to the counter. We're expected to chat to them, and find out whether they have products with another bank that could be transferred here. Can we sell them house insurance? Can we sell them a savings account? Do they have a credit card with us? Have they thought about changing their car, because we're doing a great offer on car loans?' She sighed. 'You can see the customer glaze over sometimes. They're not daft, most of them know there's a hard sell coming.'

'It must be tough.'

'Well, you know …' She trailed off, and then added 'sometimes we get lucky. We did quite well in March and April because work finished on the new housing estate and the builders gave us some leads. We got quite a bit of mortgage business out of it, and managed to persuade a few people to switch their current accounts over to us as part of the deal. Plus with mortgages we can usually swing the buildings and contents insurance as well, if we're clever.'

Rose nodded in understanding. 'Does Pandora have a performance target?'

'She will have from next month. She hasn't been with us very long. She's only trained in selling current accounts and savings accounts, and she didn't have any compliance certification until last week.'

Rose's ears pricked up. 'Compliance?'

'Well, her Know Your Customer training. You know, how to check customer ID to make sure there's no identity fraud.'

'So Pandora had never opened any accounts at the branch.' Rose was still writing when Hazel corrected her.

'No, I didn't say that. You asked me if she had a performance target. She didn't have a target, but Marge encouraged her to open some new accounts as part of her training. Marge checked the ID for her and signed it off, it was all kosher.'

'So if Pandora wasn't qualified to sell products yet, who got the commission for those?'

Hazel's cheeks flushed. 'I don't know. I suppose …' Not only had the directness of the question thrown her, it had never occurred to her until now that Marge must have taken the points for herself. She straightened in her seat, momentarily defensive. 'You'd have to ask Pandora about that when she turns up.'

'Don't worry, Hazel, I will.' Rose grinned. 'You think she'll turn up OK then? You don't think she's in any sort of trouble?'

'No, she's too precious for that. Tommy told me he saw her out running last night and she was fine. He reckons she's run off somewhere with her boyfriend.' Hazel's face had clouded now, wary that she had given too much away. 'Is that why you've come here, Rose? Because someone's taken the commission points for Pandora's sales?'

Rose looked up from her notebook and shook her head, her pale face lit by a guileless smile. 'No, not at all. Why? Do you think that's a problem?'

'Me? No, I ...' Hazel wasn't sure now what to think. 'At the beginning, you said you wanted to talk about identity checking for current accounts. I thought ...'

'Oh, that? No, that's just co-incidence.' She closed the notebook and rested her hands on it. 'I just want to look at whether the process is being followed, not who benefits from it.'

She turned away from Hazel and looked through the glass wall of the meeting room to the banking hall beyond. Tommy was a nice-looking boy, slim and fresh-faced, with a head of wayward curls. She watched him click away at his keyboard, the tousled head nodding in conversation with the customer. 'Tommy's quite friendly with Pandora then, is he?' She tried to make the question sound casual, a passing interest, a gentle tug to divert Hazel's attention away from commission points and account opening.

'Tommy? Oh, he's been mad about her ever since she started work here. They get on really well together.' Hazel sniffed. 'Mind you, I think she plays him for a bit of a fool. He'll do anything she asks of him, and she asks plenty, but I've never seen him get anything in return.'

It was eleven thirty by the time DI George Mulligan reached Market Melbourne police station, and almost noon by the time he had finished reading Dave Gilling's initial paperwork on the disappearance of Pandora Mitchell. By that time the morning's summer thunderstorms had blown themselves out, and they had used Gilling's patrol car to drive up to the top of Market Melbourne hill.

Gilling pulled off the road and onto the grass verge at the top of Larch Road and the two men sat in silence, gazing at the wet and steaming landscape. The rain had cleared the air, but the temperature was rising again rapidly and even with all the windows open it was clammy inside the car. Still, it wasn't an uncomfortable silence. Mulligan and Gilling had worked together before, when the more experienced criminal network in the nearby industrial town of Kirkby had extended its tentacles out to the surrounding rural market towns and villages, and Gilling had been secretly relieved when Mulligan had been assigned as the senior officer to investigate Pandora's disappearance.

There was probably a gap of ten years between the two men. Mulligan, the elder, was past chasing criminals with anything other than brain cells, and looking forward to an early retirement that would include an allotment and plenty of time with his numerous grand-children. Policing in Kirkby had changed, much as it had changed anywhere, and not for the better. He liked a good honest criminal, a traditional crime, an old-fashioned cat and mouse chase. These days all he seemed to get was illegal immigration, petty theft and vandalism. By contrast, Gilling still enjoyed his job. Unambitious but hard-working, he enjoyed the quiet life looking after a country patch, and was grateful to spend most of his time dealing with road traffic accidents and the occasional domestic. And he knew George Mulligan well enough to know that he wouldn't be criticised for staying in the background of the investigation providing he rolled up his sleeves and did all the hands-on graft that the older man hated.

Mulligan spoke first. 'Well Dave, she'll be a very soggy

young woman by now if she's been lying injured somewhere while that little lot persisted down.' Despite the flippant tone, he was worried. He didn't like missing person cases. In his experience they only ended one of two ways – a complete waste of time, or an unexpected death. He didn't like either result, but he'd rather have his time wasted than deal with the death of a youngster any day of the week. He rifled in his trouser pocket and pulled out a crumpled packet containing one grubby Polo mint. He offered it to Gilling fully expecting him to refuse, and then popped the mint into his mouth. 'And this is where she was last sighted?'

'More or less. We've had a confirmed sighting of her running from the direction of the bypass up the hill towards the roundabout. That was at around five to seven.' Gilling, still tired from lack of sleep, rubbed at the back of his neck.

Mulligan cut in. 'Reliable?'

'Very. A local woman, Lu Aylesbury. She's a retired journalist. Lived in the town on and off all her life. I've known her for years.'

A fleeting image of sharp eyes and chiselled cheekbones and immaculately waved blonde hair flitted across Mulligan's mind. 'Lu Aylesbury, eh? I knew her when she worked on the Kirkby Times.' His face took on a wistful look. 'I had no idea she still lived in the area. And she saw the girl?'

'Yes. She's not absolutely certain about the time to the minute, but she's confident it was within ten minutes either side of seven pm. She sounded her horn to acknowledge Pandora, and the girl waved back to her, so we're as sure as we can be that it was her.'

'Any others?'

'Yes, we had another call just before you arrived. A motorist coming up the hill from the opposite direction about seven o'clock. He says he saw her running off the roundabout and into Larch Road. He's given a description of a fit-looking blonde in green running vest and shorts. His brother was in the car with him, and he backs up the story.'

'Any news on the search?'

Gilling shook his head. 'Not yet. Maybe we're looking in the wrong place. We didn't have much to go on. We've only just learned that she was sighted in Larch Road.' He sounded defeated.

'Well that's fair enough Dave, I wouldn't beat yourself up for it. Assuming that she did run down Larch Road, then, what would be her options? Your report says she's been known to run off road.'

'That's what the family tell me. She was meant to be meeting the boyfriend in The Feathers at eight o'clock, and she would have wanted to shower and change. You'd think she'd take the most direct route from here, which would be to run straight down Larch Road into town. But there are two public footpaths off this road. One on the right about two hundred yards off the roundabout works back down the hill in parallel with the main road for about half a mile, then cuts left and crosses a farm before coming out behind the garden centre. The other one,' Gilling pointed down the hill, 'is down here on the left. It cuts down the side of The Larches residential home and along the back of the golf course, coming out near the club house. Bob Shepherd organised the golfers this morning, they've been searching the course and the footpath. I managed to get hold of the local ramblers group first thing, and they've been searching the footpath down to the garden centre.' He paused and sighed. 'Not a bloody thing, George. We've found nothing.'

Mulligan crunched on the thin sliver of mint left in his mouth, and then said 'what made you suspicious?'

Gilling looked sheepish. 'Dunno. I know the family – Danny Mitchell's a local business man, and his wife Selina is a school governor where my kids go to school. They're decent folk. They were trying to be positive, couldn't have been more helpful. They gave me photos of her, a full description of what she was wearing and carrying, said she was happy enough before she set off. I went off for a drive round myself, up and down the roads round here. Like them, I just expected to see her somewhere, sitting on the verge with a twisted ankle, feeling sorry for herself.'

Mulligan smiled. 'That's just optimism, Dave. It's natural. No-one wants to think the worst.' He became more serious. 'But you did?'

'Isn't that what they tell us to do? Assume the worst, and be glad when you're wrong?'

'I suppose so.' Mulligan shrugged. 'What about the boyfriend?'

'Nice lad. Good education, just finished university. Oxford, I think. He's a bit posh for round here. Hasn't lived here long, about five months or so. His old man is Benny Bradman.'

'Is that meant to mean something to me?'

'I thought you might have heard of him. Essex wide boy, opened a bookie's in Market Melbourne at the start of the year? We're not sure what brought him up here, but we're keeping an eye on him. Nothing known, but he doesn't seem the type to come up north looking for a quiet life.' Gilling laughed, and spoke a little easier. 'Well, that's the official line anyway. To be honest, he's a decent enough bloke. The blue rinse and church brigade aren't too happy about having a bookie's on the high street, but at least he's a real bloke rather than a shop front for a faceless multi-national outfit. He tries to get involved in the community. He's joined the golf club and the cricket club, sponsored a few local charity events, that sort of thing.'

Mulligan, thoughtful, gave the mint a final crunch. 'I didn't know bookies were sending their kids to Oxford these days.'

'Ah, that'll have been the mother's influence. The gossips reckon she was a criminal barrister, worked for some London firm. She died last year, killed in water-skiing accident. Very sad.' Gilling sighed. 'Could be why he moved, I suppose. Fresh start, and all that.'

'And now his son's girlfriend has disappeared.' The Polo mint gone, Mulligan chewed thoughtfully on his lower lip. 'Does he like the girl?'

'Dunno. I suppose I ought to ask him. Do you want me to pay him a visit?'

6

There had been one or two changes in Market Melbourne since Rose's school days. The bicycle shop had been replaced by a trendy interior design service, and the off licence that she and Janis had raided as teenagers had become a betting shop. At the end of the high street, a supermarket had replaced the old second hand car lot that had been Danny Mitchell's first business venture. Rose thought back to days when Janis would persuade her to stroll up and down past the shabby forecourt in the hope of catching Danny's attention. It had proved to some extent to be a successful ploy, but deep down he hadn't really wanted Janis. He'd just taken something handed to him on a plate, eaten too much of it, and then realised that it gave him indigestion.

Unsettled by the morning's events, Rose had escaped from the ENB to take a solitary lunch and gather her thoughts. The café across the road from the branch was busy with lunchtime trade, and she found it easy to lose herself amongst the market town clientele. Once called simply "Val's Café", a homely place to enjoy coffee and a stale scone served on a Pyrex plate, it had become "Café Valerie", a mock French patisserie serving continental sandwiches and dainty cream cakes. A string of tiny French flags draped across the front window fluttered in the breeze every time the shop door opened and Edith Piaf crooned quietly in the background. The transformation was mostly effective save for the persistence of flat provincial accents clearly audible above the music.

Pushing away an empty lunch plate, Rose topped up her cup from a small pot of surprisingly good coffee, and pulled the first edition of the local daily paper from her briefcase, spreading it out on the table in front of her.

The whole of the front page was given over to Pandora Mitchell's disappearance. A full-length photograph showed her in a green running vest and shorts, holding up a medal at what appeared to be the finishing line of a race. The headline demanded "Have You Seen Her?" and the rest of the page carried details of her disappearance the night before.

Rose studied the picture and could see the family resemblance. Pandora had Danny's blond hair, the confident tilt of the head, the perfect even teeth. And more, Rose thought, she has Selina's blue eyes, and those high cheekbones that every girl at school had envied. Poor Janis, confronted every day by the sight of that face, a face that must have unwittingly reminded her not only of the man who rejected her but also the woman he rejected her for.

She skimmed the narrative on the first page, and turned to the next. Pages two and three were also dedicated to Pandora. There was a photograph of Danny and Selina getting into a car, their heads lowered, and a map of the route Pandora was assumed to have been running when she disappeared. Halfway down page three, a short paragraph in the right hand column caught Rose's eye. "Pandora had recently started work in the Market Melbourne branch of the ENB, and colleagues will be assisting in the search for her." She wondered how much assistance Janis would be prepared to give. She re-folded the paper and pushed it back into her briefcase, then pulled out a pen and the spiral notebook she used for work, opening it at random and then leafing back to a page of scribbled notes under the heading "Friday – Clive".

The notes were succinct, as Rose's notes always were.

A dozen or so accounts opened in the last month at Market Melbourne, all using invalid ID documents. Not aware of any fraudulent use of accounts at this stage. Staff carelessness or staff collusion? Internal compliance department aware, Rose to do independent review, and hand documented findings to Clive. Work "blind", test all staff on process. Report by Friday. Discretion vital – operational and regulatory risk for the bank. (Personal risk for Clive!)

She stifled a smile. 'A suggestion of financial crime in his own beloved bank, exposure of his inadequacy in managing risk, and even worse the crime committed at the branch managed by his ex-wife. Am I getting warm?' Lu may have retired from journalism, but she hadn't lost the bloodhound's nose.

Rose added more scribbled notes to the page.

Who opened these particular accounts? Who got the commission points? Janis not pleased to see me? Collusion implies more than one person involved – are they all working together? Does Janis know what's going on? Where the hell is Pandora?

She paused and thought, and doodled a flower on the bottom corner of the page, and then added *What else hasn't Clive told me?*

'Any news about Pandora?' Jean Baker, incapacitated by a fall downstairs and temporarily resident at The Larches nursing home for a period of recuperation, was eager for a little excitement to brighten her day.

'Now how on earth did you know about that?' Marge busied herself unloading dog-eared library books from a large plaid shopping bag, and avoided both the question and her mother's gaze. 'They didn't have much I'm afraid. All the Jean Plaidys were out on loan, so I've brought you a couple of Georgette Heyers and an Antonia Fraser.'

'I do wish you'd stop bringing me all that romantic bilge. You know I don't read it. Why don't you bring me a Stephen King or a Jeffrey Archer? And I want to know about Pandora.' Jean was insistent. 'We had Dave Gilling here an hour ago, with another policeman from Kirkby. They told us all about it, and asked if anyone had seen her running past here between seven and seven thirty last night. Of course, you can't see the road from the house because of that blasted hedge at the front. But they thought it possible that the staff, or maybe a visitor, might have seen her as they were coming in or out of the drive.' She sniffed in a way that conveyed a hint of disappointment. 'You were here at the wrong time, of course. If you hadn't been late, you might have seen her.'

'If I hadn't been late, it would have meant you spending another day without your hearing aid. I told you I would have been here at seven o'clock if I hadn't had to go back for those batteries.' Marge folded the empty bag and settled herself into an armchair next to her mother. 'Anyway, I'm sure nothing bad has happened to Pandora and she'll turn up today. The police will be doing everything they can to find her. Now,' she patted her mother's arm, 'I want to talk to you about the bungalow. I have a surprise for you.'

Jean's heart sank. Marge's surprises usually involved either an unwanted gift or an unwelcome suggestion, either of which as a mother she felt duty bound to accept without question. She stared towards the open door of the lounge, willing someone, anyone, to come in and interrupt, but it was a vain hope. Those residents who weren't bed-ridden were either out with family and friends or enjoying the sunshine in the garden. Before Marge could speak, she said 'I have a surprise for you, too. But you go first.'

Marge beamed. 'You won't have to stay here for much longer. The builder rang me this morning to say they've had a job re-scheduled, and they can start work on the extension on Monday. He thinks it will only take them a couple of weeks to finish the building work, and another couple of days to do the decorating. Just think, a new bedroom and bathroom in the loft for me, and a bigger bedroom and bathroom downstairs for you, and I'll be able to come home every lunchtime and look after you. With a bit of luck you'll be home within three weeks. Isn't that wonderful news?' She rubbed her hand up and down Jean's forearm, oblivious to her mother's obvious dismay. 'Now, what sort of a surprise have you got for me?'

Rose hadn't expected to be called back to the ENB that day. She had used her allotted hour with Hazel, arranged to spend time with Tommy the following morning, and been summarily dismissed by Janis with a firm "see you tomorrow". When the call from Janis came, asking her to pop back to the branch for a meeting at 3pm, she was definitely intrigued.

She arrived to find the branch door locked, and a sign in the window advising customers that with great regret the branch was closed until 3.30 due to unforeseen circumstances. The lights were still on, but there was no-one in the banking hall. She tapped sharply on the door and Hazel appeared within seconds, trotting out through the doorway that led to the staff's inner sanctum, a ring of oversized keys dangling from her fingers.

'Janis said you were coming back.' She took hold of Rose's sleeve and pulled her into the branch, before quickly shutting the door and re-locking it. 'Sorry to drag you in, but Janis is keen to get this meeting over with as soon as possible.'

Upstairs in the staff room Marge and Tommy were already seated at a small table, nursing mugs of coffee. A third mug, presumably Hazel's, steamed in front of an empty seat. Rose declined the offer of a drink, and sat down next to Marge. 'What gives?'

Marge smiled, dimpling her plump cheeks, and said in a conspiratorial whisper 'Orders from Head Office. About Pandora.'

'Ah. Is there news, then?'

'I don't think so.'

Marge was about to elucidate when Janis, flushed and irritated, breezed into the room and shoved the door shut behind her with a jolt of an elbow. She leaned against the door for a moment, and forced a smile. 'Thanks for coming back in, Rose. I've been briefed by Head Office about how to handle Pandora's disappearance, and they want me to cascade that out to everyone at the branch. I thought you should be included, if you're going to be with us all week.' Without waiting for an answer she dropped her diary noisily onto the table, and placed both hands on the back of the chair in front of her, swaying slightly. 'Right, I need to cascade the briefing down to you as quickly as possible so that we can re-open the branch, so please let me go through all the points before you ask me any questions.' She opened the diary, licked a finger, and flicked to the relevant page.

'First of all, the Bank views Pandora's disappearance as a personal matter. The ENB's only involvement is as her employer, with an employer's natural concern for her personal welfare.' She paused, as Hazel and Marge exchanged knowing glances, and then continued to read from her notes. 'Secondly, we need to take care when handling enquiries relating to Pandora's disappearance. Some of our regular customers may be genuinely concerned and may want to know if there's any news of her. The official response to these queries is that we are equally concerned about her, and we believe the police are doing everything they can. However well you know a customer, however long they have banked with the branch, please *please* do not indulge in any idle speculation on what may have happened to her, nor pass any personal comments about her disappearance.' She paused again, waiting for the message to sink in. 'Also, please take care with any strangers in the branch, especially ones who claim to come from the media. If a journalist, or someone you suspect to be a journalist, approaches you then please refer them to me.'

Hazel opened her mouth to speak, but a sharp look from Janis deterred her.

'We may also find that other members of the public, non-customers who have heard about Pandora, may find excuses to come into the branch just to …'

Janis hesitated, struggling for an appropriate phrase and Hazel, her ability to stay silent now severely challenged, ventured to help her out. 'They'll come into the branch to be nosy. Because we've been in the news.'

Janis nodded. 'Well, yes. We think there's a small risk that the publicity might draw in a few sensation-seekers.'

'Let's hope they open accounts while they're in then.' Hazel smirked at Marge. 'This sort of publicity could be more successful than our marketing campaigns. It'd certainly be cheaper.'

Marge sniggered, and then fell silent under her manager's disapproving gaze. Janis turned to Hazel. 'That is exactly the kind of flippant remark that Head Office are concerned about. This is a serious matter, you know. Poor Pandora really is missing. There's nothing funny about that.'

Chastised, Hazel looked away. 'I know it's not funny,' she muttered. 'Poor little cow had her faults, but I wouldn't wish anything bad on her.'

Janis licked her finger again, and flicked the page of the diary over. 'Now, we are to receive a visit this afternoon from a DI Mulligan, who is the senior officer investigating Pandora's disappearance. He'll be coming to speak to me at five o'clock, and will then wish to speak to each of you briefly. That will be after hours at five thirty, to minimise disruption to the bank.' Seeing Hazel and Marge exchange a further glance, she added 'it goes without saying that the Bank expects you to co-operate fully with the police and in whatever way is necessary.'

Hazel tilted her head at Janis and opened her mouth to speak again, but this time thought better of it. Tommy stared silently at his knees, deep in contemplation, while Marge gazed into the distance and barely appeared to be listening to Janis at all.

'Now, any questions?' Janis glanced at her watch as she spoke, conveying the unsubtle hint that if there were any questions, she didn't have time to answer them.

Tommy, roused from his contemplation by the abruptness of her tone, tentatively raised his hand and asked 'what about Pandora? I mean, what you've just told us is all about the bank, and what's good for the bank. But what about her? How we will know if she's alright?' It was a simple, heartfelt question. They all turned to look at Janis.

'I don't know, they didn't say anything about that. I suppose we'll hear it on the news, the same as anyone else.' Momentarily thrown, she flipped the diary shut and lifted it up off the table. 'Well, if that's it ...'

'I have a question, Janis.' Marge leaned forward and rested her elbows on the table. 'Who is going to cover Pandora's workload? We're already a person short, with Melanie on maternity leave.'

Flustered, Janis nodded. 'Yes, sorry, I forgot to mention that. Head Office is going to send us a temp to cover branch administration while Pandora is absent. I'm afraid we'll just have to manage as best we can.'

Marge nodded and cast a sly glance towards Rose. 'And what about the review?'

It was Rose's turn to speak, and she kept it brief and to the point. 'Clive has insisted that the review goes ahead. Isn't that right, Janis?'

All eyes turned on Janis who merely scowled and nodded, knowing when she was defeated.

The meeting over, Janis sped back down the stairs to re-open the branch, leaving Marge, Tommy and Hazel to saunter into the kitchen to rinse out their coffee mugs. Rose lingered at the table in the meeting room, and taking some loose papers from her briefcase pretended to search through them for some elusive set of notes. From her seat she could easily hear their casual conversation in the kitchen, Hazel enquiring after Marge's mother, Marge expressing concerns that her mother wasn't happy at The Larches. Her mug duly rinsed and dried in readiness for her next break, Marge waddled down the stairs to the banking hall, still muttering about needing to bring her mother home as soon as possible. Left behind in the kitchen, Tommy and Hazel busied about in silence until Hazel said 'Are you alright, Tom? You look a bit peaky today.' He didn't answer her, so she resorted to teasing him. 'Not worried about the police are you? D'you think you might slip up and tell them what you've done with the body?'

There was silence, and then a clatter of cheap china mug breaking against the hard kitchen floor. 'Oh shit, look what you've made me do.' Tommy's voice broke, almost tearful. 'What did you say that for? I'd never hurt Pan. Never.'

'Oh Tommy, love, I'm sorry. I was only teasing you. What is it? What's the matter?' Hazel sounded genuinely contrite. 'You're not really bothered about speaking to the police, are you?'

Tommy gulped. 'I saw her, Haze. I saw her running up Market Melbourne hill last night. I slowed the car down and spoke to her. What if people saw me?'

Hazel's voice was soothing now. 'Well, that doesn't matter, does it? What if people did see you? You need to tell the police, it might help them to find her.'

'But what if they don't believe me? What if they know about me, that I liked her, I mean? They might think I had something to do with it.'

'Don't be daft. She'll probably turn up today and everyone will wonder what the fuss was all about.' She reached for the kettle and refilled it. 'Come on, I'll make you another coffee, to take down with you. And when the police get here, you just tell them you saw her running, and what time it was, and leave it at that. You don't have to tell them you liked her. That's between you and her.'

The coffees made, one to comfort Tommy and one for Hazel, 'since the kettle's boiled anyway', they made their way downstairs.

Rose, left behind and completely forgotten in the small meeting room, opened her spiral notebook and scribbled *Why is Tommy afraid?*

'I'm sorry if I was brusque with you this morning. I suppose it was the shock of seeing you again after all these years, and then Pandora disappearing, you know how it is.' Janis sounded sincere, and probably would have fooled anyone except Rose.

'Don't worry about it. It's been a lot to take in in one day.' Rose leaned in the doorway of the office, her briefcase propped between her ankles. 'They're locking up the banking hall now, so I'm going to get off home and leave you in peace to deal with that policeman. I'll see you tomorrow.' She bent down and picked up the briefcase.

'Well, actually …' Janis paused, unsure of her ground, and then said 'I wondered if you'd like to come round for supper this evening? Nothing fancy, just pasta and a glass of wine. Jimmy's taking the boys to football training, and Millie will be in bed by seven. I thought we could start again, catch up on the gossip?'

Momentarily thrown by the unexpected gesture of friendship, Rose hugged her briefcase to her chest and gave a gentle smile. 'You'll have to tell me where you live these days. And you'd better draw me a map while you're at it. You know I never had any sense of direction.'

7

Rose was walking down the path to Lu's cottage when her mobile rang again. She pulled the phone from her jacket pocket and looked at the display. It was Clive. She pushed the reject button and shoved the phone back into her pocket.

In the back garden Lu, curled up on a sun lounger, was reading the evening paper. Underneath a second lounger Mac sheltered from the heat. As Rose approached around the side of the cottage he got to his feet and waddled to meet her, wagging a stumpy tail. Lu put down the newspaper and eyed her niece over the top of her sunglasses. 'How was it?'

'Grim.' Rose dropped her briefcase onto the lawn and slipped off her jacket and shoes, dropping the jacket onto the end of the empty lounger. A table between the two seats held a jug of barley water and two glasses, and Rose helped herself to a drink before sitting down. 'Worse than I expected.' She gulped on the ice-cold squash. 'Janis wasn't pleased to see me, and more or less cold-shouldered me, and then she ricocheted all the way to the other end of the scale and invited me to supper this evening. Clive is being a complete pain in the arse. And just to cap it all, one of the staff has disappeared.'

Lu nodded. 'I know about Pandora Mitchell. I had to call the police and tell them I saw her last night. I passed her on my way to The Larches.' She paused, then added 'You know she's Danny's daughter?'

Rose screwed up her face. 'Do I? I've heard all about it

62

from Janis. Mind you,' she dropped onto the empty sun lounger and lifted her bare feet up onto the chair, 'I can't help feeling a bit sorry for her. You'd think Clive might have had a bit of sensitivity and stepped in. It's almost as if they put Pandora in there to wind Janis up.' She dropped her left hand to the side of the lounger and waggled her fingers. Mac licked them, and then shuffled back under the chair into the shade. Rose turned to Lu. 'You don't mind if I'm not here for supper, do you? I can't say I fancy spending the evening with Janis after the way she's behaved today, but I need to get her on side for the work I'm doing.'

'Of course I don't mind. I'll spend a bit longer with Jean this evening, and pick up a take-away on the way back.'

Inside Rose's jacket, her mobile phone began to ring again. She sat up and grabbed at it, pulling the phone from a pocket with a frown and scowling at the number. 'Bloody Clive. He won't leave me alone.' This time she pushed the answer button. 'Yes Clive, what can I do for you now?'

The voice at the end of the line was brusque. 'I've been trying to reach you for half an hour. I need you to do something else for me.'

Rose sighed. 'Depends what it is.'

'I've been speaking with a DI Mulligan this afternoon. He's investigating Pandora's disappearance.'

'I know. He's meeting with Janis, isn't he? Now, I mean, after hours?'

'Yes.' Clive paused. 'He and I have had rather a long conversation this afternoon, and I thought it pragmatic after all to tell him about your assignment. He is aware now that we have had some account-opening anomalies at the branch, and that you are there to assess whether or not the staff need re-training, and whether we need to do a full branch audit. I have told him that there is absolutely no criminal risk arising from the account opening errors, that nothing fraudulent has taken place, and that the Bank are fully on top of it.'

'And he fell for that, did he?' Rose's tone of voice conveyed her own cynicism on the matter. 'Cos I'm not sure that I do.'

Clive snapped at her. 'And what is that supposed to mean?'

'What it means, Clive, is that after going into the branch *I* don't believe that little spiel, so I'm not sure that a police officer will. What is it that you're not telling me?'

'How many times are we going to have this conversation? I've told you more than once that you have all the facts.'

'So you say.' She paused, and then asked 'so what is this "something else" you want me to do?'

'I've asked DI Mulligan to let you continue your work this week, and he has no objection providing you are able to assist him with his investigations at the branch. On an informal basis, of course.'

'You want me to work with DI Mulligan?' Rose turned to Lu as she spoke and their eyes met. At the mention of Mulligan's name Lu smiled, and drew a finger across her neck, silently mouthing 'lucky girl.'

'So will you do it?' Clive's tone was terse.

'Yes, I'll help him if I can. But if there's nothing dodgy going on in the branch, as you say, then I can't see much point in it.'

At the other end of the line Clive clicked his teeth. 'It's called "public relations", Rose. The Bank being seen to assist the police with their enquiries.'

'Fair enough. But this business about Pandora has put things on a different footing for me. The branch staff might think twice about trusting me now, it may not be so easy for me to even do the process investigation, never mind assist the police.'

'I'm sure you'll turn it round. I'll call the inspector now and tell him that you'll help. I'll ask him to call your mobile number and set up a meeting.'

'OK.' Rose paused again and then said 'Clive, in all seriousness if you do know more about this business than you've already told me, wouldn't now be the time to cough it up?'

The voice at the end of the line was cold now. 'It wouldn't be in my interests to lie to the police, Rose.'

She could almost see his narrow eyes shrinking into slits of disdain at her suggestion, and she fought back the desire to laugh out loud at his hypocrisy. After all, the whole point of her assignment was to establish whether or not his ex-wife was doing anything at the branch that would require discrete action and a few white lies to the law enforcement agencies. She composed herself, and said 'I've had a brief chat with one of the branch staff this afternoon, Hazel Grant. I'm meeting her again tomorrow, and also spending time with a young man called Tommy Fletcher. I'll tackle Marge Baker and Janis on Friday. Could you tell DI Mulligan that it would be useful if we could speak first thing in the morning, before I go into the branch?'

'I will. And Rose ...' He cleared his throat. 'If you discover anything personal about Pandora Mitchell which is useful to the police, and you consider it would be in the bank's best interests not to know about it, speak straight to DI Mulligan. Of course, if you discover anything critical to the bank, I hope you will remember that you are still in our employ and discuss the matter with me first.'

Unseen by Clive, Rose adopted her best inscrutable expression. 'How do I distinguish between the two? I mean, if for example I discover that Pandora was black-mailing your ex-wife over a spot of extra-marital indiscretion, and that your ex-wife lured her back to the branch and whacked her over the head with a banking ledger, who do I speak to first? You or Mulligan?'

There was a pause and then an audible click as Clive Barden disconnected the call. Rose placed the phone down on the table, and turned to Lu. 'How do you know DI Mulligan?'

Lu was coy. 'A good journalist never reveals her sources. Anyway, you lied to me about your work here. You said there was nothing fraudulent going on.'

'There might not be. I'm just worried there *might* be. Anyway, you knew I wasn't giving you the whole story.'

'Of course I did. I didn't expect you to break a professional confidence just because it was me.'

Rose settled back into the sun lounger. 'How about you just get off the moral high ground, and tell me a bit more about this DI Mulligan?'

Lu laughed. 'There's not much to tell, really. He's been a DI at Kirkby for years. He looks like your favourite uncle, butter wouldn't melt, but he's as sharp as a drawer full of knives.'

'Is he honest?'

'As the day is long. And he won't like it if he thinks you're keeping things from him. He blew up at me once because I had information on a case and didn't share it with him. I suppose I was too young to know any better at the time. But he isn't vengeful. I'd let him down, but he didn't cut me off after that. He forgave and forgot very quickly.'

Rose dropped her left hand to the floor again and ruffled her fingers into Mac's coat. Mac, accustomed to being a stress-reliever for human beings, ignored her and went on dozing. Eventually she said 'DI Mulligan was due to meet with Janis round about now. I hope she's honest with him.'

'Was she honest with you?'

'Of course not. But that doesn't really matter to me, because I know when she's lying and can draw the right conclusions.' Rose turned to Lu. 'She didn't like Pandora, you know. Oh, she said all the right things, but her face always gives the game away.'

'Do you think Janis is involved somehow?   In

Pandora's disappearance?'

'Truthfully? I don't know. But I'm pretty certain that there is something more dubious going on in that bank than the making of innocent mistakes, and right now I'm beginning to wish that I'd never got involved.'

In a grubby bedsit on the outskirts of Kirkby Michael Spivey opened another bottle of Cobra beer, and poured the contents into a Guinness pint glass that had once belonged to The Feathers. He preferred Guinness as a rule, but having spent more than half of Benny's forty quid on a blow-out take-away from the new Balti on the Scarborough road, he'd decided to go the whole hog and spend the remainder of the money on several bottles of Indian beer and a half bottle of Scotch.

The take-away was lukewarm by the time he got it home, and he'd shoved everything into a dilapidated oven, with the exception of the poppadum and chutneys, which he'd enjoyed with his first beer. Pleased with himself, he surveyed the low coffee table in front of him. He'd spread out the takeaway like a banquet, cramming the foil dishes together and adding a few tarnished dessert spoons for the serving up.

The television news was on in the background and the sound of a local reporter's accent and the name "Pandora" made him look up. The girl's picture filled the screen, a vibrant image of her in a turquoise halter-necked sun dress as she enjoyed last year's family holiday in the Italian Lakes.

'Poor gel.' Spivey muttered under his breath as he took a mouthful of lamb rogan josh, and a dribble of pungent sauce dripped from his fork onto his shirt. He dabbed at it absently with a piece of kitchen roll that he was using as a napkin, his attention still on the television.

The image had changed and now he was watching Danny Mitchell, drawn and tired, woodenly reading a statement from a crib sheet. Next to Danny, Craig Bradman scowled into the camera, colour high in his pale cheeks. Spivey shook his head. What the hell did that lovely gel see in a tosser like Bradman junior? He shoveled another fork-full of curry into his mouth, more successfully this time, and thought with some resentment about his afternoon.

Two bloody hours sitting outside Mitchell's palace on the Kirkby road, while the lad was in there doing God knows what. A pointless drive to Kirkby to spend another two bloody hours sat in the car outside the television studios while they filmed this appeal for the telly, and then a second pointless drive back to Market Melbourne, following them back to Mitchell's. He'd waited in the car for another half an hour and then decided not to waste any more time. Anyway, he reasoned with himself, Benny would have forgotten all about it by tomorrow. Benny was like that. Jump through this hoop today and forget the bloody hoop even existed by tomorrow.

Another face was filling the screen now, a face he didn't recognize, and he picked up the remote control and waggled it at the television to turn up the volume. The set was slow to respond but the words "generous reward of ten thousand pounds" came through loud and clear in the reporter's flat provincial tones. Spivey whistled through what was left of his teeth. Shame he didn't know where she was. He could use ten grand.

Rose was just leaving the cottage when the sleek black Mercedes pulled up outside Lu's gate. She held back for a moment and peered unseen from the doorway to see who the driver was. Somewhere to her left Mac had jumped onto the back of an armchair in the lounge, and was barking loudly through the bay window at the parked car.

The driver's door opened and the driver got out, a tall, well-built man in a sharply cut grey suit. He put a chubby hand up to his head and ran his fingers through thick black hair, looking momentarily unsure of himself, and then closed the car door and walked up to the gate of the cottage. He could clearly hear Mac's furious barking from behind the curtains, and he paused with his hand on the gatepost, staring at the front of the house.

'Looking for someone?' Rose stepped out into the porch, pulling the front door tightly shut behind her.

'I was lookin' for Lucinda.' His voice was low, his accent more East London than East Yorkshire.

'She's not here. Can I help?' Rose tried to sound casually cheery. Whoever the visitor was, she couldn't imagine Lu being on first name terms with him.

'Are you a friend of hers?'

She walked slowly down the path towards him. 'You could say that. Are you?'

He laughed and thrust the chubby hand out across the top of the garden gate. 'Benny Bradman. Pleased to meet you.'

She took the hand and shook it. 'Rose Bennett.' She let go of his hand and regarded him with interest. 'So, are you? A friend of Lu's?'

'More of a business acquaintance, really.' He leaned on the gate post. 'Me and a friend are buyin' her cottages.' Doubt fleetingly crossed Rose's face and he picked up on it. 'Well, let's say me and a friend have offered to buy her cottages, and she's thinkin' about it.'

'So you've come round to persuade her to think a bit quicker?'

'Nah, nothin' like that. I've come round to increase our offer, actually.' He thought for a moment, and then asked 'Are you stayin' with her then, Rose?'

'In the short term.'

'Just a flyin' visit then?' He grinned. 'I don't blame you for bein' cagey. Lucinda's probably told you she's turned us down.' He bent forward and lowered his voice. 'Course, if she's tipped you the nod about how much she's holdin' out for, it would be useful to know.' His tone was playful rather than threatening.

'I hate to disappoint you, Mr Bradman, but she hasn't mentioned you at all.' Rose opened the gate and edged past him, carefully closing it behind her. She leaned on the opposite gatepost and observed him coolly. 'But your name is familiar to me. Bradman? Isn't that the name of Pandora Mitchell's boyfriend? How's the search going? Is there any news of her yet?' It was a wild guess but it hit the mark. He looked momentarily stung.

'We don't know where Pan is.' He spoke quietly. 'And my lad is goin' slowly out of his mind with worry. But life goes on, don't it?' He backed slowly towards his car, his eyes still on her face. 'I'm just a businessman, Rose. These cottages are ripe for development and we've made Lucinda a generous offer. And yes, she's turned us down. But I ain't the sort to fall at the first hurdle, if you know what I mean. If you see her, tell her we'll up our offer by twenty grand. She knows where she can find me if she wants to talk.'

The residents' lounge at The Larches was always busy in the evening, but Jean had made an early claim to a couple of armchairs and a small card table in a quiet corner. Lu's daily visits were something she looked forward to.

'Well at least your Rose has done something with her life.' Jean picked up a playing card, frowned, and discarded it. 'I just despair of Marge. Fifty six years of age, never married, no men friends. No friends, come to that. No siblings. That's my fault, I suppose. And worst of all, she doesn't seem to care. There's an inherent laziness in her that just wants to shuffle up to the branch every morning, push a few papers around, and shuffle home again. She doesn't seem to have enthusiasm for anything outside of work.'

'Except for you,' Lu corrected her, and picked up a

card for herself, considering its merits in the light of the others she held in her hand. 'And I think you paint it all a bit black, Jean. She's held down a decent job all these years. She might not be a glamour puss, but she bothers to get her hair done, she keeps herself smart, and she looks after you. Maybe she's got everything out of life that makes her happy.'

'Hearing that I wanted to stay here in The Larches didn't make her happy.'

'She was probably hurt. After all, you've been happy enough to let her look after you since you retired.' Lu looked up at her friend. 'Not that I don't understand why you want to stay here. Being more or less housebound in the bungalow would be very lonely, I can see that. She'll come round when she's had time to think about it.' Lu slipped the Jack of Spades into the fan of cards she was holding, and laid it down on the table. 'Rummy.' She glanced at the wall clock above Jean's head. 'Time for another before Marge gets here?' She shuffled the cards and began to deal without waiting for Jean to answer.

Jean picked up the cards as Lu dealt them. 'She'll probably be a bit late tonight. She called me to say they had to stay behind at work to speak to the police about Pandora Mitchell.' She lowered her voice. 'Dicky Thomas - that's him behind you - he thinks she's been kidnapped. You know, so that Danny Mitchell will have to pay ransom money to get her back.'

'Oh come on, Danny's hardly Rockefeller, is he? He's only a car dealer.' Lu glanced over her shoulder to take a look at Dicky Thomas, a distinguished-looking octogenarian in a high-backed chair who was deep in conversation with a younger, oily-haired man in a brown suit.

Jean was too enamoured of Dicky's theory to let it go. 'Well, there's no suggestion of foul play, is there? No body or anything. What other explanation could there be?'

'I really don't know. Kidnapping just seems so unlikely.'

Lu folded her cards together and leaned a little closer to Jean. She tilted her head towards the brown suit. 'What's Henry Campling doing here?'

'He's Dicky's solicitor. Probably come to get him to sign something.' Jean craned her neck to look over Lu's shoulder. Henry Campling's gaze was fixed firmly on Lu's back, his eyes boring into her shoulders. 'Still trying to buy your cottage, is he?'

'He can try till kingdom come, I'm not budging.'

They resumed their game in silence, sharing the same thoughts and not needing to verbalise them. Neither had forgotten how smitten Henry Campling had been with Lu in their youth, nor how badly he had taken her lofty dismissal of him. They both knew – as did Campling himself – that the current conflict over the cottages was just another example of Henry Campling wanting something from Lucinda Aylesbury that Lucinda Aylesbury wasn't prepared to give him.

It was a short hand, and Jean was just about to deal the cards again as Marge arrived. 'Sorry to be so late, they kept me at work longer than I expected.'

'Any news?' Jean put the cards down on the table and turned to speak to her daughter.

'No, nothing. It's going to get worse, too.' Marge dropped into an armchair next to her mother. 'We're two staff members down, and now we have to go through a process review. Janis is fizzing. Some old friend of hers has turned up with orders from Clive to poke around the branch, and she's really not happy about it.'

Lu and Jean exchanged amused glances, and Jean asked 'this old friend wouldn't be called Rosy Bennett would she?'

Marge, caught off guard, flushed slightly. 'Yes. Well, Rose Bennett.' She looked from Jean to Lu, and back again. 'Do you know her?'

'She's Lu's niece.' Jean nodded towards Lu. 'Of course, I wouldn't expect you to know every child I taught in primary school. I'll always think of her as Little Rosy Bennett. She looked like a little cherub, with all those strawberry blonde curls, and she was the most stubborn little devil I ever taught. I knew what I was up against on her first day at school. I made the mistake of trying to get her out of the dressing up box before she was ready to give it up. She threw every damned shoe in that box at me, one after another. I had the bruises for weeks.'

Marge forced a smile in Lu's direction. 'I knew you had a niece called Rose, but I didn't think … well …I mean, she didn't say anything today.' She frowned, suddenly flustered. 'Would Rose know who I am? That I'm your friend's daughter?'

Lu laughed. 'I don't know. She might have put two and two together.' She put out a hand and touched Marge's arm. 'I hope you're all prepared for her at the bank, Marge. She might have grown up and changed her name to Rose, but she's still the same stubborn little girl your mother's talking about. Once she gets her teeth into the ankle, she won't let go.'

8

It didn't take Rose much more than twenty minutes to walk through the centre of Market Melbourne and out to the new-build estate that Janis called home. The development of forty or so houses had only recently been completed, a soulless collection of mis-matched Georgian-style townhouses and mock-Tudor detached homes, all built in the same incongruous yellow brick. Rose wasn't surprised to discover that Janis lived in one of the largest houses at the end of a short cul-de-sac at the centre of the development.

Jimmy and the boys were already out by the time she arrived, and Janis had put Millie to bed early. They made small talk in the kitchen over a glass of wine while Janis prepared the supper, aimless chit-chat about holidays and the price of petrol, and how little the town had really changed since they were at school.

When the meal was ready they moved into the dining room. The food was certainly nothing fancy, as Janis had suggested, consisting mainly of bagged supermarket salad leaves and overcooked ravioli in a cloying ready-made garlic and cream sauce. The conversation was equally uninspiring. Rose tried once or twice to steer talk around to the bank, the review, to Pandora, but Janis deflected each attempt by giving brief answers and then swiftly countering with a question. Yes, she did enjoy working at the Bank. How long had Rose been freelance now? No, it wasn't a problem working for the same company as Clive. Did Rose still enjoy living in Hertfordshire? No, there wasn't any news of Pandora. Had Rose never thought of marrying Mike and settling down?

The pasta course finished, Janis topped up Rose's glass of wine and excused herself from the table. 'I just want to check on Millie, and then I'll be back with dessert.'

Left to her own devices, Rose indulged her curiosity. She took her wine over to the dining room window and took in the view. Janis's home overlooked an identical house. Built as a mirror image, it gave the impression of looking out at one's own home. Rose couldn't decide if this was a deliberate marketing ploy, designed to play on narcissistic tendencies, or just a lack of imagination on the part of the architect. All the houses in the cul-de-sac were clean and neat, low maintenance, and utterly lacking in authenticity. But they weren't cheap. Even this kind of fake affluence cost money, and on a new development it was usually borrowed money. Rose took in a deep breath and smelled the unmistakable odour of overstretched mortgages and unaffordable car loans.

She turned back to the room. It was as bland as the shop-bought ravioli. An over-sized dining suite filled the centre of the room, a modern affair of chrome and tinted glass, and a matching wall unit lined the wall opposite the window. Despite the best efforts of a couple of scented candles on the table, the room still bore the faint smell of new carpet mingled with the aroma of trade emulsion. The insipid off-white walls were bare of pictures, but the central shelves of the wall unit held framed photographs, and Rose skirted the dining table to take a better look.

The display showed the Porter family indulging in various activities. On the top shelf there were photos of Janis and Jimmy, looking tanned and happy in various European holiday locations. Jimmy was good-looking, blond and muscular, and bore an uncomfortable resemblance to Danny Mitchell. On the next shelf down, a large professional portrait of an enchanting two-year-old with wispy blonde waves took centre place. This was flanked by family snaps of the angelic Millie with her parents or her grandparents dancing in attendance. On the bottom shelf, out of eye-line, were several shots showing two teenage replicas of Clive Barden in school uniform, their humourless faces old beyond their years.

Rose leaned back and, considering the collection as a whole, found it intriguing that Janis had compartmentalised her life into three shelves – life with Jimmy, life with Jimmy and Millie, and the remnants of life with Clive consigned alone to the bottom shelf.

'Admiring the photos of Millie?' Janis had silently returned and was unloading the various components of a self-assembly supermarket dessert course from a large plastic tray.

Rose, caught off guard, concurred. 'Yes, isn't she cute? Does she get on well with Joey and Jake?'

'They adore her. Of course, it's difficult for them when they go to stay with Clive and Jennifer, because she can't go with them. It makes things bloody awkward at Christmas.' Janis sighed. 'That's the problem with broken families, isn't it? It's always a balancing act.'

'Yes, I suppose it is.' Rose tried not to think about her own broken-family balancing act, and how lately the scales had begun to tip dangerously against life with Mike in the shadow of his ex-wife and kids. She sat down at the table and helped herself to a couple of miniature profiteroles, drizzling them with microwaved chocolate sauce. Janis seemed to have relaxed a little, probably thanks to the amount of wine she'd consumed, and Rose decided on another attempt to turn the direction of the conversation. 'So how did you get on with DI Mulligan?'

Janis screwed up her face. 'OK, I suppose. He wanted to know who Pandora was friendly with, whether anything was bothering her at work, all that sort of thing. Of course there isn't anything to tell. She was friendly with everyone. The staff liked her, the customers liked her, Tommy adored her … but then he's too young to know any better.'

She helped herself to profiteroles and sauce. 'To be honest, if you don't mind I'd rather talk about something else. I've had about as much of Pandora bloody Mitchell as I can take today.' She pushed a sad-looking profiterole around her plate, squidging it into the chocolate sauce, then looked directly at Rose and said 'can we talk about this review that Clive has sent you to do?'

The problem with being small, one-eyed and slightly arthritic was that no one took you seriously. Only Mac knew that there was nothing wrong with his hearing, or with his good eye, or with his judgment of who should and who shouldn't be in his garden, especially at this time of night.

He'd been alone in the cottage for two hours when he heard the noise outside that alerted him. He had no vantage point downstairs at the rear of the house from which to see what was going on. There were French windows in the dining room, and although he could see out into the garden the view was so low that all he could make out were pots and plants and the legs of the patio furniture. He tried the kitchen but knew his own limitations – he was just too short-legged to be able to jump up onto the kitchen counter and look out of the window over the sink.

He galloped upstairs, nosed open the door into the guest room at the rear of the house, and jumped up on to the bed. The bed was too far away from the window for him to be able to see out, and he padded back and forth in frustration. It would have to be the chair, the padded winged armchair that Lu had found in a junk shop and re-covered in an expensive old-rose print to match the rest of the room. He wasn't allowed to climb on it, but then Lu wasn't here to see him. He launched himself from the bed on to the seat and scrambled up the arm rest and onto the chair back, balancing precariously. It was still quite light and his one good eye could just make out a human shape moving about in what had been Frank's garden. He barked fit to burst, and the shape looked up at the window then glanced around anxiously in case the noise had alerted someone in the house.

But there was no-one around to hear Mac's appeal. After a few minutes, the shape went back to work. Mac barked for a full fifteen minutes until the shape, its task completed, gathered up its tools and faded down the garden and away into the falling dusk.

Thwarted, the dog carefully made his way down off the chair, and back down the stairs to inspect the lower part of the house. He checked each room in turn, and snuffled at the bottom of the back door for a minute or two. Completely alone again, there was nothing to do but curl up in his basket in the lounge and wait for someone to come home.

'Well, it's alright for bloody Clive, isn't it? He's not in the front line, trying to meet impossible sales targets.' Janis folded her arms defensively across her chest, and looked away from Rose to stare at a blank wall. Her right hand still grasped her wine glass, and the smooth red liquid inside quivered, betraying her trembling annoyance at Rose's explanation.

'It really isn't a big deal, Janis, I don't know why you're getting so worked up about it.'

Janis snorted into her glass, then turned wounded eyes to Rose. 'Don't you? No, I don't suppose you would. But then, all your job consists of is swanning round other people's banks, telling them they're not doing their job properly. All you bloody governance people are the same.' She snorted into her glass again and took a generous gulp of wine, almost emptying the glass. 'Do you know what life on the front line of retail banking at the ENB is like, Rose? Shall I tell you? It's all about mixed messages. I've got the regional manager on my case, phoning me on a daily basis to bitch about my branch not meeting its sales targets, and telling me to do anything I bloody well can to get some new business in. And on the other hand,' she waved the glass in Rose's direction, dangerously slopping the last inch or so of wine around, 'I've got bloody Clive sending you in to poke around my sales processes in case we're not writing the business properly.'

'No one is suggesting that you're not doing things properly. I've already tried to explain ...'

'Oh, sod your bloody explanations. I don't believe a sodding word of it, Rose.'

'Jan ...'

'No. No, you've had your say, now you can bloody well listen to me. Do you know how we're targeted, Rose? Of course you do. We're targeted on how much we sell. Not how we sell it. As long as Head Office ties performance to sales figures, branch staff will do anything they can to sell. However they can sell it. If they want us to be careful with process, they should start targeting us on accuracy and conformance to regulations, not on sales figures.' Rose opened her mouth to speak, but Janis hadn't finished. 'And another thing ... they *know* Rose, they bloody know that we take risks with account opening. They turn a blind eye to it all the time, as long as the business is coming in. They turn a blind eye, because our targets are their targets. If we don't meet our targets, they don't meet theirs. If we don't earn a bonus, they don't earn a bonus. Do you know when they send people like you along? When it looks like they might be found out. When they think the Regulators might come sniffing round. When they think there'll be bad publicity, or a police investigation, or - God forbid - another bloody fine from the Regulator.'

Rose sighed. 'I'm sorry you feel like that. I can see it can't be easy.'

'Easy? I don't ask for "easy". Just "adequate" would do for me. Do you know why we don't have electronic screening for our customers? Do you know why the ENB hasn't, like all the other banks, invested in a system that would go off and check in seconds whether a customer is on the electoral role, or the post office address file, or that the driving licence is genuine and not a fake?'

'Because they can't afford it?'

'Exactly.' Janis raised her empty glass in a triumphant gesture. 'But not for the reasons you mean. It isn't that they can't afford the capital outlay on implementing it. It's because the capital outlay would be minimal compared with the loss of business. It would mean turning customers away.'

'But it would mean a reduction in fraud. The bank's losses would be reduced if they identified fraudulent applicants.'

'Well yes, if you assume ...' Janis paused, and Rose saw the unmistakable flicker of realisation on her face, realisation that she was about to say too much. Janis reached out for the wine bottle, topped up Rose's glass, and emptied the rest of the bottle into her own. For a moment she sat staring at the glass, avoiding Rose's gaze, and then calmly said 'no, of course. You're absolutely right. Of course losses would be reduced.' She sighed. 'Hell, Rose, I'm sorry. I didn't mean to spoil the evening. It's just been a shit day, and I've had too much wine, and ...well, you know how it is.' She forced a smile. 'Can you forget what I've just said, and enjoy a coffee before you go?'

Rose nodded in understanding. 'Let's forget about work and talk about something else. And I'd love a coffee. Milky with plenty of sugar, please.'

Momentarily alone again, Rose stared into her wine glass and contemplated Janis's angry outburst. Oh I know how it is, she thought. I know now why Clive sent me rather than anyone else. I know there's a lot more bothering you than Pandora's disappearance. And I know you're hiding something. But as for forgetting what you've just said … I don't think there's much chance of that.

'How the hell am I going to explain this to Rose?' Lu had lost her customary composure, and was leaning shakily on Dave Gilling's arm for support. 'I don't want her to see it. Can't we get rid of it?'

Gilling shook his head and gently said 'no, I think she'll have to know. Are you absolutely certain you don't know of anyone local who has a grudge against her?'

'She's only been back here for twenty four hours. All she's done is have supper here with me last night, and go into the ENB branch today to attend some meetings. She doesn't really know anybody round here now, except for Janis Porter, and she's with Janis now, having supper at her place.' At her feet, Mac began to snuffle at a mound of earth, and Lu snapped at him. 'Leave it, Mac. For God's sake, come away from it.' She bent down and scooped him up from the ground, tucking him safely under her right arm, and brushing his muddy paws to remove the dirt.

Gilling put an arm round her shoulders. 'Tell you what, why don't you go in and make us a brew? I'll radio in to the station and tell Bob I'm going to stay with you until Rose gets back?'

Lu nodded, and retreated from Frank's back garden back towards her own cottage, taking Mac with her. Gilling took his radio from his jacket pocket. 'Bob, are you there? I'm at Lu's now.'

Bob Shepherd responded in his usual laconic tone. 'What's the problem?'

'Dunno, really. A nasty piece of spite by the look of it. Lu's badly shaken up. I'm going to stay around until her niece gets back. Give me a call if you need me?'

'OK. Is it criminal damage?'

'It's criminal something, but I'm not sure what.' Gilling switched his torch back on and shone it at the ground, lighting up the mound of earth. In the middle of the garden, where Frank had latterly grown his first early potatoes, someone had dug over the ground, pulling the loose soil up into the unmistakable shape of a crude grave. At the head of the mound a small bunch of yellow petrol-station chrysanthemums, still in their cellophane wrapping, leaned against a make-shift cross fashioned out of two pieces of thin plywood. Gilling lifted up his torch and shone it on the cross. 'What do you make of this, Bob? Someone's dug a grave in old Frank's garden. They've laid flowers on it and there's a wooden cross at the end, with writing on.'

'What does it say?'

'That's the really spiteful bit. It says "RIP Little Nosy Bennett."'

9

Rose woke early on Thursday morning, roused by the sound of Mac barking loudly in the room below. She stretched out a hand to the bedside table and fumbled for her watch. It was only six thirty. She lay back on the pillows and closed her eyes, folding a sleepy arm over her head.

The previous day began to replay in her head. The grave, Pandora's disappearance, Lu's cottages, Benny Bradman, Janis's angry outburst ... how did it all fit together? Did it fit together at all? Oh come on Rose, she thought, get a grip. You're here to look into some process errors, that's all. Janis is angry with her ex-husband. Lu is dealing with a couple of dodgy property developers. Pandora probably had a row with her boyfriend. It's co-incidence, that's all. Co-incidence and bad timing.

The guest room in Lu's cottage was directly over the kitchen, and she heard the outer door from the kitchen to the garden open and close. The short disappointed bark that followed indicated that Mac had been left alone on the inside. What the hell was Lu up to now? Was it something to do with that damned grave?

Out of bed, she leaned on the armchair by the window and pulled one curtain aside, letting a shaft of morning sunlight into the room. Peering out she could see Lu disappearing into Frank's garden with a spade and a soil rake, a black bin bag tucked under her arm. Off to destroy the evidence, then. She sighed, and let the curtain drop.

She'd offered to do the job herself, to save Lu from any more distress, but Lu had refused, and Rose knew it was pointless trying to argue with her. They were both cast in the same mould, but the cynicism and stubbornness that characterized them was amplified in Lu. She was best left to get on with it.

Rose consoled herself with a long hot shower before daring to venture downstairs in search of breakfast. By the time she reached the kitchen, Lu was back indoors and making scrambled eggs with a bad humour. Mac at least was welcoming, and he trotted over to sniff around her feet before scuttling off into the lounge out of Lu's way.

'Can I do anything to help?' Rose knew the answer was likely to be no, but she asked the question anyway.

'You could go home to Hertfordshire. I really don't think you should stay here now, do you?'

Rose sat down at the kitchen table and helped herself to coffee. 'Of course I should. Apart from anything else, I'm not going to bale out and leave you to deal with a couple of property vultures on your own.'

'It's nothing to do with the property. I told you that last night.' Lu clattered two plates of over-cooked scrambled egg on to the table, and flopped down on the chair opposite her niece. She was still rattled, and it showed in angry red blotches on her chiseled cheeks. 'The cottages are nothing to do with you. If it was Bradman and Campling why would they put your name on a makeshift grave?'

'Maybe I just upset your friend Mr. Bradman by asking him about his son and Pandora.'

'Did you tell him your name was Rosy?'

'No. I think I introduced myself as Rose.'

'Couldn't be him, then, could it?'

'Why not? He certainly didn't appreciate my line of questioning. Easy enough for the word "nosy" to cross his mind. Maybe he likes a bit of rhyming slang. They go in for that in the East End, don't they?'

Unconvinced, Lu shrugged. 'I suppose so.' She took a slice of cold toast from the rack and set about buttering it. 'They've never threatened me, you know. Benny Bradman has been round here a couple of times before. He made the initial approach actually, came here to the cottage and made a very generous offer in person. But I don't want to move. I like living here, especially now I've got Frank's cottage, and I don't see why I should give up my home just to line their pockets.' She wrinkled her nose, and some of the tension eased from her face. 'To be honest, I quite like him. In fact,' her face became almost mischievous, 'if I was twenty years younger ...'

'He looks like a cheap gangster.'

'I know, isn't he fun?' Lu smiled, her good humour returning. 'It's all show, though. I don't think he's the type to threaten somebody in that awful way.' She poured herself coffee, and took a sip. 'The thing is, I can't think of anybody who would. It would have to be someone who knew you as Rosy Bennett.' She looked up at Rose. 'I suppose if it was to do with the bank, rather than the cottage, it could have been Marge.'

'Marge? Marge at the ENB?'

'Yes, Marge Baker. You know she's Jean Baker's daughter?'

'No, I didn't.' Rose was intrigued. 'And if Marge knew that her mother used to teach me at primary school, she certainly didn't let on.' She stifled a laugh. 'Oh come on, a middle-aged assistant bank manager moonlighting as a grave digger? And why would she want to threaten me?'

'She was at The Larches last night when I went to visit Jean.' Lu frowned. 'She was quite lost for words when Jean told her you were my niece. Maybe she doesn't like you poking around at the bank.'

'Then she only has to say so. She doesn't have to dig up the back garden.'

'She was there when Jean and I were talking about you. She heard Jean call you Rosy. Jean said she still thinks of you as Little Rosy Bennett.'

It wasn't a suggestion that Rose could take seriously, and she gave up trying to suppress her laughter. 'Tell you what, when I get into the branch this morning I'll take a look at Marge's fingernails. If she's got mud under them, I'll buy you lunch every day for the rest of the week.'

The investigation into Pandora's disappearance was going too slowly for Dave Gilling. He felt a father's distress at the disappearance of the teenage girl, although she was older than his own girls by some three or four years, and at least once during the night he had woken from disturbed sleep and felt the need to check that both girls were in their beds. He knew the fear was irrational, even in his sleeplessness at three in the morning, but he couldn't quell it.

There were too many things about this business that he didn't like. Talking to the girl's parents was up there at the top of the list. Seeing the hope flickering in Selina Mitchell's eyes when he entered the room, feeling her desperate gaze on him as he cleared his throat and tried to speak, watching the eager anticipation on her face dissipate as he told her he had no news. That he'd come to ask for information, not give it.

He hated invading their privacy, too, snooping into their affairs, trespassing on their grief. He knew it was necessary, but that didn't make it easier, nor did the calm and cooperative way in which they responded to his requests. Pandora's bank details, her mobile phone account, permission to search the house, they had provided everything asked of them without a murmur of complaint. He'd explained that these were all just routine requests, that there was no suggestion of foul play or of any involvement by the family, all the normal platitudes designed to reassure the grieving family. They appeared to think the explanations unnecessary, just nodding and accepting his words at face value. There was something unnerving about their acquiescence, their refusal to take offence at his requests, their repressed emotions. Maybe he should mention it now, to George Mulligan.

'Alright Dave? Where are we up to?' Mulligan, just arrived at the Market Melbourne station, took off his jacket to reveal a crumpled shirt and tie. He hung the jacket it on the back of his chair before sitting down opposite Gilling and rolling up his wrinkled shirt sleeves. 'Have we had any more sightings?'

'No, nothing new has come in overnight. She's been missing for about thirty-six hours now. I called in to see the Mitchells again last night, and they've heard nothing either. There's been no response to the televised appeal, apart from a few cranks trying to claim the cash prize.'

Mulligan screwed up his face. 'Can you get onto Danny Mitchell this morning for me, and ask him to stay away from the press until we've had a chance to talk? Don't piss him off, tell him I'm happy with what's been put out so far, but we ought to agree a media strategy that works in line with the investigation. This reward he's offered is going to muddy the water – it's too early to bring in any useful information.'

'Are you genuinely happy with the media coverage, or is that just for his benefit?'

Mulligan considered the question. 'Well, it's got Pandora's name and face into the public eye. The local TV stuff has been useful for that, and showing her at the Great North Run last year was a bonus, given that she was dressed in exactly the same outfit when she disappeared. What we don't want is lurid speculation. At least one of the nationals has got onto it, looking at this morning's papers. I don't want them using Pandora to invent sensationalist fiction just to boost their circulation figures.' He leaned back in his seat. 'How are the Mitchells coping?'

'OK, all things considered. They're not easy people to

read.' Gilling gave a shrug. 'I suppose people cope in different ways. Danny seems to be bearing up reasonably well, but Selina's losing it a bit. The doctor's given her something to keep her calm.' He referred to the paperwork on the table in front of him. 'They've given permission for her bedroom to be searched, I'll arrange for that today. And they've given me some more photographs.' He ticked the items off his list as he went. 'They've confirmed that they've contacted every friend or relative who might know something, and drawn a blank. And we've checked all the local hospitals and other police stations in the area.'

'Nothing turned up as a result of the PNC posting?'

Gilling paused and then shook his head, deciding not to confess that he'd forgotten to update the Police National Computer until first thing that morning. 'I've notified all the usual missing persons agencies as well, nothing back from them.'

Mulligan scratched at his ear. 'Was the boyfriend there last night?'

'No, he'd already gone home.'

'You made a note in your initial report that the boyfriend - Craig, is it? - that Craig claimed she was concerned about something at work.' Mulligan helped himself to Gilling's dog-eared copy of the report, flicking through it until he found the page he wanted. 'She called Craig in the afternoon and said something about an argument at work, and that she needed to speak to him about it that evening.' He looked up at his colleague. 'Do we know what that was about?'

Gilling shook his head. 'Sorry George, I didn't follow it up. I asked Danny Mitchell last night if he knew what it was about, but he told me that it was probably nothing. He said if Pandora wanted to talk about work, she would have gone to him or Selina first.'

Mulligan tutted. 'A teenage girl talk to her parents before she talks to her boyfriend? I thought you had teenage daughters yourself, Dave?' He dropped Gilling's report on to the desk. 'Does Danny think he's lying?'

'He didn't give that impression. He didn't seem to think it was important at all. Do you want me to follow it up?'

'No, I'll do it. I need to have a chat with young Craig, this'll give me a good excuse. For today, can you push things forward with the search? I've put a request in at Kirkby for a managed search team. We need to get some dogs out to cover the lanes that have already been searched unofficially. Can you liaise with the Kirkby team? And see if you can rustle up some of the locals to do an unofficial search of a wider area while that's going on, maybe a mile or two further out than we've already looked at. There's still the possibility that she ran further out of town than we originally thought.'

'Do you want me to go back to the Mitchells?'

'No, I'll do that later today.' Mulligan noted the relief on Gilling's face at this news. 'And I'll tackle Craig Bradman about this problem at work.' He tapped on the desk. 'And talking of work, I've got a meeting lined up this morning with someone who might be able to help us.' He slid a hand down into his jacket pocket and fished out his notebook. 'The ENB have an independent consultant in there at the moment who's agreed to be my eyes and ears for the next couple of days.' He leafed impatiently through the pages of his notebook. 'It's a bit of luck, really, her not being a bank employee. No misplaced loyalties to deal with.' He found the page he was looking for. 'Her name's Rose Bennett.'

Dave Gilling straightened in his chair. 'Lu Aylesbury's niece?'

It was Mulligan's turn to pay attention. 'Is she indeed? Well let's hope she's as smart as her aunt, then. Have you met her?'

'Yes, I met her last night. I knew she was doing some work for the bank, but I never thought ...' Gilling chewed on the end of his pen. 'It wasn't exactly a social introduction. I'd better tell you about it before you go.'

'Well, it's good to see that we're all here for this morning's huddle. That makes a change.' Janis fixed Tommy with a disapproving stare.

On the receiving end of the barb, Tommy felt his pulse quicken and his face start to grow hot. Was she going to start with him today? He turned to look at Hazel, hoping to see a supportive smile, but Hazel was busy picking at a loose fingernail. He wondered if she was deliberately avoiding his gaze.

Across the table, Janis had pulled out her desk diary and started to scribble. She spoke again without looking up. 'Hazel, would you like to start us off this morning?'

Hazel flinched, and swore under her breath as the offending fingernail snapped away from the strand of cuticle holding it in place. She looked up. 'Ouch, that was sore.' She rubbed at her finger to ease the pain and forced a smile in Janis's direction, but Janis remained stony faced. 'Well,' she began, 'I can't say yesterday was a brilliant day. Mrs. Henderson was in again, but I've given up with her now. She keeps failing the affordability checks on personal loans. Marge took her off my hands, so hopefully that will be the last time she comes in wasting our time.'

Marge, at the other side of the table, gave an inscrutable smile.

Hazel took in a deep breath. 'Apart from that, it was pretty slim pickings. We were disrupted because of the Pandora thing, of course, and I had to spend time with Rose Bennett. But,' her voice took on a more positive note, 'I did find time to do some prospecting in the afternoon. I've made a list of standard current account holders who might be interested in moving to a premium current account, and I've already called five of them to invite them in to the branch to talk about it. Two of them have made appointments for next week, the other three are thinking about it.' She paused, and then added 'and of course I'll be making more calls today to invite other customers in.'

Janis frowned, and gave a sigh. 'Better than nothing, I suppose.' She turned to Marge. 'Cheer me up, Marge. Tell me that Mrs. Henderson wasn't a complete waste of time after all. Did you manage to sell her anything, or have we lost all hope?'

'Oh you know me, Janis. I enjoy a challenge.' The older woman's cheeks dimpled into a self-satisfied smile. 'I'm pleased to say that we'll be able to give Mrs. Henderson an eight thousand pound loan for some home improvements. In addition, she's taking critical illness cover and income protection for herself and Mr. Henderson, and as she happened to mention that her son Peter is celebrating his eighteenth birthday at the weekend I took the opportunity to suggest a credit card application for him now that he's old enough.' She folded her hands into her lap. 'Mrs. Henderson agreed it would be useful for the household to have access to some extra credit. Just for emergencies, of course.' She turned to Hazel. 'I hope you don't mind me stealing your thunder Hazel, but you did ask me to take her off your hands.'

All eyes turned to Hazel. 'But I couldn't get the system to accept her loan application.' Stunned by Marge's success, she turned to Janis. 'I don't know what I did wrong. It wouldn't even give her two thousand when I tried it, never mind eight.'

Janis didn't respond, but Marge put out a plump hand and laid it on Hazel's arm. 'I'm sure you didn't do anything wrong Hazel, that loan system can be very temperamental. I think I've just learned to persevere until it sees sense and approves the application.'

Hazel opened her mouth to speak, but Janis put up a hand to stop her. 'I'm sure you and Marge can chat about this after the huddle. We only have a few minutes left, and we haven't heard from Tommy yet.' She looked across at him. 'And how did you get on yesterday?'

Tommy's body stiffened with renewed anxiety. 'Not very well.' The words came out almost as a whisper. He coughed to clear his throat. 'I couldn't concentrate. I kept thinking about Pandora.'

Janis closed her eyes and licked her lips. 'Pandora's disappearance is no excuse to avoid doing your job, Tommy. Did you make any sales at all yesterday?'

'No.' He couldn't look at her.

'Did you attempt any sales?'

'No.'

'Did you undertake any prospecting activity?'

Why was she asking him? She already knew the answer. 'No, I didn't.' He felt a stinging at the back of his eyes, and he blinked hard to make it go away. 'But Hazel didn't sell anything either.'

Janis took in a sharp hiss of breath. 'We're not talking about Hazel, we're talking about you. I can't remember the last time you actually sold anything, Tommy. I can't remember the last time you were anywhere near making your sales target. You seem to forget that you are part of a team. We have a branch target to achieve. You cannot go on relying on your colleagues to carry you.' She clicked her tongue. 'Do you realize, Tommy, that you are in danger of being demoted? That if things don't improve, your pay scale may be revised downwards?'

Did he realize? Of course he realized. He wasn't an idiot. He knew he was a whisker away from a pay cut, from disciplinary action, probably even from losing his job altogether. He turned to look at Hazel, and was relieved to see a sympathetic smile. He turned back to his manager. 'I'll do better today, Janis. Maybe Hazel could give me a hand with some prospecting?'

Janis sighed. 'Well, it's not ideal, but I suppose it will have to do.' She pulled a loose sheet of paper out from the back of her diary. 'Next month, there will be a special sales drive on a new product for the bank. The ENB are introducing a new investment product designed for the elderly.' She ran a finger along the paper, seeking out the relevant details. 'It's a funeral plan, available for the over fifties. Three levels of benefit … bronze, silver and gold … and each one sold will earn you between eight and twelve hundred commission points depending on the details of the sale.' She looked up at her team. 'Market Melbourne has a mature population, there should be good sales potential for this one. I suggest you all start thinking about prospects today, and we can discuss your ideas at tomorrow morning's huddle.' She paused, and then turned her gaze to Tommy. 'I'd like you to be the branch's main point of contact for this product, Tommy, and I'll be looking for you to identify a significant customer base. You can start a list of target customers this afternoon, twenty sounds about right to be going on with. Have it ready for tomorrow morning's huddle.'

Twenty names? Of old people? Tommy's stomach lurched. 'But Janis, I don't know any old people. Can't Marge do it?'

Janis rolled her eyes in exasperation and brought them to rest on Tommy's face. 'Oh for goodness sake, use some initiative for once. You've got grandparents, haven't you?'

'Cancelled? Are you sure?' Lu perched on the arm of the sofa with the phone against her ear. 'But I thought Marge was desperate to get the work done?'

'Nope. Definitely cancelled.' At the other end of the line, the builder's voice crackled with irritation. 'She called me this morning, just after eight. She's sorry for the inconvenience, she says, but they don't need the work doing now because her mother's not coming back to live there.'

'But that's marvelous news. Jean was only telling me yesterday that she wants to stay in The Larches. It sounds like Marge has agreed after all.' She hesitated, realizing her lack of tact. 'Of course, that's not necessarily good news for you. Sorry, Geoff, I didn't think. Well, I know it's a lost contract for you, but I'm more than happy for you to reschedule the work you're doing for me. Next week will be fine for you to start knocking the doors through. I've got my niece staying with me at the moment, and she's going to help me clear the place out. I'm sure we can get it done by Monday.'

'Thanks Lu, I appreciate that. See you next week, then.'

The call disconnected, Lu began to dial the number for The Larches, and then decided against it. She'd be seeing Jean at lunchtime anyway. She went out into the hall and called upstairs to Rose. 'I'm off into Kirkby to do some shopping, and then I'm going to The Larches to see Jean. I'll take Mac with me.' Without waiting for an answer she whistled for the dog. 'Coming for a ride in the car, Mac?' Mac appeared from the kitchen, tail wagging, and she swept him up with one hand, tucking him securely under her arm. 'Let's get out of Rose's way. We don't want to cramp her style in front of Mr. Mulligan, do we?'

10

'You've just missed Lu, I'm afraid. She's popped out to do some errands. I think she thought that she ought to leave us in peace.' Rose led DI Mulligan through into the lounge.

'That's a shame.' The policeman sounded disappointed. 'She's told you we're acquainted, then?'

'Oh yes, I've heard all about you. Just the good bits, of course.' She smiled impishly, and gestured towards an armchair. 'Take a seat. Can I get you a tea or coffee?'

'Neither for me, thanks. I've had four teas this morning already, and at two spoons of sugar a go I think my doctor would have something to say about it.' He patted a paunchy stomach, making the folds of flesh quiver under his crumpled shirt.

'You should try fennel, it's good for the digestion.' Rose sat down on the sofa, and picked up her half-finished drink from the coffee table. 'I suppose the taste takes some getting used to, though.'

They sat in silence for a moment, each observing the other, each trying to size up the other without looking too obvious. DI Mulligan was just as Lu had described him, homely and avuncular, and as far removed from a policeman as Rose could imagine. Easy to fall into the confidence of such a man, if you weren't careful.

It was Mulligan, his own inspection of Rose complete, who broke the silence. 'It's good of you to meet with me, Rose. We could do with a bit of help on this case, and that's a fact. I take it you're familiar with the details of

Pandora's disappearance so far?'

'Out running, didn't come home, not been seen since Tuesday night. No word from her since, family worried sick, I should think?'

'That about sums it up. Have you ever met the girl?'

'No. I knew her father a long time ago, around the time I left school. I haven't spoken to him for the best part of twenty years.'

Mulligan nodded in a way which suggested he already knew all about Rose, and Danny, and Janis. 'She's a nice girl, by all accounts. I had a chat with some of her bank colleagues yesterday afternoon. They all speak very highly of her.' He frowned. 'I understand from Clive Barden that you're investigating some mistakes that were made at the branch here? Was Pandora going to be part of your investigation?'

'Yes, but not specifically. I'll be speaking to all the staff while I'm here.'

His eyes narrowed, and a hairline crack appeared in the benign veneer. 'Clive said something about fake ID documents.'

Rose met his gaze with inscrutability. 'Did he? Then you know more than I do, Mr. Mulligan.' He may have been bluffing but she wasn't going to take any risks. She paused and smiled, and chose her words carefully. 'I've been briefed by Clive that a number of accounts have been opened incorrectly at the Market Melbourne branch, using invalid ID. This suggests that staff are becoming careless. I'm not aware that any of the ID presented was fake.'

'Isn't that the same thing? Fake, invalid, what difference does it make?'

'Quite a lot, actually.' She settled back into her seat. 'Fake implies that the ID documents are forgeries. Invalid implies that they are genuine documents, but invalid for the particular applicant.'

'Meaning?'

'There are two elements to identifying a new customer.

Firstly, you have to assure yourself that the person named in the application form exists, and so you ask for genuine identification documents and check them for authenticity. Secondly, you have to be certain that the person in front of you is definitely the person to whom the documents relate. If there is any doubt about this, we would say the documentation was invalid, even though it is a genuine document. To give you an extreme example, if Lu tried to open an account using my old non-photo driving licence and my latest credit card bill, both documents would be authentic, and prove that Rose Bennett exists, but a decent bank clerk checking the ID documents would spot that the date of birth on the driving licence wouldn't be right for someone of Lu's age. The implication there would be that Lu was trying to fraudulently open an account in my name.'

Mulligan was interested. 'So the staff here at Market Melbourne haven't been checking ID documents properly?'

'That's the implication. I've been asked to go through the account opening process with all the staff here. If they make mistakes during the review, I'll report all the mistakes made back to Clive, and recommend that staff be re-trained in the process, and that stronger internal conformance checks are put in place to ensure that the problem doesn't happen again.'

'And if they don't make mistakes?'

Rose grinned. 'If they don't make mistakes, it opens up the possibility that the clerk or clerks who accepted the invalid ID *may* have been colluding with the applicant to open the account fraudulently. That they knew the documents were invalid, but still accepted them.'

'What happens then?'

'I'll tell Clive that I think he has a problem that needs official investigation, and Clive will contact the appropriate authorities. It usually means a police investigation. I don't get involved in that side of things, because I need to stay anonymous to do this kind of work.'

'So basically you're the scouting party. You go in to the branch, sniff around, and if something stinks you tell Clive?'

'That's about it.'

'And Pandora may have been involved in these account openings?'

'I don't know.'

Mulligan looked doubtful. 'You don't know? Surely Clive briefed you on who opened the accounts before you went into the branch?'

'No, I usually work blind on this sort of thing. More regulations. It's an offence to tip off a criminal, isn't it? If I don't know who made the mistakes, there is no danger of my accidentally tipping them off that we're on to them. Always supposing that a crime has been committed, which at the moment we don't know.'

Bemused, Mulligan gave a deep sigh and scratched at his ear. 'It all sounds dubious to me, Rose. A crime may or may not have been committed, Pandora may or may not have been involved, the police may or may not be invited to look into the matter. Am I missing something?'

She laughed. 'No, that's pretty much how it is. Can you see the other aspects to the problem? We can't just come out and accuse someone of a crime when they may have made a genuine mistake. And if it is a genuine mistake, the police have no place in what is essentially internal bank business. The staff members involved will be retrained, and the applicants who presented invalid documents will be asked to come back to the branch and provide further identification. If they refuse, or if other suspicious activity starts on these accounts, then Clive will have to inform the police, because he's bound by regulations to notify you if a crime is suspected. But at this stage, there is no evidence of suspicious activity.'

'And what would you call suspicious?'

'Evidence of laundering, large and irregular deposits to

the account, patterns of behaviour outside of the norm such as money suddenly being transferred abroad on a regular basis, that sort of thing.' She paused while he thought about it, and then said 'I've been given no evidence that Pandora was definitely involved in this, if that's what you're thinking. She wasn't even qualified to open current accounts on her own until a few days ago.' Rose paused, considering whether to share more, and decided against it.

The policeman just grunted. 'Fair enough. Shall we talk about what I need you to help me with, then?' He rubbed again at his ear. 'You've been put into the branch by Clive to listen and watch and sniff out whether or not anything dodgy is going on there. I'd appreciate if you could try to do the same for me, with respect to Pandora. Now I'm not saying her disappearance has anything to do with your work on these accounts, but it may be that one or more of her colleagues might be able to help us.'

'I thought you'd already spoken to them?'

'Yes, I have, and I'll speak to them again in due course. But alongside of that, I'd be grateful if you could keep your eyes and ears open. You see Rose, people are sometimes unnecessarily frightened of talking to the police. They might be afraid to tell us what they know for all manner of reasons. It seems to me that we're in the same boat – you don't know if a financial crime has been committed, and we don't know yet if Pandora's disappearance is the result of a crime, or just an accident. We have no body, no clues, no evidence of a crime at all.'

'But you think it's suspicious?'

'The official line is that we're keeping an open mind. Some people choose to go missing, and don't want to be found. Not many go missing in the middle of a training run, without a mobile phone or means of accessing money. Unofficially we have to assume the worst. If we don't explore every avenue and it turns out that someone has harmed her, well I'd never be able to forgive myself.'

Rose thought about Pandora, and how unlikely it was that she would want to leave a happy and comfortable family home and a boyfriend she evidently cared for. DI Mulligan was right to be concerned. 'So what do you want me to look out for?'

'There are a few things I need to check out. Was anything bothering her at work? Are any of her colleagues aware that something was troubling her outside of work? How did she get on with the other branch staff? Was she particularly friendly with anyone? I've already asked her colleagues these questions, and I'll be asking again over the next day or two. But I'm a policeman. They may not be as open with me as they would be with you. And you'll hear the gossip that goes on behind the scenes. You might pick up on something that we couldn't possibly hope to hear about.'

Rose smiled. 'I can do that for you, keep my eyes and ears open. Anything else?'

'There are a couple of things I should mention which it might be worth keeping in the back of your mind, although you may know them already. Pandora has a boyfriend, Craig Bradman. His father is Benny Bradman, the local bookie.'

'Yes, I saw Craig on TV last night, when Danny did the appeal.'

Mulligan put a hand up to his face and rubbed thoughtfully at his chin. 'We understand that she was quite friendly with her colleague Tommy Fletcher at the bank. He on the other hand is not too friendly with young Mr. Bradman. It would be useful to hear Tommy's side of things.'

Rose answered with an inscrutable nod. 'Anything else?'

'Should there be?'

Her smile was guileless. 'No, I just wanted to make sure I have all the facts.'

'Well,' Mulligan glanced at his watch, 'I'd better make

tracks. I'm due to see young Craig at eleven. And I know you need to get into the branch to start your review work.' Mulligan pushed himself out of the armchair and picked up his jacket. 'Thanks for your time, Rose. It's much appreciated.' As they walked down the hall towards the front door, he asked 'do you know Clive Barden well?'

'Well enough to know that Clive's primary interest is Clive.'

Mulligan laughed. 'You've got you aunt's cynicism, I see.' He opened the door, and turned to stare at Rose. He was serious now. 'Dave Gilling told me about that business with the grave last night. Aren't you worried about that? I thought you might have mentioned it to me.'

For a brief moment, Rose dropped her guard. 'Of course I'm worried, but only for Lu. There are people who'd like to see her move on from here, but she doesn't want to go. I think I know who was responsible for that, and it's got nothing to do with Pandora and the bank.'

The air in Campling's office was as stale as ever. Benny Bradman opened the sash window, lifting the lower pane as high as it would go, and leaned against the frame, as close to fresh air as he could get in the first floor room. He had plenty of vices himself, but smoking wasn't one of them, and he'd never been able to understand its attraction. At least Campling didn't smoke when he had clients with him. He was musing on the solicitor's need for such an addiction when Campling, seated at the desk behind him, stopped jotting figures on to a piece of paper and turned to face him. The nicotine-stained leather chair squealed as it swiveled, and Benny winced at the noise. 'Blimey Henry, have you never heard of WD40?'

Campling ignored the question. He balanced the single sheet of white A4 on his thigh, and rested his hand on it. 'So you didn't manage to speak to Lucinda Aylesbury last night?'

'Nah, she was out when I got there. I spoke to some friend of hers, Rose she said her name was.'

Campling's eyes darkened. 'Rose Bennett?'

'Yeah, that's the one. Know her, do you?'

'Not personally, no. She's Lucinda's niece.'

Benny raised an eyebrow. 'Family, eh? I didn't know that.' And that, he thought, would explain why she was protective. 'I got the impression that old Lu ain't thinkin' of goin' anywhere soon. I told Rose to let her know we'd up the offer by twenty grand, but I ain't holdin' me breath.' He sniffed. 'Henry, I ain't a quitter but I think we've played this one long enough. I reckon we should let it go. Leave the old bird in her cottage, and find another plot to develop.'

'Out of the question.' Campling's retort was sharper than he had intended. He coughed, clearing his throat, and spoke in a more reasonable tone. 'We've invested a considerable amount of time and effort in this proposal, and the numbers stack up.'

Benny leaned down and grinned into Campling's oily face. 'You're lettin' this get to you, Henry. Is it personal? Not prepared to be beaten by a little old lady?' He chortled to himself. 'Not that there's much of the little old lady about old Lucinda. I'll bet she was a looker when she was younger, eh? Was she?'

The tart expression on Campling's face was enough to confirm the suspicion. 'I have known Lucinda Aylesbury for many years. She's always been difficult.'

Benny's grin broadened. 'Blimey, it *is* personal. You sly old dog, Henry. What would Mrs. Camplin' think?'

The solicitor refused to be riled. 'The site is still good for our original plans.' He handed the piece of paper to Benny. 'I asked our surveyor to take a look when Lucinda was out yesterday. He has confirmed that if the cottages are demolished, we should be able to fit in two rows of two-storey terraced houses, with five in each block.'

Benny cut in. 'Five? That's too many. We said four.

We'd never get access to all the properties if we built that big.'

'I wasn't proposing to decrease the access. If we shave the room sizes …'

'Oh be reasonable, Henry. There ain't anythin' to shave. These things will be rabbit hutches as it is.'

'It would significantly increase the profit.'

'It might do, but I ain't in the habit of sellin' shoe boxes. We agreed these would be starter homes for families, it ain't reasonable to cut down the room sizes that much.' Benny glanced down at the piece of paper. 'It's all a moot point, anyway. Lucinda ain't goin' to budge.'

'Then as you said yourself, we'll have to be more creative. If she won't budge for money, then we'll have to come up with something else. I'll give the matter some consideration, and come back to you with my suggestions by the end of the day. Now,' Campling swiveled the chair back to face his desk, turning his back on Benny, 'any news of Pandora Mitchell?'

Benny turned back to the window and stared out at the high street below. 'Nah, the silly little tart is still missin'. Our Craig's mopin' about at Danny Mitchell's all the time, he won't tell me any more than he told us yesterday. I'll be honest with you, Henry, I didn't want him to throw his life away on the girl, but I didn't want it like this. I don't wish the girl any harm, and if I'd known just how miserable our Craig would be, well I would've made more of an effort with her, and that's a fact.'   Down in the street below, he recognized a mane of red hair as it disappeared through the door of the ENB. Rose Bennett. What had brought her up to Market Melbourne, then?   Funny how she arrived just as Pandora disappeared.

He was about to ask Henry Campling if he knew any more about Lucinda's niece, when he spotted another familiar figure, this time heading towards his own betting shop. He muttered under his breath. 'About fuckin' time.' He turned back to Campling. 'I'll have to go, Henry. I

need to get back to the shop. I'll catch up with you later.'
He was gone before Campling had time to object.

For Michael Spivey, Benny's sudden departure couldn't
have been more timely. As Benny dashed across the road,
dodging between slow moving cars, Spivey slithered into
the front door of Campling's offices and up the narrow
staircase to the first floor. He tapped on the door.

'Come.' Campling's response was brusque. He looked
up as the door opened, expecting to see his secretary. At
the sight of Spivey he stiffened, and sat back in his chair.
'Ah, it's you.'

Spivey closed the office door, and walked over to the
desk. 'Sorry I'm a bit late, Mr. Campling. I meant to come
earlier, but we was a bit busy at the shop."

'That's quite alright, Michael.' Campling opened the top
right hand drawer of his desk and took out a thin wad of
bank notes. He counted out fifty pounds in ten pound
notes, and handed them over to Spivey. 'Will you be
available to do another errand for me this week?'

Spivey shifted uncomfortably. 'Tomorrow afternoon. Is
that alright? Benny owes me half a day.'

Campling consulted the calendar on his desk. 'Friday?
Yes, that should be alright.' He looked up at Spivey,
expecting him to leave. Spivey seemed immovable. 'Was
there something else?'

'In the pub last night. That Tommy bloke who works
in the Bank with Pandora, he was telling people that
Pandora was sweet on him, that she wanted to dump Craig
so she could go out with him.'

Campling sat back in his chair and steepled his fingers.
'Go on.'

'He'd had a bit to drink, and he started saying that he
thought Craig had done her in, because she didn't fancy
him any more.' Spivey paused, and licked his lips. 'Should I
tell Benny?'

Campling reached into the top right hand drawer for a second time. He pulled out several more notes and handed them to Spivey. 'Keep it to yourself for now, Michael. We don't want to upset Benny unnecessarily, do we?'

11

It came as no surprise to Rose that Hazel's grasp of the ENB's account opening process was text-book perfect. Rose took her through a selection of scenarios, from the simple to the complex, and she took every one cheerfully in her stride.

'How did I do then, Rose? Or aren't you allowed to tell me?'

'You did just fine, Hazel. Nothing to worry about there.' Rose completed her scribbles on a page headed "Hazel, Thursday morning", and looked up at the pixie face across the table. 'I suppose if you do most of the work, you'll get most practice.'

'We don't sell enough for anybody to get much practice.' The pixie face scowled. 'And you never know which way management are going to swing next with sales strategy. One minute we're told to sell to anybody with a pulse just to get the business in, and the next minute we're told to be squeaky clean and do everything by the book.' She glanced at Rose. 'You work with the people at Head Office, so you shouldn't be shocked by that.'

'No, I'm not shocked. But selling products and sticking to the regulations aren't mutually exclusive, you know. You should be able to do both at the same time.'

'True. But we don't get bonuses for sticking to the regulations.'

Rose nodded. If Hazel and Janis were telling her the same story, then clearly it was a common problem at the bank, and something openly discussed in working hours.

She closed her notebook and glanced at her watch. Hazel had breezed through the questioning, and they had another ten minutes of the allocated hour left. She rested her elbows on the table and folded her hands under her chin. 'Off the record, do you feel under pressure to sail close to the wind when you're selling?'

'Off the record? Sometimes. But it's not worth it. I know people in other branches who've done it, and they've been found out in the end. Head Office might pat you on the head while you're making the sales, but they'll drop you like a hot potato if you slip up and you're found out. I'd rather miss my bonus than lose my job.'

'Fair comment.' Rose turned and looked out through the glass wall of the meeting room into the empty banking hall. Marge and Tommy were seated at the counter, and appeared to be chatting amiably. At the end of the counter Janis was in conversation with a tall, groomed, attractive woman wearing a bank uniform and impossibly high heels.

Hazel followed her gaze. 'That's Elizabeth. She's Pandora's temporary replacement.' She chuckled to herself. 'I don't think Janis likes her. She's too efficient by half.'

Rose had to agree that Janis looked distinctly uncomfortable in Elizabeth's company. Elizabeth was standing to attention, her back erect, her manicured hands folded neatly on the counter in front of her, her eyes fixed firmly on Janis. Janis in turn was flicking through a procedures manual, avoiding eye contact. She looked harassed this morning, pale and lined, and older than her years. Her greeting of Rose had been polite but abrupt, all the familiarity of the previous evening swept away by the new day, and she had almost bundled Rose and Hazel into the glass-walled meeting room to get them out of the way. Rose turned back to look at Hazel. 'Did Janis get on well with Pandora?'

The question hung in the air while Hazel considered her choice of answers. Eventually she said 'as well as could be expected.' She picked at a fingernail, and eyed Rose accusingly. 'You were going to tell me about Janis and Pandora's dad.'

'There's probably no more to tell than you already know, Hazel.' Rose gave a shrug and took her elbows off the table, and leaned back in her chair. 'They met when we were still at school. Well, Janis and I were at school. Danny had already left to start up a garage on the high street with his older brother. He and Janis got engaged, had a row, split up. That's about all there is to tell.'

'Apart from the wedding.' Hazel leaned forward over the table. 'Is it true that she went berserk at the wedding, and beat up Danny's wife?'

Rose leaned forward to meet her. 'Not really. She'd been ill for a while, and she got a bit upset, that's all.' Her eyes met Hazel's disappointed gaze. 'Oh bloody hell, Hazel … alright, yes it was sort of true. She went to the wedding, got upset, and decided to have a pop at Selina. But she wasn't well. Don't forget that.'

Hazel's smile was ghoulish. 'Was there blood?'

'Yes, Hazel, there was blood. All over Selina's wedding dress. But it wasn't Selina's, it was the bridesmaid's. And it wasn't Janis's fault, the kid had a nosebleed. Are you satisfied now?'

Hazel grinned. 'I've heard that from somebody else, but I didn't really believe it.' She glanced through the glass wall again. 'No wonder Janis had it in for Pandora.' She winced and took in a short sharp breath. 'Oops, shouldn't have said that, should I?' She turned back to Rose. 'You didn't hear that.'

If Rose was pleased at Hazel's slip, she didn't let it show. She just shrugged and smiled. 'Hear what?' She waited for Hazel to catch on, and then said 'you'd be surprised at how deaf I can be, especially if you know anything else interesting that you shouldn't tell me.'

The pixie face ran a gamut of emotions and settled on resignation. Hazel leaned across the table again and lowered her voice. 'Promise you won't tell Clive?' A simple nod from Rose seemed enough reassurance, and Hazel launched into her tale. 'We thought at first that Janis was going to be alright about Pandora being here. The first couple of weeks were fine. Then Janis began to find fault with her. Nothing big, just little things … asking her not to gossip with Tommy so much, making sarky comments about her boyfriend, that sort of thing.'

'She doesn't like Craig?'

'Oh, it's not that she doesn't like him. I think she's jealous. He's quite a catch for a young girl like Pandora. He's fit, he has a rich dad, he's been to a posh university, has a plum job lined up in London … I think Janis resents the fact that Pandora has everything going for her, including Craig. Janis made some snide remark one day about Pandora taking after her mother, and marrying Craig for his money.'

'And how did Pandora react to that?'

'She was quite cool about it. I told her she shouldn't let Janis speak to her like that, but she just said she thought it was really sad that Janis still felt bitter about her dad after all this time.'

Rose was impressed. 'Quite a mature outlook for a nineteen year old.'

'That's what I thought. That's why I never thought she'd go for Tommy. Poor love, he's quite smitten with her, but he's a bit too immature. He's a harmless enough lad, but she's just out of his league.'

'Does Pandora know how Tommy feels about her?'

'Oh yes, he makes no secret of it. But she's not going to finish with a lad like Craig Bradman to go off with Tommy.'

'Unless she turns up, Hazel, she's not going to be going off with anybody.'

Hazel frowned. 'No, it's not good, is it? Poor little mare.'

'Did you like her?'

'Yes, I did, funnily enough. She was a bit spoiled, but she pulled her weight and that was alright by me. When Mel went on maternity leave Janis dumped a lot of the admin work on her, but she never complained. She was interested in the job, too. She would have enjoyed her session with you, if she'd been here to do it. She had her KYC training on Monday, you know? She came back full of it, asking me all sorts of questions about dodgy ID. She said how are you supposed to know all the different things to look out for, and I just told her it's a matter of common sense really. The knowledge builds over time, and once you get a bit more experienced you'll know what to look for. Best thing to remember is that ninety-nine percent of applicants are honest, so there's not much to worry about.' Hazel's face clouded. 'Just her luck to get one of the one percent that isn't.'

For a moment Rose thought that she had mis-heard. 'Run that by me again.' She put out a hand and laid it on Hazel's arm. 'Are you saying that Pandora had to deal with a fraudulent applicant?'

Hazel's eyes took on a wary look. 'It might be nothing. She might have made a mistake, you see.' She looked out into the banking hall again. Janis and Elizabeth appeared to be deep in conversation. She turned back to Rose. 'It was on Tuesday afternoon. She refused to open an account for a customer because of his ID documents, and Janis went ballistic. How dare Pandora presume to turn a customer away? Who the hell did Pandora think she was? All that kind of thing. I think if ...'

Behind Hazel, the door of the meeting room opened and Marge leaned into the room. 'Sorry to disturb you, ladies, but Janis has asked if Hazel could come back into the banking hall. It's almost ten past twelve.' She looked meaningfully up at the wall clock over their heads.

'Sorry Marge, it's my fault. I kept Hazel talking. We'll wrap up now.' Rose smiled amiably at the incomer until she took the hint, and backed out of the room. She turned

110

to Hazel. 'Much as I'd like to know more, we'd better call it a day for now. Perhaps you can tell me more about it later?'

Hazel shrugged. 'As you like.' She got to her feet and strolled to the door, and as she opened it she turned back to Rose. 'If you want to know more about that account, you don't need to wait for me. Ask Tommy when you see him. He knows all about it.'

'You know I'm not meant to run reports for you without authorisation from Clive.' Stan Wilkins was enjoying giving Rose a hard time from the other end of the line. 'Haven't we had this conversation before?'

'Yep, just before the last time you caved in and ran the report for me anyway.'

Stan sighed. 'And I suppose it's trivial, is it, like last time?'

'Far too trivial to waste Clive's time with. Oh come on, Stan, it's just a little report. Ten minutes work at the outside for an IT expert like you.'

'You can forget the flattery. It doesn't work.'

'OK, it's not trivial. It's important. I wouldn't ask otherwise.' He didn't answer, so she continued pleading. 'Look, I'm at the Market Melbourne branch, and there's a problem with the account opening. All I need is a report of all accounts opened by the same staff member in the last sixty days. She's probably only opened half a dozen accounts, if that.' Still silence at the end of the line. Rose laid it on thick. 'She's a nice kid, Stan. Only nineteen. Only been with the Bank a few months.' She could sense a slight thaw in the ice at the other end of the line. 'You wouldn't want a nice kid to get into trouble just because I couldn't help her with a few process errors, now, would you?'

Stan sighed, defeated by her persuasion. 'Go on, then. Tell me what you need.'

Rose raised her eyes heavenward in thanks. 'Details of

all current accounts opened by the staff member in the last sixty days. Time and date of opening, name and address of applicant, ID taken, reference data for ID documents, and ID authoriser – she wasn't KYC-qualified.'

At the other end of the line Stan was scribbling. 'OK, that shouldn't take long. What's her staff number?'

Rose cringed. 'I don't know.'

'Rose ...'

'Oh come on, it's only a cross reference to the HR files. You can look her up.' Silence. She adopted her best persuasive tone. 'If you could email that to me by ...'

'No. No emails. You know better than to ask for that. I can't send account data to an open email account. Running reports without authorisation is one thing, but I'm not breaking data security rules.' He paused, and then said 'you're at the Market Melbourne branch? Right, they get a delivery of internal mail from Head Office between four-thirty and five-thirty every day. I'll print your report, and put it in the internal mail this afternoon. Be there to collect it.'

'Can you put it in a sealed envelope and mark it "private and confidential"?'

'Don't push your luck.'

'Thanks Stan, I really appreciate it.'

'Sure you do. What's the girl's name?'

'Pandora Mitchell.'

'Pandora Mitchell.' He repeated the name as he noted it down. 'Pandora Mitchell? Wait a minute, Rose. Isn't Pandora Mitchell that girl who's gone missing?' The question came too late. Rose had already hung up.

'They've been here for about an hour and a half.' Jean pointed out of the sitting room window at the array of police vehicles lining The Larches' driveway. 'Dave Gilling called the matron this morning and asked if they could park here while they conducted the search. We've had cars and vans and police dogs, and dozens of police officers. They're searching all the lanes off Larch Road again. Dave called in to speak to us when they arrived, and said there's nothing for us to worry about, they've just come to do a more detailed search.'

Lu sat down in the chair next to her friend. 'There's been no more news of her, then?'

Jean sighed. 'No. It's such a shame. Such a lovely young woman.' She stretched up in her seat, trying to get a better view out of the window. 'Marge called me earlier to say she can't visit at lunchtime because none of the branch staff are getting a lunch break today. That detective is going back into the branch to speak to them again.'

'George Mulligan? Yes, he's been speaking to Rose this morning.' Lu placed a hand on Jean's arm. 'At least Marge has changed her mind about you staying here. Geoff Wilton rang me this morning, about the building work on the cottage. I hope you don't mind, he told me about Marge cancelling the alterations on the bungalow.' She rubbed Jean's arm. 'You must be pleased about that.'

'Pleased?' Jean pursed her lips. 'You don't know the whole story. Marge hasn't just cancelled the building work. She's taken it into her head that we should sell the bungalow to Henry Campling.'

'Campling? Whatever for?'

'Marge says he'll pay a much better price than a private buyer, because of the money he'll make from knocking it down and building more houses on the plot, and it will save us having to pay for marketing and estate agents.' Jean bit her lip. 'I don't think she's really thinking about it, Lu. She's angry with me for saying I want to stay in The Larches. She says if we can get a really good price there is another alternative to me staying here, but she won't say what it is. You know,' Jean looked away out of the window into the distance, 'sometimes she worries me. She's never had a life of her own.'

Lu thought for a moment, and then rubbed again at her

friend's arm. 'Marge has lived the life she wanted to live, Jean. She's been happy staying with you. There are mothers out there with children they never see who would swap places with you in a heartbeat.'

Jean forced a smile. 'I suppose you're right. But Henry Campling? How could she suggest selling our home to that weasel? You must know how I feel. You hate him as much as I do.'

'I know, but this is different from my situation. In your case it might make sense. You don't want to stay in the bungalow anyway, and if Campling will pay a good price and give you a quick sale, well why not? Just because he's a weasel is no reason not to take advantage of him. He'd be quick enough to do the same to you.'

'He'd knock my house down, Lu. The house I've lived in for over fifty years.'

Lu took hold of Jean's hand and squeezed it. 'I'm sorry, I didn't think. Then don't sell it to him. If that matters to you more than a quick sale, put the house on the market and sell it to a nice young couple who'll make a home of it.'

'And what about Marge?'

'Well, it's not up to her, is it? The bungalow belongs to you.'

'I know, but it's her home too. And her inheritance. And she's agreeing to sell, even though she doesn't want me to stay in The Larches. I'll have to see to it that she has somewhere to live. Maybe a normal sale wouldn't raise enough money to give us both what we want.'

'Nonsense. She's only agreeing to sell because she thinks there is an alternative to you staying here which suits her better. Didn't she give you any idea of what was in her mind?'

Jean shook her head. 'No. She said it was time that we had an adventure, and she wanted it to be a surprise.' She pursed her lips and shook her head. 'I don't want adventures and surprises. I want an easy life, peace and quiet, and good company. I can get all of that here.'

'Then you're going to have to tell her that. Maybe it is time now for her to make her own way and have an adventure or two. But you don't have to go with her. Why not let Marge look after Marge, and think a little bit more about yourself for once?'

12

The Feathers didn't do much lunchtime trade, except of the passing kind. Local people seemed to favour the town's cafes if they wanted to lunch out, leaving the bar vacant for use by traveling salesmen and the occasional displaced policeman.

After his meeting with Craig Bradman, George Mulligan had strolled to The Feathers, ordered steak pie and chips, and settled himself into a corner table with a pint of local bitter. Only two other tables were occupied, and he hoped it wasn't the food that put people off. He opened up the early edition of the local rag, and spread it out on the table in front of him. He had no intention of reading it, merely of giving the illusion, so that he didn't attract attention to himself by staring into space as he took time out to think. The open pages were full of pictures of Pandora, many of them showing her in childhood. So much for his request to Danny Mitchell to hold back from the media.

He sipped from his pint and looked idly round the bar. It was an old-fashioned pub, with dark varnished tables and chairs, and grubby flock wallpaper. The walls were hung with framed prints of Market Melbourne in the 19th century, and the shabby carpet still held the aroma of stale smoke even though the days of smoking in public bars were long gone. So this was where Craig Bradman courted Pandora Mitchell. Did that say something about them? It wasn't the smartest of places for an attractive and intelligent young couple to spend their evenings, so what was the appeal? Were they part of the crowd here? Was it just local and convenient, somewhere close for a drink that didn't involve taking the car? Or did they come here for another reason? To bait young Tommy, for example?

He looked down at the newspaper, focusing his gaze on the left hand page without really looking at the words. It had been a long morning, and his head buzzed with facts and theories. He could have done with someone to talk things through with, but he was beginning to realize that Dave Gilling was too close to these people to be rational about them. Still, he supposed there was nothing wrong with not wanting to think the worst of people. Though maybe that's why Gilling had never progressed beyond PC. There was nothing wrong with not wanting to think the worst of people - unless you were a policeman, in which case you didn't have the luxury of choice.

He turned his gaze to the right hand page and focused loosely on a picture of Pandora, aged 12, in school uniform. There was still no sign of her, and still no firm clue as to why she disappeared. Everyone – local police included – was still hoping for a happy outcome. Everyone except me, he thought. My gut says she's dead. But why? And how? It would be easy, just because she's young and pretty, to say "abduction, sexual assault, disposal of body", but there's no evidence. Yet. Except … now I know that somebody is lying.

He recalled his conversation with Craig Bradman, and the earnest look on the lad's face as he told of his last conversation with Pandora. 'She'd argued with Janis about something at work, and wanted to know what I thought she should do. We were going to talk about it later in the pub.' So why didn't Janis Porter mention this yesterday? Was she afraid to admit that she'd argued with the girl?

He sipped on his pint. Let's call that lie number one, then. But which of them is lying? Thinking about it, none of the other branch staff mentioned an argument on Tuesday either. So if Janis is lying, they all must be lying too.

Then there's lie number two, he thought. When asked if she had any particular friend at work, all her female colleagues at the Bank told him she was friendly with Tommy, that the two of them spent a lot of time together at work. Tommy himself had been bashful about this, blushing at the suggestion. Yet according to Craig, Pandora was irritated by Tommy. They had struck up a friendship when she joined the Bank, but Tommy wanted more and his attentions were becoming more persistent. Is this just Craig's view of the world again, or are the bank staff colluding to cover up for Tommy, to draw suspicion away from him?

Colluding? That's the second time today that word's come up. Now when was the first time he heard it? Rose Bennett, that was it. She talked about the bank staff possibly colluding with criminals to open fraudulent bank accounts. He chuckled to himself. She's a piece of work alright, talking about collusion with a straight face, when she herself is colluding with Clive Barden to keep the bank's dirty linen under wraps. Still, she's offered to help, even if her contract to the Bank binds her to some sort of confidentiality agreement. If she's half the girl her aunt used to be – and at first sight it looks like she might be – she won't let that stop her from finding a way to do the right thing.

And thinking of Rose Bennett, just exactly what is she doing here? Is the problem she's investigating as harmless as she makes out, or is there more to it?

He was about to consider his conversation with Rose when a young waitress crashed out of the bar's kitchen door carrying a large earthenware plate of homemade pie and chunky hand-cut chips, garnished with the obligatory spoonful of canned peas and a lonely sprig of parsley. She rolled up to Mulligan's table and smiled. 'Pie and chips?'

'Please.' He looked up at her to return the smile. Somewhere underneath those tattoos, he thought, there's a pretty girl trying to get out.

She dropped the plate onto the table. 'Sauces?'

He shook his head and she breezed back into the kitchen, pausing only to bestow the same smile on a thin, seedy-looking customer leaning on the bar.

'And just one last question, Tommy. If you're presented with an old-style driving licence, the one that doesn't come with a photograph, what data would you check to make sure it's valid?'

Tommy frowned and leaned forward against the table. 'I'd check that the name and address on the licence matched the name and address on the application form. I'd check that the date of birth matched, too.' He paused, waiting for Rose to write down his answer. 'I'd check that the licence looked kosher, did the paper look too new and clean if the issue date was old, that sort of thing.'

Rose nodded. 'Anything else?'

'I'd check that the licence number looked correct.'

'And do you know how to do that?'

'We have a reference card in the branch, but I'll have a go without it.' He smiled awkwardly, and then closed his eyes to concentrate. 'The first five characters are the first five letters of the surname, and if the surname is less than five characters they pad out the blanks with a nine. The next six numbers are the date of birth scrambled … third digit of the year of birth, then two digits for the month, then two digits for the day, and then the fourth digit of the year of birth.' He opened his eyes and frowned again. 'I think the first digit of the month has five added to it if it's a woman, so February would be seven, instead of two.' His eyes closed again. 'Then you get the first letter of the Christian name, then the second letter or a nine if there is no middle name, and then the last five digits are random-generated somehow. I don't know how.' He opened his eyes and looked expectantly at Rose.

Rose observed him with interest. 'That was impressive. I haven't come across many people who can do that.'

'Was I right?'

She laughed. 'I haven't got a clue. I'd have to get the reference card out.' She added more jottings to the spiral notebook. 'Anything else?'

'I'd check that the name and address matched the name and address on any other pieces of ID given. Sometimes we get one piece of ID with a full name on it, and the other with a common name – you know, Catherine on one, and Kate on the other.'

'And how do you know what's OK to accept?'

He shrugged. 'Common sense, I suppose. If everything else matches, it would be OK. If one said "Catherine Smith, Flat A, 321 the High Street, and the other said "Kate Smith, Flat B, 321 the High Street", then I'd ask for another piece of ID.'

'Would you think it suspicious?'

'I might do. I depends what they'd put on the application form. If the customer had said her address was just 321 the High Street, but she didn't say which flat, then I might think some of the ID was stolen. Then I'd ring Head Office and ask for advice.'

Rose completed her notes, and looked up at him. 'Thanks Tommy, that's been good work.' She smiled, and he blushed slightly at the compliment, shaking the tousled head modestly.

'So I did OK, then?'

'You did more than OK. But there's nothing wrong in making a few mistakes with this sort of thing, you know. Sometimes mistakes show us that we're asking too much of staff, and that we need to think of better ways of doing things.' She glanced up at the wall clock. Tommy's grasp of the process had been even better than Hazel's and there were twenty minutes of the allotted hour left. She closed the spiral notebook and patted it with both hands. 'Well, I don't know about you, but I'm glad that's over and done with.'

'It wasn't as bad as I expected.' He answered her, but seemed distracted by something happening on the other side of the glass wall. Out in the banking hall, a paunchy middle-aged man was being led into Janis's office. 'Is that that policeman again?'

'DI Mulligan? It looks like him.'

'Do you think he'll want to speak to everyone again?' Tommy's face had clouded, and he shifted uncomfortably in his seat.

'I don't know.' Rose crossed her fingers under the desk. 'Maybe he's come back to ask Janis about what happened on Tuesday. You know, when Pandora refused to open that account.'

Colour flushed into Tommy's face and he turned sharply to look at Rose. 'How did you know about that?'

'Hazel told me when we were chatting this morning. She said you knew more about it than she did, and that you'd be able to tell me about it.' She waited while he gave the matter some thought. 'It's off the record, Tommy. Hazel told me you were fond of Pandora, I wouldn't want you to tell me anything if you thought it would cause her a problem. But maybe it would help find her. Have you thought about telling DI Mulligan what happened?'

'No. Not the policeman. It's nothing to do with him. It's bank business.' His objection was a little too fierce.

Now that's an interesting point of view, Rose thought. Were those Tommy's words, or were they his manager's? Had Janis briefed them all not to tell what went on? She decided to try a different tack. 'Well, what about telling me? I'm not a policeman. And I'm here to deal with bank business. On behalf of Clive Barden.' She hoped Tommy would be more impressed by the mention of Clive's name than most people were. 'In fact, Clive's very worried about Pandora, and we all want to do everything we can to help find her.'

Tommy hesitated, and the expression on his young face

flitted through suspicion, doubt, reservation and uncertainty before settling for acceptance. 'Well, if Hazel thinks I should tell you …' He glanced out into the empty banking hall again, where Hazel was sitting behind the counter playing with her false fingernails. She saw him looking at her, and waved to him cheerfully through the glass wall. He turned back to look at Rose. 'What did you want to know?'

'Why did Pandora refuse to open the account?'

He looked down at the desk, avoiding eye contact. 'The bloke opening the account just didn't seem right for the details on the application. He'd brought a utility bill in his name for the address on the application form, and a rent book for the same address. But the address on his driving licence was wrong. He said he'd only moved a few weeks earlier, and hadn't got round to updating his driving licence.'

'Was it a photo licence?'

'No, one of the old paper ones. Pandora was suspicious because she recognized both the addresses. The new address, where he claimed to be living now, is an old block of flats on the road into Scarborough from Kirkby. She said she knew about it because it's being renovated, and her Dad was thinking of investing in a couple of the flats as buy-to-lets. They're only priced at around seventy thousand. Not up to much, even when they've been done up. It's the location, you see. It's near a fish factory.' He wrinkled his nose to stress the point.

'And the address on the driving licence?'

'It was for an address in Kirkby Park, on the outskirts of Kirkby. The cheapest houses come in at around half a million. She asked him if he'd owned that property and he said yes. So how come he's now renting a small flat in a poor location?'

'Maybe he's hit hard times. It can happen, you know. Maybe he's getting divorced, and his wife has the house, and he's had to find somewhere cheap to live while they get things sorted out.'

Tommy shook the tousled head again. 'I know that can happen, Rose. But not in this case. This bloke was a bit seedy looking, to be honest. He didn't look to me like he could ever have lived in Kirkby Park, never mind own a house there. And why would somebody who's moved to Scarborough come to Market Melbourne to open their bank account?'

'Perhaps he works here. Can you remember what his occupation was?'

He shook his head. 'Pandora didn't tell me.'

'So, thinking the applicant was lying, she refused to open the account?'

'She went to Marge first, to ask what to do if a customer had incorrect documents that looked suspicious. Marge spoke to Janis, and Janis went crazy. She told Pandora to authorize it, and Pandora refused, so she authorized it herself. After the customer had gone, she took Pandora into her office. She was shouting so loud we could hear her out in the banking hall. Who did Pandora think she was to refuse to open an account for a customer, how dare she contradict her manager, didn't Pandora know how bad things were at the bank, didn't she know how important it was to sell whatever business we could? We were all really embarrassed by it.'

'Did Janis ask you not to tell anyone about it?'

He blushed. 'Yes. She said it would be bad for the Bank if people found out that Pandora hadn't done her job properly.'

Rose shook her head. How typical of Janis to do the wrong thing and then try to shift the blame onto someone else. 'And did you believe her, Tommy? Do you really think that's why Janis didn't want people to know?'

'No. We all think it's to do with the bonuses.'

'Bonuses?' Rose was lost now.

His blush deepened. 'Well, if we don't sell, we don't meet our targets. If we don't meet our targets, we don't get our bonuses. And if we don't get our bonuses ...'

She finished the sentence for him. '… then Janis doesn't get hers.'

13

George Mulligan tried a reassuring smile, hoping to put Janis at ease. 'I just wanted to let you know that so far there still hasn't been any news, but we are broadening the search to take in a wider area, in case Pandora ran further afield than we originally thought.'

He watched her closely for a reaction but she simply nodded, her face impassive. The efficient, business-like woman he'd met yesterday had vanished overnight. There was still a briskness about her, but the calm and confident air of managerial authority had gone and she looked defensive and agitated.

'Also, I wondered if I could have a quick word with young Tommy while I'm here?'

'I'm afraid Tommy is busy at the moment. He's with an external consultant, and can't be disturbed.'

'Perhaps I could wait?'

She was about to object when Mulligan's mobile phone began to ring. He pulled it from his pocket, and barked into it. 'Mulligan.' He paused, and then said 'I'm at the ENB, Bob, with Janis Porter.' He smiled at Janis. 'Just hanging around hoping for a chat with young Tommy Fletcher.'

At the other end of the line, Bob Shepherd took the hint. 'No need to answer more than yes or no, George. We've just had a call from a lady out walking her dog up on Market Melbourne hill. She's found a silver necklace matching the description of the one Pandora Mitchell was wearing when she disappeared. She recognized it from the newspaper report last night. A box-link silver chain with a charm in the shape of a letter 'P'. Dave's gone to take a look. It's not where we've been searching. Larch Road is off to the right at the roundabout. The chain was found in a lay-by a couple of hundred yards further on, as if she'd run straight across at the roundabout.' He paused. 'When you've finished with Janis, can you call Dave on his mobile? He'll be waiting to hear from you.'

'Yes, fine. Thanks for letting me know, Bob.'

Mulligan disconnected the call. 'Sorry about that. Now, we were talking about Tommy, weren't we?' There was no more time for kid gloves. His tone hardened. 'I'm afraid I'll have to insist on speaking to him this afternoon. If he really can't be disturbed until the consultant has finished with him, then I'll just have to wait here in your office until he's available.'

In the small staff room above the banking hall, Rose nursed a mug of coffee and contemplated the last half hour. Tommy had been whisked away into Janis's office to meet with DI Mulligan. Rose had tried to speak to Janis, to give her an update on the day, only for the reticent Janis to retreat into the glass-walled meeting room with Marge. Even the gregarious Hazel was out of bounds, commandeered by Elizabeth to help with the end of day cashing up. Rose wanted to leave for the day, but the internal mail still hadn't arrived from Kirkby, and she couldn't risk Stan's report falling into the wrong hands.

She sipped on the coffee and wondered what the report would reveal, if and when it arrived. It should at the very least show the one account that Pandora opened on Tuesday, with Janis clearly named as the person who authorised the ID documents. Would Tommy overcome his prejudice and his fear of Janis, and tell DI Mulligan what had happened on Tuesday? If not, she would have to find a way of letting the policeman know without breaching the bank's confidence.

The sound of light footsteps trotting up the narrow staircase heralded the arrival of Hazel, her pixie face pink-cheeked and full of curiosity. She presented Rose with a large buff-coloured envelope. It was addressed to Rose and fastened loosely with a Velcro tab, the kind that could be opened and resealed without evidence. Rose took it from her, and forced a smile. 'Thanks, Hazel. I can be on my way now.'

'Something interesting?'

'Something interesting to me, hopefully.' Did they already know? Had someone opened the envelope before her? She ripped opened the Velcro tag, and peered into the envelope. Inside was a second envelope, an ordinary Manilla one, tightly sealed. She hoped her relief wasn't too visible to Hazel. She pushed the envelope into her briefcase, and got up from the table. 'Shall I just leave the mug in the kitchen?'

'I'll take it for you.' Hazel picked up the mug and smiled mischievously. 'Something to do with the review?'

'It might be.' Rose's own smile was equally puckish. 'Then again, it might not be.' She moved away from the table and towards the staircase. 'Whatever it is, I don't think I can face reading it tonight anyway. Definitely one to save for tomorrow.'

Outside in the street the late afternoon sunlight was balmy and comforting, and her shoulders relaxed under its warmth. A slow walk back to the cottage would go a long way towards easing the tension that had built up during the day. She turned right and headed down the high street. What passed for a rush hour in Market Melbourne was already underway, and traffic was building. There was a buzz about the place as cars parked, doors slammed, and evening shoppers on their way home from work darted in and out of late-opening stores.

She called into the local newsagents and bought an evening paper. The coverage of Pandora's disappearance was becoming increasingly lurid, and the front page now cried "Who Has Taken Her?" She shoved the paper into her briefcase and resumed her walk. As she reached the corner, a disturbance across the road caught her attention. A fracas was breaking out in the doorway of Benny Bradman's shop. A fair haired, good looking young man was being pushed out of the door and on to the street by an unpleasant looking character with greasy thinning hair. 'Now piss off, and go home.' The young man, shaking and anxious, stepped back towards the door and as he reached the threshold Benny Bradman appeared and pushed him roughly back onto the pavement.

Instinctively, Rose stepped back and tried to lose herself behind a carousel of dog-eared paperbacks outside a nearby charity shop. Bradman took hold of the man's arm and steered him firmly towards a funeral-black Mercedes saloon parked a few yards further down the street, opening the passenger door with a flick of a key fob. The young man seemed to wilt under Bradman's influence, and he climbed into the car without objection. Bradman slammed the door shut behind him, and got in behind the wheel. As the car sped off, Rose peered into it to get a better look at the passenger, hoping she had been mistaken. But she hadn't.

She'd only seen his likeness in the photographs for a few moments, but there was no doubting that the passenger was Jimmy Porter.

'Bob, it's Dave. I'm at the Mitchell's now.' Gilling leaned back against his patrol car and faced the house as he spoke. 'I've shown them the chain. Selina Mitchell says it looks identical to the one Pandora wore. It was a birthday gift for her eighteenth. And it's not a mass-produced piece. She thinks she's still got the receipt, so we should be able to trace it through the jeweller.'

Bob Shepherd's voice crackled at the other end of the

line. 'Have you spoken to George Mulligan yet?'

'No. He still hasn't called me. I've left a couple of the search officers standing guard over the place where the chain was found, but if he does think it's a scene of crime we'll need to get a move on if we're going to do a proper inspection of the area today. It's nearly six o'clock now. He can't still be with Tommy Fletcher, can he?'

'Dunno. Maybe he's on to something. Not much more we can do if he's not answering his phone and not picking up text messages.' Bob Shepherd sniffed. 'Are you knocking off at six?'

'I'm meant to be. But I think I'm going to go back up to the lay-by. There's something not right about this chain. If it is Pandora's, how did it get there? If she'd lost it in a struggle, or if it had come off her neck accidentally while she was running, it would have been broken, wouldn't it? I would have expected either the chain or the catch to be broken. But it's completely intact. And the charm, the letter P, it was still on the chain. It just looks like it's been taken off, and the catch refastened so that the charm doesn't fall off.' He frowned as he spoke, and turned his head slightly, towards the Mitchell's dining room window. Selina Mitchell was leaning against the frame, watching him through the glass. Her face was expressionless, but her eyes burned into him. He put the mobile phone to his other ear and turned away from her gaze, opening the car door with his free hand and leaning on it for support. 'I reckon this chain's been planted, Bob. It's been put there deliberately to make us think she ran straight on at the roundabout.'

Bob Shepherd drew in a breath. 'It's not for us to come up with deductions like that, mate. It might not even be her chain. And even if it is, it's up to Mulligan to come up with the theories.'

'Maybe. But right now he's not here to deal with it. I'm going back up there to take a look.

14

It was only a short drive from the outskirts of Market Melbourne to The Boar, and Rose followed Lu's directions easily. Straight up Market Melbourne hill, straight across at the roundabout, follow the main road for three or four miles to Hillingham, then turn right at the crossroads. The pub was on the right at the far side of the village.

George Mulligan was already waiting for her, relaxing at a table in the beer garden with a half pint of bitter and the latest edition of the Kirkby Evening Press. He stood up as she approached the table. 'What can I get you, Rose?'

'Just a tonic, please, ice and lemon.' She nodded towards his half-empty glass and her smile was playful. 'Are you meant to do that on duty?'

He smiled back. 'Not really, but every so often I need to indulge my inner rebel.'

She sat down at the table and surveyed her surroundings while he went to the bar. When he'd suggested The Boar as a meeting place she had a fleeting recollection of a tatty country pub, a place from her childhood where doorstep sandwiches full of home-roasted ham were served with hand-made chips, and where teenage boys brought their underage girlfriends to sample illicit half pints of snakebite in the beer garden. Danny had brought Janis here long before there was any talk of marriage, with Rose tagging along like a spare part because Janis wouldn't go anywhere without her.

The place had changed now beyond all recognition. Bought over by a large brewery some years back it was aiming squarely for the aspirational market and hitting its target with ease. It was barely six o'clock and already the car park was crammed full of high-spec cars, and affluent-looking families and couples of all ages filled the tables both inside and out. It would suit Janis down to the ground now, in her new incarnation as matriarch of a typical middle-England family. Except these days, Rose mused, she wouldn't want me in tow.

Mulligan wasn't long at the bar, and he soon returned with two tonics and a couple of packets of crisps. 'I didn't know if you were hungry.'

'Starving.' Rose helped herself to the salt and vinegar. 'Sorry to ask you to meet me again so soon. Just that something's come up that I thought might be important.'

He frowned. 'Don't apologise, Rose. I'm just glad that you're willing to help.' He sat down. 'I take it you've turned something up at the ENB?'

'Mm. Possibly more than one thing, actually.' She munched on a crisp and eyed him thoughtfully. 'I'm quite happy to tell you what I've found out. But you didn't hear it from me.'

His own expression was non-committal. 'As far as I can, I will keep this strictly between us.'

'Well, that'll have to do then.' She leaned her elbows on the table, and rested her chin in her hands. 'Has anyone spoken to you about an argument between Pandora and Janis on Tuesday afternoon?' She watched his face. It remained impassive, but a knowing glint in his eyes told her that he knew what she was talking about. She nodded, and said 'I don't know what you've heard, but several colleagues at the branch have confirmed to me that Pandora refused to open an account for a suspicious applicant on Tuesday afternoon. And Janis wasn't very pleased about it. In fact she was so displeased, she overrode Pandora's decision, and authorized the identification documents herself.'

'And do you know why?'

'No. Not with any certainty. The consensus at the branch seems to be that Janis is worried about sales figures, and doesn't like turning customers away. If that's the case, then of course that's a matter for the Bank to sort out. I'm only telling you about it so that you know Pandora may have had something on her mind when she disappeared.'

'I appreciate that.' He sipped on the remains of his beer. 'So the staff are happy to lie for Janis, then, are they?'

'It would seem so. But I wouldn't read too much into that. These are hard times in banking, they're probably just worried about hanging onto their jobs. She didn't want them to tell me about it, either. She's probably worried that Clive will get involved.'

'Don't they get on?'

'About as well as any ex-husband and wife.' The surprise on Mulligan's face confirmed her suspicion that Clive hadn't shared that particular fact with him, and she gave a wry smile. 'Like I said this morning, Clive's very good at looking after Clive.'

Mulligan nodded in comprehension. 'So that's why he brought you in. He needs to keep any trouble under wraps because his ex-wife is running the branch.'

'Quite.' Rose sat back and took her arms off the table, folding them in her lap and tilting her head to one side. 'I need you to take the next piece of information at face value, and not jump to the conclusion that Pandora has come to any harm as a result of what I tell you. It may have nothing at all to do with her disappearance. I don't know enough about the circumstances at this stage.'

He nodded. 'Go ahead.'

'I've learned today that Pandora was involved in opening nine accounts in the last two months, all of which have been highlighted as using invalid identification documents. The last in the sequence is the one I've just told you about, the one Janis authorized. The other eight were opened before Pandora got her KYC training, and were all authorized by the same member of staff.'

'But it wasn't Janis?'

'I'm sorry, I can't tell you that yet.' Rose was adamant in her refusal. 'I'm only part way through my review work, and I need more information.'

'Rose, this might be critical.'

'And it might not be. I can't accuse someone of doing something fraudulent until I have all the facts. It may have been a genuine mistake.'

'Once I admit, but eight times? Was it the same mistake?'

'No, it wasn't. But people can be careless.'

'There are regulations.'

She laughed. 'Spoken like a man who thinks that all regulations are followed. Banking these days isn't what it used to be. It's all about sales. Selling financial products. That's why it's called "retail banking". Half the junior bank staff at the ENB have no previous banking experience, most of them started off behind the counter in a chain store or a supermarket. To them, selling a bank account is like selling a pair of jeans or a washing machine. It's a commodity, and selling it earns them more money.'

'What you've just told me suggests to me that Pandora was being used by someone to open fraudulent accounts.'

'I don't disagree. But you'll have a job proving who was pulling her strings.'

'Wouldn't that be the person who authorized the accounts?'

'It doesn't have to be. If Pandora knew that one of her colleagues was always careless, or didn't care about the regulations, she could have arranged herself for the accounts to be opened, knowing that that person could be relied upon to just rubber stamp the ID documents.'

She was moving too fast for him. 'Pandora? Why would she want fraudulent accounts opened?'

'Maybe she was doing it for someone else. What about her boyfriend, or maybe his father? What if Pandora happened to mention that things at the Bank are a bit lax at the moment, because they are desperate for new business? Benny Bradman is a bookie, dabbling in property development. That's a prime way of laundering illegal earnings, by the way. Inflating the value of a property, so that a dummy purchaser pays over the odds. What if he had some cash sloshing around that needing cleaning up?'

Mulligan was slow in following. 'But if I pay two hundred and fifty thousand for a property that's only worth two hundred thousand, I lose fifty thousand. Don't I?'

'If the money wasn't yours in the first place, because it should have been paid to the tax man, you're not losing anything. And some fraudsters will gladly lose twenty percent of their illegal earnings if the other eighty percent can be laundered clean. After all, it's a better rate of return than paying forty percent tax.'

'But what about the regulations on source of funds? Wouldn't the Bank ask you to confirm where the purchase money came from, if it's cash and not a mortgage?'

'Of course. But that evidence can be provided by your accountant or solicitor. Which relies on the assumption that all accountants and solicitors are honest. It's not only bank employees who collude, you know.' She sipped on her drink. 'But it's all speculation, Mr. Mulligan. Just a possibility. That's why I can't tell you who authorized the accounts.'

'These were current accounts, weren't they? There was nothing to do with property?'

'Yes, that's true.' She thought for a moment. 'But current accounts are handy for laundering too. You can deposit money more or less no questions asked, so long as you remain within certain guidelines. It's easy to make regular deposits, especially if you mask them as salary payments. It's also easy to transfer money out. You can take out cash on a regular basis, set up small standing orders to transfer money to other accounts, the possibilities are endless.'

'Suppose Craig Bradman did ask Pandora to open those accounts, why would she refuse to open the one on Tuesday? Why have the argument with Janis?'

'I've been thinking about that. One possibility is that Pandora was getting cold feet. Before she had her KYC training, she wasn't held accountable for the checking of ID documents. That responsibility lay with the colleague who authorized the documents. But once she'd had that training it would be too risky for her. If she was found out, she could be prosecuted. Maybe she tried to tell Craig that she couldn't open any more accounts, and maybe he refused to take no for an answer.'

'So her only option was to refuse to open the account in the branch.' He chuckled to himself. 'And then Janis Porter let her own emotions get the better of her, and wrongly authorized it anyway.' He shook his head. 'But like you say, it's all speculation.' He finished his half pint of bitter, and pushed the glass away from him. 'Have you met Craig Bradman?'

'No, but I've met his father.'

'You don't like him much, then?'

'Do you?'

He laughed. 'There you go again Rose, just like your aunt, answer a question with a question. Yes, I do like him, as it happens. I've only met him the once, earlier today. But he seems to me to be a fairly straightforward bloke. He has a shady reputation, which I understand he sometimes encourages, but that can be deliberate. After all, I have my own reasons for leading people to believe I'm just a plodding copper.'

Rose grinned. 'Oh well, I guess there's nothing like a double bluff to keep people on their toes.'

It hadn't been easy for Stan Wilkins to wangle a late night

working at the office. He always joined his colleagues for a few pints after work on a Thursday, and his decision to give it a miss this week in favour of completing "an important piece of work" had caused consternation in some quarters and hilarity in others.

A couple of older colleagues, intrigued by his uncharacteristic desire to work late, had concluded that Stan had been asked to do some more confidential work for Clive Barden, and had decided to suck up to the boss instead of standing his ground and leaving work at his usual time.

Meanwhile, a couple of younger colleagues had devised a far more entertaining theory, based on Stan's growing fancy for one of the new cleaning staff who frequented the office after hours. They had hovered by Stan's desk and made teasing remarks about his yearnings for the lovely Magda, playfully suggesting that the regular team outings to the pub on a Thursday would make a good smokescreen to put the shrewish Mrs. Wilkins off the scent.

He took these jibes in good part, but stood his ground against any attempts to persuade him to change his mind, masterfully shuffling pieces of paper around his desk and clicking away at his keyboard in mock concentration. Eventually the joke paled, and the lure of cold beer and a sunny pub courtyard grew, and in ones and twos his team-mates wandered off towards the office staircase without a backward glance.

He waited until they were all out of view before getting up from his desk and sauntering over to the vending machine, shoving a few coppers into it and selecting a black coffee, extra sugar, extra strength. The office was open plan, a hundred or so desks partitioned into team areas, and as the machine dispensed his coffee he glanced around to see if anyone else was working late. At the other end of the room, a couple of young Polish girls were divesting a large cleaning cupboard of its contents, but he couldn't see anyone else around. The vending machine whirred and clicked decisively, and he lifted the thin plastic cup carefully out of its holder and carried it gingerly back to his seat, the hot liquid burning his fingers through the thin brown plastic.

He put the cup down on his desk, shoving aside printed listings of computer code, and gathered up a scattering of loose papers containing his afternoon's labour. He'd worked hard this afternoon to complete both his outstanding work for the day and a little something just for his own interest. He'd known that his note to Rose, carefully pinned to the front of the report he'd printed for her earlier, would elicit a response. "If you'd stayed on the line at lunchtime, instead of being so quick to hang up on me, I'd have told you that Clive Barden had already asked for an almost identical report two days ago. So to save a bit of time, I've just run the same report again. Everything you asked for is there, along with a flag to show whether or not there has been any transactional activity on the account. I'm surprised you didn't ask for this at the time. But I guess you'll be back on the phone this afternoon, when you see what the flag is set to."

Rose had called him just before five. And he didn't blame her. All of the accounts opened by Pandora had been flagged as potentially fraudulent, and eight of the nine were already being used. It had been easy to second guess that Rose would want to know what kind of transactions were going through the accounts, and by the time she called him he'd already started to code a new report to show payments in and payments out. It didn't take long to complete and test, but he had to wait until the office was empty before he could run it against the live files and print off the results. The misuse of real customer data was a dismissible offence, and while there was a thrill in helping Rose in her work, it wasn't enough of a thrill to risk losing his job.

He clicked at his computer keyboard, calling up the

program and the job instructions he'd prepared earlier, and then submitted his request. The job only took seconds to run. He glanced around to make sure no-one was watching, and then clicked again at the keyboard to open up the report. His screen filled with lines of data, page after page of payment details. He leaned closer to the screen, resting his elbow on the desk, and his chin on his upturned hand. His eyes scanned down the right hand column of figures, and he smiled to himself, nodding in appreciation. Crafty buggers, he thought, they certainly know how to play the game. He tapped at the keyboard and the screen flickered, and then presented another set of data. More of the same.

He picked up his coffee and sipped on the cooling liquid. To print, or not to print, that was the question. He frowned in contemplation, sipping again on his coffee, and glanced idly over at the printer bay in the corner of the office. Magda, the prettier of the two cleaners, was flitting around the desks to the right of the printers, flicking her duster ineffectively over the computer equipment and technical manuals that covered them. He waited until she had moved away, and then sent just three pages of the ten-page report to the printer. He crossed the office in the time it took for the printer to spew out the pages, and deftly removed them, pausing only to smile shyly across the office at Magda before heading back to the safety of his desk.

He glanced quickly at the sheets of paper, and then folded them repeatedly until they formed a thin packet, small enough to fit discretely into the back pocket of his jeans. It was only a sample of the transactions made so far, but it would be enough for Rose to get the picture. Without further delay he shut down his computer, grabbed his rucksack from under the desk, and headed for the staircase. Behind him, Magda flicked her duster over his desk and hissed 'good evening to you, Stanley' in her best broken English. She had never spoken to him before. He didn't even know that she knew his name. He turned and gave her a bewildered smile, and as he descended the stairs he quietly cursed Rose Bennett for the umpteenth time that day.

15

'So let me see if I've got this right. Pandora Mitchell opened fraudulent accounts that are being used for money-laundering, and you haven't told George Mulligan about it?' Lu emptied the remnants of a bottle of Pinot Grigio into her glass. 'I'd better get another bottle from the fridge. I don't think one is going to be enough for this conversation.'

'You're twisting my words. I said Pandora opened *potentially* fraudulent accounts which *may* be being used for money-laundering.' Rose sighed. 'And that is exactly why I haven't told Mr. Mulligan yet. Because he'll do exactly what you've done, and jump to a dangerous and unproven conclusion.'

'But what if it's the right conclusion, Rose? What if it's got some bearing on Pandora's disappearance? You can't play God with this one.'

'I'm not playing God.' Rose sipped on her own glass of wine. 'Look, a number of suspect accounts were opened with invalid ID. I've told Mulligan about that. And I've told him that Janis and Pandora argued when Pandora refused to open a ninth account after she'd had her training. But I can't tell him yet that most of those accounts had their addresses changed shortly after opening. And I can't tell him about the transactions. Not yet. If the police start asking questions, and the branch staff are colluding with someone over these accounts, there is a danger that they'll be tipped off.'

'They won't be tipped off if he only speaks to Clive

about it.'

'If Mulligan speaks to Clive about it, Clive will know I've given him confidential bank information, and he'll take me off the case before I've finished the review. It's critical that I do the reviews with Marge and Janis tomorrow. I can't complete my report without it.' She sipped again on her wine. 'And don't forget that Mr. Mulligan has asked me to help him out by digging for gossip while I'm in the branch. I can't do that if Clive takes me off the case, can I? What I learned today from Hazel and Tommy was valuable for Mulligan. Maybe tomorrow I'll learn something from Marge and Janis that will be even more useful.'

Lu shrugged. 'I suppose you have a point. But I don't understand why Clive hasn't already reported this money laundering business to the police, if he knows about it. Surely the Bank has an obligation to report criminal activity?'

'Of course. Anyone who works for the ENB has a responsibility to report anything that they think looks like suspicious activity. But you have to be pretty sure that something suspicious *is* happening before your set the hares running.'

'I thought you said large sums of money were being paid in and out of these accounts on a daily basis?'

'They are. But Clive is playing a very clever game. He asked Stan to let him know whether anything had been paid into or out of each account. That's all. The answer to that question is just yes or no. There's nothing suspicious about that. Clive doesn't want to report anything to the police until he knows whether or not Janis is involved.' Rose huddled further into her armchair. 'Stan's really put his neck on the block producing this report for me. He can see what Clive is up to, and he doesn't think much of Clive's determination to cover his own backside.' She smiled. 'He even drove all the way out from Kirkby to Market Melbourne this evening, to bring me the print.'

Lu still wasn't satisfied. 'So what is the definition of "suspicious" then? I would have said that money being paid into fraudulent bank accounts was suspicious enough to warrant making a report.'

Rose wrinkled her nose and shook her head. 'There are no clear guidelines on what is and isn't suspicious activity. I tried to explain this to Mr. Mulligan this morning. Broadly speaking, suspicious activity on an existing account is anything which deviates from the normal pattern of behaviour. So maybe someone suddenly starts transferring large sums of money abroad when in the past they have just used their account for salary receipts and mortgage payments and day-to-day spending. To identify where this might be happening, the ENB has to keep an eye on what its bank accounts are being used for. It runs a report every month to flag up any large payments in or out of accounts, money being wired to and from foreign countries, that sort of thing.'

'What, on everyone's accounts?'

'Even yours, Lu.' Rose smiled. 'The report lists all transactions in or out of personal bank accounts held with the ENB which exceed a threshold. Let's call it ten thousand pounds. This threshold is known to all bank staff, so where criminals are colluding with staff they might know about this ten thousand pound threshold, and they keep any transactions on the account to just below the threshold in order to avoid detection. To counter this practice, the ENB runs an additional report every month to look for transactions over a different threshold, a lower one. They might look for transactions over seven thousand, for example. Only senior managers know when these secondary reports are run, and what the threshold is set to. To limit the risk of it becoming common knowledge.'

Lu was appalled. 'So if I knew that the secondary threshold was seven thousand I could pay in six thousand, nine hundred and ninety nine pounds every day and I would never come up on the report of suspicious activity?'

'That's about it.' Rose sipped again on her wine. 'Of course, you would have to know about the secondary threshold. And you would only know about that if you were a senior manager at the ENB.'

'Or if you were in collusion with a senior manager at the ENB?' Lu frowned. 'Does Janis know about that secondary threshold?'

Rose laughed. 'I see you're on top form this evening. I don't know, to be honest, but whoever has been using the accounts opened by Pandora certainly knows about it. All the transactions were just under the current secondary threshold.'

'And there is no other check? They don't run a report every month, say, to see if anyone has banked multiple transactions which would add up to a suspicious amount?'

'Not at the ENB. Every bank has its own policy. You have to remember that monitoring this sort of thing costs the Bank time and money. Every item that comes up as "suspicious" has to be investigated by a human being. And the ENB is in business to make a profit for its shareholders, not carry out investigations for the law enforcement agencies. Actually, money laundering is a particularly interesting case in point, because providing no one finds out about it there is no risk of the Bank losing money. You'll find that the ENB puts a lot more effort into investigating fraudulent credit applications than they do into money laundering. That's simply because with a fraudulent credit application they risk losing their own money.'

'So did Janis authorise all nine accounts?'

'I can't tell you that.' Rose frowned again. 'To be honest, I wish I didn't know the answer to that myself.'

'Well, a trouble shared is a trouble halved …'

'You're incorrigible.' Rose wasn't to be persuaded. 'You'll just have to trust me when I tell you that it's better if you don't know, at least not yet. I need to finish the review.

Once I've done that, and I'm off the case, I promise I'll tell you everything.'

'Sorry I've been out of touch, Dave. It's been one of those days.' George Mulligan, trying hard to sound contrite, balanced his mobile phone in the crook of his neck, leaving his hands free to operate a can opener as he spoke. 'I had to go back to the ENB to talk to young Tommy Fletcher this afternoon. That prompted me to go and see Bradman, and then I've been up to The Boar to have a chat with Rose Bennett.'

'S'alright, George. I understand.'

'Understand? You couldn't have a word with my wife, could you? I got back too late for supper again, and she's cleared off to her sister's for the evening. I wouldn't mind if she'd left me anything worth eating.' He twisted the can opener as he spoke, and the can lid came away with a clatter. 'Bugger.'

At the other end of the line Gilling laughed. 'Beans on toast again, is it?'

'I should be so lucky. She hides the beans when she's really mad at me, and just leaves me a can of tomato soup.' He put the can opener down, and licked a smear of the cold glutinous liquid off his fingers. 'Anyway, tell me about the chain.' He poured the soup into the pan, and set it on the gas, then leaned against the kitchen counter. 'Your text said you thought it was planted.'

'I do. It was lying on the road, easily visible. The lady who found it had just parked up there to walk her dog, and she saw it as she was getting the dog out of the back of the car.'

'Could it have come off in a struggle? Maybe if Pandora was pushed into a car?'

'No chance. It wasn't broken or damaged, and the catch had been fastened to make sure that the charm didn't fall off the chain.'

'Are we sure it's Pandora's?'

'A hundred percent. The jeweller is a good sort. He went back to his office this evening to check the paperwork. He's confirmed that it was a limited production piece, and that Selina Mitchell ordered it as a gift for Pandora's eighteenth birthday. Only seven letter P charms were made. The charms were all hallmarked, including the maker's mark, and they carried an edition number. Pandora's was number five. I drove over to see him this evening, after I'd dropped the chain off at Kirkby for tests. He's confirmed from the hallmark that it's Pandora's chain.'

'How could he do that, if you'd already left the thing at Kirkby?'

'Digital photography, George, you ought to try it some time. It's quite popular here in the twenty-first century.'

Mulligan snorted. 'Cheeky bugger.' He lifted the pan off the stove and swilled the soup around, too weary to search out a spoon and stir the thing properly. 'What about the actual chain, rather than the charm?'

'Yes, we checked that too. He's confirmed it's the original chain.'

'So the assumption is that someone removed the chain from around Pandora's neck, and re-fastened the clasp to keep the charm on the chain, before deliberately planting it at the layby.'

'That's my guess. It looks to me like someone has taken her, and planted the chain to make us think we're looking in the wrong place.'

'Did you have anyone in mind?'

Gilling clicked his teeth. 'Well, there are a few obvious possibilities aren't there? Craig Bradman, for one. Tommy Fletcher. An unknown assailant.'

'And you think she'd let them take the chain off without a struggle?'

'She might not have been conscious.'

'True.' Mulligan flicked off the gas, and swilled the

soup around one more time before pouring it into a bowl. 'But you've forgotten one. Who is the one person most likely to be able to get that chain off Pandora's neck without damaging it?'

Dave Gilling wasn't always the sharpest knife in the drawer, but even he could see where Mulligan's train of thought was heading. He didn't like the idea, but he had to admit it was a possibility. The obvious answer to that question was Pandora Mitchell herself.

'I've been thinking about what you said earlier, about Janis arguing with Pandora. Shouldn't Pandora have completed a Suspicious Activity Report when she refused to open that bank account?'

Rose sighed, and shifted in her chair. She had failed to dissuade Lu from opening a second bottle of wine, and the drink had made her sleepy. 'Can't we just drop this? I thought we were going to start clearing out Frank's cottage tonight?'

'No we can't drop it, and don't try to change the subject. I'm being serious. If Pandora thought the applicant was fraudulent, shouldn't she have completed a report?'

Defeated, Rose turned to face Lu. 'Yes, strictly speaking she should have completed a report. And if she'd made it into work the next day, she probably would have done.'

'But what if that's what they argued about? Not just that Pandora wouldn't open the account, but that she wanted to submit a report, and Janis didn't want her to?'

'I think you're letting your imagination get the better of you.'

'Do you? Or do you just not want to entertain the thought of Janis being involved in Pandora's disappearance?' Rose didn't answer, so Lu continued with her train of thought. 'And what if that's what Pandora wanted to speak to Craig Bradman about? Did she want his advice on whether or not to blow the whistle on Janis?'

Rose rubbed her forehead with fingers. She wanted sleep, not another in-depth discussion about the ENB, but she had to admit that there was something in Lu's suggestion that made her uncomfortable. 'I have to be honest. There is something about Janis's behaviour that's bothering me. I can't fathom just exactly why she was so insistent that Pandora should open that account in the first place. I thought at first it was because she didn't like Pandora, and was just angry that the girl had challenged her, but there's something else.' Rose sat up and uncurled her legs from the armchair's soft folds. 'According to both Tommy and Hazel, Janis is getting pretty worked up about the poor sales figures for the branch, and the impact it will have on her bonus. I wondered at first whether Janis had money worries, and was so desperate to maintain her bonus that she would be prepared to sell bad business to make sure that her income didn't drop.'

'I thought you said she was doing well these days?'

'Maybe I did. I think what I meant was that it looked as though she was doing well. Oh, she's got the big detached house, new furniture, foreign holidays, even a new car on the drive ... but that's not necessarily with her own money. She could be up to her eyes in debt for all I know. Maybe she's feeling the squeeze. Bank staff aren't immune from financial problems, you know. They have the same challenges as the rest of us.' Rose frowned. 'And there's something else. I saw her husband today, on the high street. I recognised him from some photos she showed me. He was with Benny Bradman.'

'I didn't realise they were friends.'

'They're not. At least, it didn't look like a friendly encounter. Bradman virtually threw Jimmy out of the betting shop, then strong-armed him into a car and drove off with him.'

Lu whistled. 'And you think he's involved in all this

somehow?'

'I don't know. I can't get it straight in my head. I keep wondering if Pandora knew what she was doing, opening those accounts. What if Benny Bradman wanted accounts to use for laundering money, and Pandora told him that business was bad at the bank, and that her colleagues weren't being as vigilant about account opening processes because they just needed new business? Maybe she was doing him a favour because he's Craig's dad, and then when she'd had her KYC training she couldn't take the risk any more?'

'I can see how that theory would work, but Janis authorised that ninth account. She insisted that Pandora should open it.'

'I know. And maybe Benny Bradman knows that as well. Maybe he's worried that Janis knows what they've been up to. Think about it … Pandora called Craig to tell him about her argument with Janis. Easy enough for Craig to tell his father about it.'

'And Jimmy?'

Rose shrugged. 'I don't know. Perhaps he's putting pressure on Jimmy to make sure that Janis keeps quiet.'

'What are you going to do?'

Rose thought for a moment, and then smiled. 'I'm going to take a shower. And then I'm going to make a coffee and call Mike, and check out how things are at home.'

Not to be thwarted, Lu stretched out a foot and gave her niece a gentle kick in the shin. 'I meant about Janis.'

Rose shrugged. 'I'll try talking to her tomorrow. If she is involved in any way, she's going to need all the help she can get. Although I'm not sure she'll be willing to accept any help from me.'

16

Hazel bounced her right hip against the door into the banking hall, nudging it open, then turned and backed carefully through the gap, teasing the door further open with her backside as she went. As always she'd overfilled her coffee mug, and the warm sweet liquid lapped dangerously close to the mug's rim, threatening an overspill. Struggling to keep the coffee away from the sheaf of papers held tightly in her other hand, she slowly turned forward and shimmied left away from the doorframe, holding the door in place with her right foot until she had enough clearance to let it swing shut without risk to either the papers or her clean uniform. She glanced up at the wall clock, then put the papers down on the counter and took a sip from the coffee. It was only twenty five to nine and already the day was shaping up to be a bad one.

Let down by her child minder for the third time in month, she'd had to call on her mother yet again for emergency childcare. Then, reversing into her parking space in the small car park behind the branch, she had misjudged her position and scraped the car's flank against a concrete post. She'd blown into the rear door of the branch swearing all kinds of damnation against "whoever put that stupid ruddy bollard there", and been stopped in her tracks by the sight of Janis.

It was a sight she had found genuinely shocking. God knows, she'd never liked the woman, and it had been a struggle to somehow rub along for several years as work

149

colleagues without anything more than a false camaraderie and an occasional grudging respect. But Hazel wasn't the vindictive type. A careless change in Janis's appearance, the emergence of dark roots under the bleached hair, an unfortunately choice of lipstick, black circles under the eyes after a late night, any of these might have prompted a characteristically bitchy remark from her. But if anything, today Janis was more tightly groomed than ever. Her naturally curly hair had been ironed sleek, her make-up was immaculate, her nails freshly painted, and unless Hazel was mistaken her usual costume jewellery had been replaced by a matching set of tasteful white gold pieces. And still her cheeks were gaunt, her eyes hollow, her pain visible. She had opened the door to Hazel and retreated into her office with barely a word.

Now, alone in the banking hall, Hazel could only muse on what might be causing Janis such distress. It couldn't be Pandora. Janis didn't give a toss for Pandora. If anything, Hazel guessed, she was glad to be rid of her. No, there had to be something else. Clive, perhaps? A row with Jimmy? Her imagination was about to concoct one or two possible alternatives when a sharp tap on the outer door caught her attention, and she looked across to see Marge and Tommy grinning at her through the glass.

'Is Janis here yet? I need to see her.' Tommy pushed past Hazel as she opened the door and made straight for the manager's office without waiting for an answer.

'Yes she is, but I don't think she'll want to see you just now.' Hazel's words bounced off his back. She turned an inquisitive eye on Marge as she lumbered through the doorway.

Marge shook her head and smiled wryly. 'He has something important he needs to tell Janis. He's been bending my ear with it all the way down the street.' She clicked the door lock shut with a plump hand. 'Something to do with that policeman who was here yesterday, and Rose Bennett.'

'Something to do with Pandora?'

'Mm, possibly. I should think he'll tell you all about it when he's seen Janis.' Marge bustled past Hazel and headed for the stairs to the staff room. 'Will you and Tommy be alright on your own for a bit after we've opened up? Elizabeth won't be in until ten today, and I've got my review with Rose Bennett at nine thirty.' She paused, and turned to look back at Hazel. 'Only I thought I ought to mug up on the account opening process before I meet with her, if you don't mind holding the fort.'

Hazel shrugged. 'No problem. I was going to do a bit of prospecting, but I can get things ready to open up before I start. Will Tommy be long with Janis?'

'I shouldn't think so.' Marge smiled sagely and turned back towards the stairs. 'I don't think Janis is going to be too pleased at what he has to tell her, and I can't imagine he's going to want to hang around for the fall out. Anyway,' she glanced at her watch, 'we haven't got much time for the huddle this morning, so the sooner he comes out, the sooner we can get on with it. It's going to have to be a quick affair.'

Hazel watched Marge disappear up the narrow flight of stairs. A quick affair? It would certainly be that, if it took place at all. Having seen into her manager's soul that morning Hazel couldn't imagine that selling funeral plans was high on Janis's list of priorities.

'They didn't hold out much hope of finding anything on the chain itself, but there was a possibility of something on the charm.' Dave Gilling dropped the fax onto the desk in front of George Mulligan. 'They've found some smudges, possibly made by the woman who found it, and some particles of grit embedded in the chain that were probably acquired in the lay-by. In fact,' he put his hands on the chair back and leaned over the desk, 'apart from that the bloody thing is spotless. It's been cleaned. They've found traces of a commercial jewellery cleaning fluid all over it.' Gilling pulled the chair away from the desk and sat on it, resting his elbows on the table. 'So what do you think now, George? Do you still think Pandora might have planted the chain herself?'

Mulligan grinned at Gilling. He'd barely set foot in the Market Melbourne station that morning before Bob Shepherd had warned him that Gilling was getting too involved, and Bob wasn't wrong in his judgment. Still, there was nothing wrong with a bit of commitment. 'I think all this overtime is wearing you down, Dave. When did I say she'd planted it herself?'

'Last night, on the phone.'

'Ah, no. I said she was the one person who could definitely take the chain off without damaging it. She might have taken it off before taking a shower, or before dressing if it didn't match the outfit she was going to wear. That doesn't mean she planted it. Just that the undamaged chain was off her neck and available for someone else to plant under our noses when it suited them.'

Gilling pulled a face. 'It's all conjecture anyway.'

'Of course it's bloody conjecture. Conjecture is ninety five percent of my job.' Mulligan hitched up his crumpled shirt sleeves and leaned across the table to look directly into Gilling's face. 'We're going to have to make a decision soon on how to proceed. It's pretty obvious now that we're not going to find her sitting on the roadside with a twisted ankle. That only leaves two possibilities. She's either done a bunk, possibly because of something that happened at work, or she's been abducted and possibly harmed.' He watched the expression change on Gilling's face and put up a hand to pacify him. 'I know you don't like the idea that someone's taken her, or harmed her, any more than I do. But we have to face facts. We've been diddling about for two days now, and she still hasn't turned up.'

'So what do you suggest?'

'Well, whichever of the two possibilities it is, there has to be a motive. The strongest motives I can see relate to her work at the Bank and to her relationships with Craig Bradman and Tommy Fletcher. The problem is,' he tapped his frustration out on the table with a stubby finger, 'those motives cut both ways. If she's done a bunk, it could be because of the bank, or because of her relationships with Tommy and Craig. If she's been taken, it could be because of the bank, or because of her relationships with Tommy and Craig.'

'You think Tommy or Craig might have taken her?'

Mulligan shook his head. 'To begin with, I think Tommy Fletcher is full of bullshit.' He relaxed and leaned a little further over the table. 'When I was in The Feathers yesterday lunchtime I overheard one of the barmaids laughing with a punter about young Tommy, and his fantasies about Pandora. Apparently he'd been shooting his mouth off in there on Wednesday night about Pandora wanting to dump Craig Bradman so that she could go out with him. Everything points against this being likely. By all accounts Pandora is pretty keen on Craig, and even Tommy's colleagues at the Bank think she's out of his league. I went back to the ENB yesterday afternoon to have a chat with him. I wanted to let him know that it's not a good idea to go around saying things that aren't true, in case he gets himself into more bother than he can handle. He didn't like the lecture, but I think he got the message.'

'Would Craig Bradman hurt her if he thought there was any truth in what Tommy was saying?'

'He might. But I really don't think there'd be any need. I admit that the workings of a teenage girl's mind are mostly beyond me, but if I put Craig and Tommy in a line up I don't think there'd be much of a contest.' Mulligan frowned. 'But then there's no harm in keeping an eye on those two lads, is there? You could argue that either of them might have a jealous streak. Tommy might have

153

come on a bit heavy if she was always playing hard to get, or then she might have gone to ground to avoid Craig if there was any truth in the rumour that she was keen on Tommy.'

'But where does the ENB come into this?'

'Ah, well, that's something else that came up yesterday. Rose Bennett is on to something at the bank. I'd like to be able to tell you what it is, but ...' He grinned at Gilling across the table. 'I can't tell you, because she won't even share it with me. She says she has to finish her review today before she can give me more details.'

'But it provides another motive for Pandora's disappearance?'

'It might do. And again, Pandora may have chosen to disappear, or she may have been quietly put out of the way.'

'By either Tommy or Craig?'

Mulligan nodded. 'Or possibly by someone else.'

Gilling, completely baffled by the twists in Mulligan's train of thought, shoved back his chair and stretched his legs out under the table. 'Tommy Fletcher isn't the only one full of bullshit, is he George? From what I can see, you haven't got a bloody clue.'

Rose gave what she hoped was a reassuring smile, and laid a hand gently on Marge's arm. 'It's fine Marge, don't worry about it. We all have off days.'

Marge reached into her skirt pocket for a cotton handkerchief and pulled it out to dab at her eyes. 'I feel so silly. I mean, it's not like I haven't had enough practice at opening accounts. I've been doing it for the best part of forty years.'

The younger woman shrugged. 'Maybe it's stage fright. Some people are fine doing their job, but get nervous when they feel they're being tested. There isn't really any other way for me to do these reviews, except to talk you through some examples. I can't really sit in and watch while you open an account for a customer. It would be a bit tricky to explain if something was wrong.' Especially, she thought, if something was as spectacularly wrong as the session we've just had.

Marge didn't have any difficulty with the basics of checking a customer's identification documents. She knew what documents were acceptable, how many needed to be presented, and how to check the obvious pieces of data like name and address. Beyond that, she was a regulatory nightmare. Rose had tried several scenarios out on her, and was in no doubt that providing a prospective customer produced a couple of documents with near enough the same name and address on them, Marge would be happy to approve the application. Only at the end of the session had Marge appeared to realise that she hadn't passed muster. Rose had pragmatically asked how she would feel about taking a refresher course, and Marge's plump face had crumpled to the edge of tears.

Rose let her dab at those tears for a few minutes, and took the opportunity to consider. She tipped her notebook towards her, so that Marge couldn't see what she was writing, and scribbled her verdict at the bottom of a page headed "Marge – Review". *Missed nine out of ten opportunities to spot that ID was invalid. Habitually careless? Would training help?* She thought for a moment, and then added a final comment. *Exceptionally careless today for my benefit?* She closed the notebook, and laid her pen on top of it.

'I suppose you've got a lot on your mind at the moment. It can't be easy with your mum being in the nursing home.' Rose adopted a more casual tone. 'I knew your mum, you know. She taught me at primary school.'

At the mention of her mother, Marge visibly brightened. 'Yes, she told me the other evening.' She gave a nervous giggle, and said 'she said you were the most stubborn child she ever taught.'

'I'm honoured. That's one hell of a compliment.' Rose

smiled. 'I must pop up to The Larches and see her before I go back home. Is she going to be in there much longer?'

'Not if I can help it. She keeps telling me that she wants to stay there permanently, but I know she doesn't really mean it. She's just trying not to be a burden on me.' Marge sighed, and pushed the slightly soggy handkerchief back into her pocket. 'I don't think she's happy there at all. I've been quite at my wits end trying to decide what to do for the best.' She paused, and then said 'Actually, I think what's happened this morning may have been a blessing in disguise. Perhaps I don't need retraining after all. Perhaps what I need is early retirement.'

'Retirement? Good heavens, Marge, my reviews have had some interesting results over the years, but I've never driven anyone into retirement.'

Marge's round face dimpled. 'Oh, you're not driving me to it. I've been thinking about it for a while. We've had a good offer for the bungalow, you know. Mum thinks we're selling so that she can stay in The Larches, but … well, there's no reason why we couldn't put the sale proceeds towards buying somewhere more suitable, and the ENB allow staff to take early retirement after the age of fifty, if they choose to.' She gave a thoughtful smile. 'I've always fancied the Lake District. Lots of fresh air and rolling countryside, and plenty of tea rooms to visit. Mum loves her afternoon tea. It would be quite an adventure.'

Rose wasn't sure whether Marge was teasing her or being serious, so she opted to play along. 'Well, the Lake District would be lovely, but wouldn't it be rather expensive? Properties in some of these rural locations are at quite a premium.'

'Oh, I think we could manage. I'd get quite a good pension you know, with so many years' service, and I've been saving hard to build up a bit of extra cash for retirement. And we're quite frugal in our habits. I think we'd be fine, so long as we weren't extravagant.'

'Well, it sounds like a grand idea, but I hope Clive and

Janis don't blame me if you go through with it. They're struggling as it is without Pandora.'

She hadn't deliberately dropped that particular name into the pool of conversation, but it certainly prompted a reaction. Marge's face began to crumple again. 'Poor Pandora. Whatever can have happened to her?' She fished out the handkerchief and dabbed at her eyes again. 'She's such a nice girl. A little thoughtless sometimes, but mostly a lovely girl.'

'Thoughtless?' Rose was intrigued. The image of Pandora she'd formed from her conversations with Tommy and Hazel was that of a careful pragmatist, especially in her handling of Janis.

Marge's ample cheeks flushed pink. 'Yes. Sometimes she could speak without thinking. She was quite rude to Janis, you know. And Janis only had her best interests at heart.'

'I think I heard something about that. An account that Pandora didn't want to open, and Janis disagreed with her?'

'Yes. Janis was really only trying to help me, I think. I'd already told Pandora to open the account, you see. I couldn't see anything wrong with the documents.' She lowered her voice almost to a whisper. 'I'm not sure whether I should tell you this or not, Rose, but under the circumstances ... well, I think I might have made a mistake. With the documents, I mean.'

'The documents? For the account that Pandora wanted to open?'

'Well, not just that one.' Marge twisted the handkerchief between her plump fingers. 'Actually, I authorised quite a few accounts for Pandora when she was doing her training. I suppose ... what if I made mistakes with those accounts, too? Do you think I should say something to our audit department?'

17

Janis's frame of mind was evident from her body language. She had rolled her chair slightly back from the desk in a subconscious effort to distance herself from the conversation to come, and her arms were firmly folded across her body in self-defence. Any pretence of friendship, any hope that Rose had nurtured of their being able to work together, was long gone.

Unlike Hazel, Rose hadn't been surprised today to see the change in Janis. She didn't take any pleasure in seeing Janis look so strained, but she instantly recognized the sleek hair and careful grooming as her old friend's first line of defence. What did she used to say when they were teenagers? When the chips are down, make sure you're wearing your best underwear? If Janis was already wearing her battle armour, then clearly a battle was expected.

Rose forced a smile, and pretended she hadn't noticed. She cleared her throat, and thumbed through the spiral notebook resting on her knees. 'There are just a few things I need to go through with you this morning.' She ran a finger idly down the page. 'I've done my review with Marge this morning, as you know. Unfortunately, there were quite a few issues with Marge's answers. In fact, Marge has admitted to me that she thinks she may have made mistakes with live applications, including some accounts that she authorized for Pandora when she was doing her training.' She looked up at Janis, inviting a response, but none came.

She kept her eyes on Janis's face, and said 'I've also

finished my work with Tommy and Hazel, so the only thing left to do before I draft my report is spend some time with you.'

'With me?' Janis arched an eyebrow, but her face remained otherwise impassive.

'Yes. Because of the results of Marge's review this morning, I'm afraid I'll need to review your own understanding of the process for authorizing ID documents.'

'That's out of the question.'

Janis was clearly struggling to stay in control of her emotions, but her tone was sharp, and Rose was impressed by her will power. She nodded and said 'I didn't expect you to like the idea. But I'm afraid that's the way it is.' She turned to a clean page in her notebook. 'How would this afternoon work for you?'

For a few moments, they sat in silence and then Janis spoke through clenched teeth. 'I am the manager at this branch, Rose. I appreciate that you have to do your job, but I do not open accounts for customers, and I do not intend to submit to being tested by you on the subject.'

'Marge will have to undergo retraining, and until that is complete you will be the only senior authorizer at this branch. As part of my review I have to confirm that a competent person is overseeing account opening at this branch.'

'It's out of the question.'

'I'm afraid Clive will back me up on this.'

'I don't give a toss what Clive will do. Clive can put me on disciplinary if he likes. I don't have to submit to this, and I don't intend to.'

Rose laid her notebook down on the desk. 'Janis, don't you think it's time you told me what's going on here? I don't want to be rude, but you look awful this morning. You look exhausted.'

'Millie had a bad night, that's all. I haven't had much sleep.'

Rose nodded. As lies went, it was a pretty weak one. 'Have I done something to offend you? I thought we were getting on OK until today. I thought we had an agreement to work together on this?'

Janis's face contorted into a sneer. 'And that agreement included DI Mulligan, did it?'

'Mulligan?' Rose was caught off guard. 'What's Mulligan got to do with it? I'm talking about us working together on the review? We agreed that I would do the review, and share my results with you before I share them with Clive, so that we can work together to put things right.'

'Well, that was before I knew you were working with the police.' Janis was beginning to lose some of the self-control. 'You were seen, Rose. Tommy Fletcher saw you last night, drinking with DI Mulligan at The Boar. And I thought I could trust you.'

'Who said you can't?'

The question was ignored. 'What do you think Clive would say, if he knew that you were passing information to the police, betraying the bank's confidence?'

'You needn't worry about that. It was Clive's idea that I should assist the police.' Rose smiled. 'Are you surprised? DI Mulligan approached Clive about Pandora's disappearance, and Clive asked me to brief him on the work I'm doing here at the branch. Mulligan just wanted to understand whether it was relevant to his investigations. I think I've put his mind at rest. I've told him that my understanding from you is that Pandora didn't have any problems at work, so her disappearance is unlikely to be work related. That's right, isn't it?' She watched the colour drain from Janis's face. 'Unless something else has happened that changes that?'

'Such as?'

Rose leaned across the desk, and her tone hardened. 'Shall we stop playing games, Jan? I know that Pandora was bothered about something at work. And I think that you know damn well just exactly what it was that was bothering her. I think you're lying, and I think you're up to your neck in something that you wish you'd never started.' She leaned a little closer and lowered her voice to a whisper. 'And I think it involves ignoring bank regulations and selling bank accounts to anything with a pulse, to make sure you get your bonus.'

'How dare you?' Janis hissed through her teeth. 'How dare you come in here and start accusing me?'

'How dare I? Because we were friends, Janis. Because I'm probably the one person who *could* come in here and accuse you of it. And to try to help you out of the hole you've dug, if only you'd let me.' Rose sighed and backed away, leaning back in her chair. 'I hoped you might have the sense to admit you've been doing something you shouldn't. If you make a clean breast of it now, I can still help.' Janis didn't respond, her face a frozen mask of inscrutability. Rose waited for a moment, hoping that even now Janis might decide that honesty was the best course of action. But she couldn't wait forever. She closed the spiral notebook and reached down to slide it into her briefcase. 'OK, suit yourself. I can't force you to do a review. I'll let Clive know you're not happy about it.' She closed the briefcase and lifted it up on to her lap. 'I'll let you have a full copy of the report before I submit it to Clive. I realize now that you've decided not to work with me to sort any problems out, and that's up to you. But just so you know, I'm going to recommend to Clive that all accounts opened by Pandora should be fully investigated because there is a risk of fraud. Clearly Marge hasn't been as vigilant as she should have been in checking Pandora's work.' She stood up. 'And I do mean all accounts, Janis. Not just the ones authorized by Marge.'

Across the desk, Janis sat erect in her chair, her hands clenched to the chair arms, her eyes fixed on the wall behind Rose, every effort spent on resisting Rose's attempts to reach her.

Rose walked to the door and put her hand on the handle, then turned and looked back at Janis. 'Just one last thing, Jan. I saw Jimmy last night. With Benny Bradman.' Janis's eyes widened slightly, but still she didn't speak. 'To be more precise, I saw him being thrown out of Bradman's shop.' She paused. 'Is Jimmy in some sort of trouble?'

Tears were beginning to well up in Janis's eyes, but Rose couldn't feel any sympathy. She'd seen Janis's tears of self-pity before. Janis wasn't contrite for what she'd done, she felt no concern for Pandora's disappearance, she was just frightened for her own skin. Nothing had really changed in twenty years.

Rose shook her head, frustrated by the display of stubbornness. 'Fine. Go ahead and stew in your own juice. But while you're deciding what your next move is going to be, you might want to bear one thing in mind. DI Mulligan isn't the only one who's not going to rest until Pandora turns up. I think her disappearance is connected to what's been going on at this branch, and I'm going to be helping the inspector every step of the way until we find her.'

Benny Bradman picked up the framed photograph from his desk, licked his index finger, and rubbed with it at a smudge on the glass. He liked smudges. He never tired of looking at his wife, and smudges gave him an excuse to pick up the photograph and study it. 'What the hell would you do, then, Trina? How would you get our Craig out of this one?' He sighed, and placed the photograph back in its place. She'd been gone for nearly a year, and it still felt like the pain would never go away.

He leaned back in his seat and folded his hands behind his head. 'Silly little tart is still missin',' he muttered under his breath. 'Our Craig is almost permanently camped out at Mitchell's place, and now that nice Mr. Mulligan has been on the phone tellin' me that by the end of the day it could officially be a murder case.' He laughed under his breath.

'You'd like George Mulligan, Trina. He does his homework. He knows all about you. Knows all about how to try reelin' his suspects in, too. Crafty old bird, droppin' me the hint that it could be a murder case, tryin' to wind me an' our Craig up.' He stroked the frame's edge with his fingers. 'I don't half wish you was here, girl. I know our Craig had nothin' to do with it, but I ain't got your brains when it comes to dealin' with the law.'

He thought for a moment, and then picked up the phone and jabbed at the keypad. 'Sal, is Spivey down there? Send him up, will you?'

Footsteps sounded on the stairs almost before Benny had returned the phone to its cradle. The door opened, and Spivey's greasy face appeared in the opening. 'You want me, Benny?'

'Still ain't learned to knock, then?' Benny sighed and, casting another glance at the photograph on his desk, mumbled 'believe it or not, I did this for you.'

Spivey was in the room now, hovering at the other side of the desk. 'You did what for me?'

'I weren't talkin' to you.' Benny closed his eyes in momentary contemplation, and then turned the full force of his gaze onto Spivey. 'What happened when you followed our Craig on Wednesday night?'

'What happened?'

'Yes, what happened? Am I talkin' Greek? I told you to follow our Craig, and I'm still waitin' to hear what happened.'

Spivey licked his lips. 'Well, Boss, I followed him to Mitchell's in the afternoon, and then when they went to Kirkby, to do the telly thing, I followed them there and I sat outside in the car till they come out.'

'And then what?'

'I followed them back to Mitchell's and sat outside until about ten. He never went anywhere else.'

Benny closed his eyes again, and sighed. 'You're lyin'.'

'I ain't Benny, straight up, I stayed there till ten. I didn't think there was much point in staying longer than that, he weren't going to get up to much at that time of night.'

'Well if you ain't lyin' Michael, you ain't much of a guard-dog. He was back home havin' supper with me by half past eight. He even had time to pick up the pizzas on his way home.'

Spivey squirmed, and shifted his weight from one leg to the other and back again. 'I never saw him, Benny. Honest. He must have come out of another door. Jeez … you mean I was sitting out there for nothing all that time?'

'Not for nothin', no. You was doin' it 'cos I paid you to.' Benny shook his head, and flicked his fingers towards the door. 'Go on, piss off. You're a waste of space.'

Spivey backed away from the desk, and put a hand out behind him to open the door. 'Before I go … well, it's Friday, and you said I got a half day owing. Can I …. I mean, is it alright if …if I take my half day today?' He watched Benny's face fold into a scowl, and meekly added 'please?'

Benny growled. 'Two o'clock. No earlier. Otherwise I might forget why I took you on, and feed you to Mulligan.'

Rose's request had been brief, but to the point. 'I'm going to have to file my report to Clive by the end of the day, and at that point I'll be officially off the case as far as the ENB are concerned. I'd like to talk to Craig Bradman before I complete the report. Can you arrange for me to meet him, with you as chaperone? I need to know exactly what Pandora told him about her argument with Janis before she disappeared.'

George Mulligan clicked his teeth. Cheeky mare. Whose bloody investigation was this, anyway? He chuckled to himself. What an ignominious end to thirty-five years of policing – playing personal assistant to a private investigator.

He flicked through his notebook until he found Craig

Bradman's mobile number. He dialed the number and Craig answered almost immediately. It only took a couple of minutes to set up the meeting. Craig accepted the invitation without question, but he couldn't meet any earlier than mid-afternoon. 'Three o'clock, at The Boar. See you there.'

Mulligan punched a text into his mobile phone and sent it to Rose. 'Craig tied up in Kirkby until two thirty, will meet us at The Boar after three.' She responded immediately with a simple 'OK'.

He knew Rose was trying to help, and it was help that he welcomed, but it wasn't in his nature to give up so much control. All this waiting about was making him edgy. He felt a sudden need to be close to Pandora, to put himself in her footsteps, to re-establish his connection with the missing girl. He dropped the mobile phone onto the empty passenger seat beside him, started up the engine, and turned the car back towards Market Melbourne.

18

Café Valerie was always busy on a Friday lunchtime, and Rose and Lu had to content themselves with the smallest table in the darkest corner of the room. At least it gave them some privacy, and they huddled over their plates speaking in hushed tones for fear of being overheard.

'And that's why you didn't tell me last night who authorised the accounts? Because it was Marge?' Lu was beginning to understand her niece's reluctance to share all the facts.

'I know how friendly you are with Jean. I didn't want to worry you unnecessarily. I needed to do the review with Marge first, to see for myself how likely it was that she had authorised those accounts on purpose.'

'And?'

'She was absolutely bloody useless, Lu. Forty years in the bank, and she could barely demonstrate a grasp of the basics.'

'Do you think it could have been an act? To give you the impression that she doesn't know what she's doing, when really she does?'

'I don't know. I don't know if she's that clever. She was so spectacularly bad.' Rose shook her head, and pushed her plate away. 'Maybe she's always been that useless, but no-one's really noticed because Market Melbourne is such a piddling little branch. I guess that's why I changed my mind about discussing it with you. I need to know more about her. I thought maybe you could help me out.'

Lu's brow puckered in contemplation. 'I don't really

know her that well. Oh, I know her to say hello to, pass the time of day, that sort of thing. But my friendship has always been with Jean, so anything I know about Marge has come from her. Jean does talk about her lot. To be honest, I think she worries about her. She doesn't think it's healthy that she's never married or moved away from home. I think a lot of people think Marge has been self-sacrificing, living with her mother all these years, but it's not quite like that. It wasn't what Jean wanted. She's quite determined to stay in The Larches now. Despite her accident, she's really enjoying living there. She's got company all the time, and they're quite a feisty bunch of old fogies, you know. She's taken quite a shine to Dicky Thomas. He was in a prisoner of war camp during the war, somewhere out in the east. Jean thinks he's quite a hero.' She paused in thought, and then said 'she and Marge have been talking about selling the bungalow. She wants to use some of the sale proceeds to stay in The Larches, but Marge has other ideas. Trouble is, she won't share them with Jean. All she'll say is that it would be adventure, and she wants it to be a surprise, whatever that means.'

'It'll be a surprise, alright. Marge told me that she thinks Jean is staying in The Larches for her benefit, so as not to be a burden. She's talking about taking early retirement so that when the bungalow is sold, she and Jean can move away somewhere else and enjoyed a shared retirement.' Rose leaned a little closer to Lu. 'She's talking about moving to the Lake District.'

'Oh hell.' Lu's dismay was genuine. 'I suppose I'm going to have to warn Jean about that, am I?'

Rose shrugged. 'That's up to you, I guess. Are you going to see her today?'

'Later this evening. She's been invited out this afternoon, to take afternoon tea with Dicky and his daughter.' She rolled her eyes. 'Young love, eh?'

Rose laughed softly. 'Nothing wrong with that. You ought to try it yourself. Shall I put in a word for you with

Mr. Mulligan?'

'No, thanks. I never make it a habit to re-tread old ground.'

Rose's laugh was louder this time. 'And I thought your relationship was purely professional.' She sipped on her coffee. 'Could I come with you to visit Jean? If not tonight, then maybe over the weekend? I'd like to see her before I go back home.'

'You're definitely not going home until Sunday evening, then?'

Rose looked away. 'You know I'm not going home until Sunday evening, Lu. Don't go there.'

'I'm not trying to pry about you and Mike, I just want to know that everything is alright.' Lu sighed, defeated yet again by Rose's obstinance. 'Well, yes then, if you're going to be here at the weekend I'm sure Jean would be delighted to see you.' She paused again to think for a moment, and then said 'Rose, talking of old ground, about that grave in the garden … you thought it was funny when I suggested Marge might have been responsible. But what if she has something to hide?'

Rose shook her head and smiled. 'It wasn't Marge. I still think that was about your refusal to sell the cottage. In fact,' she glanced at her watch, 'you've just reminded me that I have a little errand to do on that score this afternoon, and not a lot of time to do it in.'

Rose stepped tentatively into Benny Bradman's shop just as the 1.20 at Kempton Park was starting. She'd never been into a betting shop before, and she glanced around to get her bearings. A couple of punters perched on high aluminium bar stools at the front of the shop, mugs of coffee in front of them, their eyes fixed on the wide-screen TV hanging above their heads. At the other side of the shop, two mousy-looking girls sat behind a glass-fronted counter, waiting for customers. In the window that fronted onto the street, three leather armchairs surrounded a small coffee table that held copies of the Racing Post and a couple of the tabloid dailies. In many respects, it didn't look that different from the inside of a bank. Except that banks made their profit by selling easy credit to customers and gambling on whether or not they would get it back, while bookmakers were shrewd enough to let the customer do the gambling.

At the far end of the shop, Benny Bradman was in conversation with an oily, briefcase-carrying man in a badly cut brown suit. Their conversation appeared to be earnest, their heads lowered. Benny was the more animated of the two. He seemed to be disagreeing with the other man, shaking his head, and grinning his dismissal of some suggestion that didn't please him. Rose stepped quietly forward down the shop, trying not to draw attention to herself. As she reached the counter Benny looked up and opened his mouth to speak, and she saw his face brighten unexpectedly as he caught sight of her. He laid his hand on the oily man's arm and said 'well here's an unexpected surprise. Look who it is, Henry.' He stepped forward and put out his hand, taking hold of her hovering fingers and shaking them enthusiastically. 'Nice to see you again, Rose. Come in for a flutter? We don't get many ladies in durin' the week.'

Rose stifled a smile. 'Actually I was looking for Craig. I thought I might find him here.'

Benny frowned. 'He ain't here this afternoon, he's doin' an errand for me over in Kirkby.'

Rose was relieved that Mulligan's information had been correct. Craig out of the way, and an open opportunity to quiz his father, was exactly what she'd been hoping for. She sighed her disappointment as convincingly as she could. 'Will he be back later?'

'I should think so.'

Behind him, Henry Campling edged forward. 'Aren't you going to introduce me, Bradman?'

Benny rolled his eyes. 'Where's me manners today? Haven't you two met? Sorry Rose, this is my solicitor, Henry Camplin'.' He jerked his head at the oily man. 'Henry, this is Rose Bennett. She's Lu Aylesbury's niece.'

Henry Campling's face registered first recognition, and then mild disdain. He shook her hand with a limp, moist handshake. 'Ah, the infamous Miss Rosy Bennett? Of course I've heard of you. You're doing some work in Market Melbourne for the ENB, I believe?'

Rose gave her most engaging smile. 'That's right. And I've heard all about you from my aunt. You're into property development, I think?'

Campling smiled, revealing uneven nicotine-stained teeth. 'Indeed, yes. Bradman and I work in partnership, don't we Bradman?' Beside him Benny merely smiled and nodded. 'So,' Campling continued, 'you're looking for Craig? Are you and he acquainted?'

'Not yet. I'm hoping he can assist me with the work I'm doing for the ENB.'

Campling frowned and shot a warning glance at Benny. 'Presumably this has something to do with Pandora Mitchell? Frankly, Miss Bennett, I think I should advise you that I am representing Craig in the matter of Miss Mitchell's disappearance. And I think the police would take a very dim view of an independent investigator interfering in the case.'

'I'm sure they would. Always assuming that I am working independently, and not assisting with the official investigation at their request.' She let the point go home, and then added an extra barb. 'They would probably take as dim as view as I take of the kind of lowlife who would dig a grave in my aunt's garden, just to frighten her out of her home.'

Benny frowned. 'Somebody did that to Lucinda? Blimey Rose, I can see why that would upset you. What sort of scumbag would do that, eh Henry?' He nudged Campling with his elbow, but Campling's attention was elsewhere, his face etched with contempt. Rose and Benny both turned and followed his gaze to a weasel of a man lurking behind the shop's counter. The weasel looked up at them, and his eyes flicked from Campling to Benny, and then settled on Rose. Benny shouted to him. 'This is Rose Bennett, Michael. Have you met?'

The weasel turned pink. He tried to look at Rose again, but some invisible impediment seemed to restrict his movement. He lowered his head, and mumbled into the collar of his shirt, then faded away down the counter to avoid any further dialogue.

Benny watched him knowingly for a moment, and then turned to Rose. 'You'll have to excuse Michael, he's a bit shy around the ladies.' He turned back to Campling. 'I think we're done, ain't we Henry? Thanks for droppin' in. I'll give you a call later about those plans.'

Campling opened his mouth to object, but Benny had already dismissed him, and with a hand laid against her back, he was gently steering Rose towards the stairs to his office. 'Tell you what Rose, why don't you bob up to my office for mo? It's just up there, see, at the top of the stairs. I'd like to hear a bit more about this grave business, if you have time to tell me.'

'And you think I had somethin' to do with that?' Benny appeared to be genuinely hurt.

'You were at the cottage on Wednesday evening. And you knew no-one was in. I told you that Lu was out for the evening, and you saw that I was just leaving.'

Benny sighed. 'I'm a lot of things, Rose, but I ain't the sort to threaten a lady. If that's how I'm comin' across, then I need to do somethin' about my image.' He leaned back in his chair. 'Well, I can promise you that I had nothin' to do with it, and I'm sorry if you think otherwise. I can't do nothin' about your opinion of me, except wish that it was a better one.'

He thought for a moment, and then said 'now that I know what a dim opinion you have of me, d'you mind tellin' me exactly what you want to speak to my son about?'

'I don't mind at all. I've been told that Pandora had an argument with her manager at work on the day she disappeared. I've also been told that she called Craig and spoke to him about it. It's possible that she shared information with Craig that might be relevant to the work I'm doing for the ENB.' It wasn't quite the truth, but it was how she wanted Benny Bradman to see things.

Benny's eyes were wary now. 'Information?' He bit into his lip, contemplating his response, and then leaned across the desk. 'Are you really workin' with DI Mulligan, or was that comment just for Henry's benefit?'

'I'm engaged by the bank, but I've been asked by them to assist DI Mulligan with his enquiries.'

'You think the work you're doin' at the Bank has some bearin' on Pandora's disappearin' act?'

Rose paused. She was dangerously close now to giving too much away, but it had to be a risk worth taking. Did it really matter if she broke the rules to get closer to Pandora? In her book, there was only one answer to that question. 'It's possible that Pandora made some mistakes in her work. That some of the bank accounts she opened for new customers may have been fraudulent. She wasn't very experienced, you see.'

'And you think my Craig might know somethin' about it?' Benny sat back in his chair, and examined her face more carefully. His gaze made her feel uncomfortable. He glanced at a framed photograph on his desk for a moment, and then looked back at Rose. 'I love my son, Rose. He's a good lad, a clever lad. An honest lad. As for Pandora, well I didn't think much of her, but she weren't the dishonest type either. If she's got herself caught up in some trouble, the only advice she would have had from my boy is to get herself out of it, and quick.' He stood up, and held out a hand across the desk. 'I think we're finished here. Thanks for droppin' in. I'll tell Craig you were lookin' for him. Now, why don't you let me show you out.'

Rose stared at his outstretched hand. This wasn't how she had expected things to pan out. She'd hoped for a reaction, a heated debate, maybe a slip on Benny's part that would confirm her suspicions that he was involved in some way. She hadn't expected to be summarily dismissed. Did this mean she would have to consider the possibility that her judgment of Benny Bradman had been wrong? Unless …

She got to her feet and let him usher her to the door of his office, then turned to speak to him again. 'I believe you know Jimmy Porter, Benny. Is he a friend of yours?'

This time his reaction wasn't a disappointment. Benny's eyes widened, and then narrowed into slits. 'No, Jimmy Porter isn't a friend. My dealin's with Jimmy Porter are personal business, Rose. Personal to me, and personal to him. If you want to know the nature of our business, I suggest you ask Jimmy to tell you that himself. Tell him he has my blessin', if he's got the bottle to tell you. He'll know what that means.'

As Benny walked back to his office, Spivey appeared from the kitchen at the back of the shop. 'I'm off now, then. You said I could go at two.'

Benny turned and grabbed hold of Spivey's lapel, yanking him up onto his toes. 'Where are you goin'?'

Spivey shrank under Benny's grip. 'It's my half day, you said I could go.'

'Go where?'

'I've got an errand to do. Making a bit of pin money in me spare time, that's all. That's alright isn't it? It's my half day.'

'Supplementin' your income with a bit of moonlightin'? That's very enterprisin' of you, Michael. Is that what you were doin' on Wednesday night, when you were supposed to be keepin' an eye on Craig?' Spivey squirmed, and Benny lifted him a little higher, until their faces were almost touching. 'Well, is it?'

'Henry said you wouldn't mind. He said it would be alright to leave Craig round at Mitchell's.'

'Henry? What the hell's it got to do with him?'

'I've been doing a few jobs for him, that's all. He said it would be alright. He said you wouldn't mind.'

'Did he, now?' Benny slackened his grip on Spivey's lapel and set him back on his feet, straightening out the front of his shabby jacket with stubby fingers. 'So you're runnin' errands for Henry on the sly, are you? Well, now I know about it, I'll be keepin' an eye on you. And if I find out that any of these errands involve a spade and bunch of flowers, you'll be diggin' another grave to order, and this time there'll be a body to go in it.'

19

The car park at The Boar was surprisingly empty when Rose arrived, save for George Mulligan's green Toyota and the large black Mercedes she had seen Benny Bradman throw Jimmy Porter into yesterday evening. The sight of the Mercedes made her momentarily panic, and she took in a deep breath to steady herself. For God's sake Rose, pull yourself together. Craig has probably just borrowed his father's car, that's all. She parked up next to Mulligan's car, grabbed her briefcase from the back seat, and braced herself to apologise for being late.

The inside of The Boar was as quiet as the car park. In one corner, a large table was occupied by the remnants of a lunch party, the last few stragglers from an office outing. In the opposite corner at a smaller table, George Mulligan had divested himself of his jacket and was enjoying a half pint of lager. Beside him, a fresh-faced young man in a crisp blue shirt and silk tie was talking earnestly. The young man was as pale-skinned as Benny Bradman was tanned, and Rose could only guess that his auburn hair and freckles had been inherited from his mother.

'Sorry if I'm a bit late.' Rose approached the table and dropped her briefcase onto the floor beside an empty chair. She looked straight into Craig Bradman's face and held out a hand. 'You must be Craig?'

The young man smiled and shook her hand warmly. 'That's right. And you must be Rose. DI Mulligan was just telling me a bit about your work at the bank.' His face was open, as guileless as Rose had ever seen. 'I don't know what I can do to help you, but if there's any chance of finding Pan ...' His voice trailed off, but his eyes were full of hope.

Rose sat down opposite the two men, and eyed a glass of slightly flat tonic water. 'Is that for me?'

Mulligan grinned. 'You should have been here at three o'clock, it was still fizzy then.'

She pursed her lips. 'Point taken.' She turned to the younger man. 'Thanks for giving us some time, Craig. I guess Mr. Mulligan has already told you that I've been looking into the work Pandora was doing just before she disappeared?'

Craig nodded, and his face saddened. 'She was worried about work, Rose. I've already told DI Mulligan that.'

'Can you tell me exactly what she was worried about? I believe she called you from work on the afternoon she disappeared?'

'She'd had a row with Janis Porter, because she refused to open an account. She told me that she thought the customer was trying to use stolen identification documents.'

'Did she actually say she thought the documents were stolen?'

'Yes, she seemed quite certain about it. She said she couldn't have opened the account because of the documents, and she asked Marge Baker for advice. She thought that the right thing to do was to refer the application to Head Office, and they would pragmatically refuse to open the account. But Marge disagreed with her. She asked to see the documents, and when Pan showed them to her she said there was nothing wrong with them. Pan didn't believe her, and she went to speak to Janis about it. Janis agreed with Marge, and told her to open the account. When Pan refused, Janis authorised it herself, and she asked Marge to take over with the customer.'

Rose looked across at Mulligan. 'This all tallies with what I've heard at the bank.' She turned back to Craig.

'And was that an end of it?'

Anticipating his reply, Mulligan nodded. 'We've been through all this, Rose. Craig gave us a full statement about this the day after Pandora went missing.'

Craig's face took on a slightly sheepish look. 'Actually, there was something else.' He looked from Mulligan to Rose, and back again. 'Sorry Mr. Mulligan, but Pandora asked me not to tell anyone.'

The inspector turned his eyes heavenward. 'Bloody hell, Craig, she's missing. This girl you care about so much has been missing for two full days, and you still haven't told us everything?'

Craig turned appealing eyes on Rose, hoping to find an ally. 'I thought she'd hurt herself when she was out running. I thought we were going to find her straight away. I was respecting her confidence. This is to do with work, not with her going missing.' He watched as Mulligan and Rose exchanged glances. 'You're not going to tell me that she's disappeared because of work?'

'We don't know, Craig.' It was Rose who spoke first to calm him down. 'But we need to know what she told you, if only to eliminate that possibility.'

Colour had flushed into Craig's face, and he suddenly looked more like a frightened schoolboy than a confident Oxford graduate. 'She went back to see Janis a second time after the customer had gone. She tried to tell her that she thought some other accounts had been opened with stolen ID, and that Marge had authorised them.'

Rose put up her hand. 'She actually said that to you, Craig? That she thought the ID was stolen, but that Marge had authorised it?'

He nodded. 'She asked Janis about completing some form for the police, I can't remember what she called it.'

'A Suspicious Activity Report?'

Craig shrugged. 'It could have been. I can't remember. Whatever it was, Pan said that Janis went crazy when she suggested it. She tried to make out that Pan was mistaken, and that she'd better just let it drop.' He sighed. 'But Pan wasn't like that. If something was wrong, she wouldn't let it lie. She told me on the phone that she was thinking about submitting the report herself, but she was scared about it rebounding on Janis and Marge. She didn't want to get them into trouble. She wanted to talk it through with me in the pub, but she said she was going for a run first to try to clear her head.'

Rose laid a hand gently on his arm. 'Did you tell anybody at all about this conversation, Craig?'

Craig shook his head. 'Not even Danny or Selina.'

'And your Dad?'

'No. I didn't tell him, either.'

'Your Dad doesn't like Pandora very much, does he?' Rose thought she already knew the answer to this, but Craig's view would be interesting.

'He doesn't dislike her. He doesn't think she's good enough for me.' He rolled his eyes, as if to say "what does he know?" 'I don't really care what Dad thinks. He'll come round in the end.'

Mulligan had listened in silence for a while, and now he rubbed at his forehead with his hand. 'Craig, where was Pandora when she made this call to you?'

'She was still at work. I think she was in the staff room. Sometimes she went up there to call me on her mobile.'

Rose was ahead of Mulligan. 'So she could have been overheard by anyone else at the branch.' She picked up the glass of lifeless tonic and took a sip from it while she pondered on Craig's story. It was all hearsay, of course. And yet it more or less tallied with Tommy's version of events.

Across the table, Craig's dejected face spoke of his concern for Pandora Mitchell, and Rose suddenly felt a pang of guilt. If this young man had been guilty of colluding with Pandora, of persuading her to open fraudulent accounts, of having a hand in her disappearance, it would have given her – and Mulligan – a neat solution and let the ENB off the hook. But the only thing he had to be guilty about was respecting Pandora's wishes, and keeping their conversation private. What had Benny said? "He's an honest lad." Well, like it or not it looked like this was one point on which she was going to have to agree with Mr. Bradman.

There was nothing scenic about the view from the windows of Bellevue Mansions. Half the flats in the building fronted on to the main road from Kirkby to Scarborough, overlooking a large modern retail park and an endless line of heavy traffic, their white plastic window frames already beginning to stain grey from the exhaust fumes. These were the lucky ones. The remaining flats, positioned to the rear of the block, shared a panoramic view over the sheds and hangers of the local fish processing plant. On this side, the window frames had more chance of staying white, but they would also remain firmly shut at all times. Even then, the stench of mackerel was so invasive it had begun to pervade the rubber seals around the windows.

Spivey parked his car in the car park at the rear of the building, as close to the back door as he could. Out of the car the smell didn't seem too bad today, but he knew from experience that it could insinuate itself into your clothes in a matter of minutes, so the shorter his walk from car to door the better. Last time he'd been here the barmaid at The Feathers had ribbed him all night about the need for a new aftershave.

He pulled a large bunch of keys from his trouser pocket as he walked up to the building, and used the largest on the ring to open the back door. The fire hinge at the top of the door was still stiff from newness, and he had to push against it with his shoulder to get it fully open. Inside, the faint aroma of mackerel blended unpleasantly with the smell of paint and cheap nylon carpet, and he sniffed in disgust. Why didn't somebody put an air freshener in the hall? No wonder Henry was having trouble selling these flats.

Still, at least the lack of occupants meant that the place wasn't getting grubby too quickly. He wiped his shoes on the doormat and trotted up the carpeted staircase to the second floor, then along the hall to the door of flat 2b. He rattled the keys again, looking for the right one, and let himself in, closing the door quietly behind him. The air in the hallway was stuffy, and slightly fishy.

He'd brought a document folder with him, a dated faux-leather thing in black, with a gold-coloured zip running round three sides, and he laid it down on the hall table. He'd bought the folder in the charity shop in Market Melbourne for a few pounds when Henry first asked him to help out with the flats. It was less conspicuous than a briefcase, but he thought it showed that he took his job with Henry seriously, and when he wasn't working for Benny he carried it around with him like a badge of office.

On the carpet below the hall table, three white envelopes lay under the letterbox. He bent down and picked them up, and examined each in turn. One for Hills, and two for Smith. He unzipped the document folder and shoved the envelopes inside, then quickly re-zipped it and tucked it under his arm. He turned and stepped further into the hall, and pushed open the lounge door. The room was empty, save for a badly fitted beige carpet. He looked around, assured himself that all was as it should be, then closed the door. He repeated the exercise on first one bedroom, and then the other, and then checked the bathroom and the kitchen. Everything looked just how he'd left it after last week's visit.

He let himself out of the flat, making sure that the door was firmly locked behind him, and then let himself into the flat next door. This flat also had a small table next to the letterbox in the hall, but the clutter of unopened white envelopes under the letter box was larger. He bent down and scooped them up, then rifled through them quickly, sorting them into name order, before unzipping the document folder again and shoving them inside. He carried out the same inspection on the flat, muttering to himself as he went. Lounge OK, bedroom, yes, second bedroom, yes, bathroom OK, kitchen? He squinted into the kitchen, in the direction of the sink. Was that tap dripping? Bollocks. He'd better tell Henry.

Outside in the hallway he made sure the door was locked, and then turned toward Flat 2d. His pulse quickened a little, and he licked his lips nervously, glancing around him to make sure no-one was around to watch. All of the flats on this floor were unoccupied, and he knew his anxiety was irrational, but better safe than sorry. He rifled through the bunch of keys for a third time, and unlocked the door to Flat 2d. Two white envelopes lay on the carpet under the letterbox, and his stomach churned with anticipation. He stepped into the flat, and closed the door behind him, then picked up the envelopes. He could barely contain his excitement. He hadn't expected it to be so quick. He felt at the packets. The smaller of the two contained what felt like a cheque book, and he pushed it unopened into his inside jacket pocket. The larger, A4 packet felt stiff, maybe some kind of folder? He started to unzip the document folder, then thought better of it, and just tucked the packet under his arm.

He turned and stepped forward towards the doors at the other side of the hall, opening each in turn to check that everything was OK in the lounge, the bedrooms, the bathroom, and finally the kitchen. The kitchen in this flat was slightly different from the others. The others had a small window overlooking the main road, but this flat was on the corner of the block, and light flooded into the room through a large picture window over the sink. He stepped through the kitchen door and looked around. Yes, this one was a bit different, and not just because of the window. He had a connection with it now. His post had been sent here, like it was his home. He indulged in a momentary fantasy of Henry agreeing to sell it to him. Well why not? Henry knew he'd be good for the money. He had a regular income from Benny and he made a bit doing odd jobs. He wasn't afraid of work. He ran a finger over the counter top and looked down at the thin layer of dust deposited on his finger. He ought to bring a duster next time, keep the place tidy.

An urgent vibration from his mobile phone brought an abrupt end to his daydream. He pulled the phone from his pocket and looked at the display. Bollocks, it was Henry Campling. Even though Campling was thirty miles away in Market Melbourne, he couldn't help feeling that he'd been caught in the act. He quickly scurried out of the kitchen, and out of the front door of the flat, letting it slam closed behind him before he answered the call. 'Mr Campling. Yes, I'm there now. Well, I think the tap's dripping in 2c, but apart from that no problems. No, no problems at all.'

20

'There's something wrong with Janis, isn't there?' Tommy thumbed through a wad of ten pound notes as he spoke, mentally keeping count as he cashed up his till for the day.

Hazel, half way through counting a wad of twenties, winced and started her count again. To say there was something wrong with Janis was the understatement of the day, and for once she really didn't want to gossip about it. There was an atmosphere in the branch that unsettled her, had unsettled her all day, and right now all she wanted to do was cash up and get home to her kids. She answered him with a grunt, and kept on counting.

'Do you think it's got something to do with Pandora? Do you think I made things worse by telling her I'd seen Rose Bennett with DI Mulligan?'

Hazel stopped counting and turned to him. 'No Tommy, I don't think it's got anything to do with Pandora. If you really want to know what I think, I think Janis has been doing something here at the Bank that she shouldn't have been doing. Don't ask me why, because I don't know. I just ... well, I just *know*.'

His eyes widened. 'Janis wouldn't break the rules. Would she? Why would she need to?'

'I don't know. Maybe she needed the money.'

'Needed the money? You mean, she needed her bonus?' He frowned. 'But Janis earns a packet. I know we joke about her going on about the bonuses, but I thought that was just 'cos she liked to spend it. She can't be short of money.'

'Why not? That's how it is with some people. The more they have the more they spend, and the more they spend the more they want. Not everyone is as sensible as you and me, Tommy. Janis is used to having plenty of money, and you know yourself how sensitive she's been about the bonuses these last few weeks.'

'Jimmy must earn good money. He's a supervisor, and he gets a shift allowance.'

'Yes, but just because he earns it, doesn't mean he shares it all with Janis.' She clipped a wad of notes with a large paperclip, and pushed them into a bag in readiness for the safe.

She wanted Tommy to stop talking about Janis now. Because she wasn't sure her manager's problems were just to do with money. When Janis opened the door to her this morning, Hazel saw into her soul. No-one could look that bad, that numb, that frightened, just because their bonus was going to be a bit short this month.

Tommy stopped counting bank notes and turned to look at her. 'Is that why Rose Bennett came here? To snoop on Janis?'

'Maybe. But don't think of it as snooping. Rose is OK. She's done right by you and me, hasn't she?' And now she's gone, Hazel thought. The review is finished, and Rose has gone.

And now the trouble is going to start.

Benny turned the ignition key, and the engine of Craig's ageing BMW coughed and spluttered into life. He pulled the car away from the kerb and tucked into the queue of traffic just three or four cars behind Michael Spivey. It was almost the end of August, and Scarborough still buzzed with holidaymakers and day trippers. Behind his sunglasses, with his shirt sleeves rolled up and his elbow resting casually on the rolled down window, Benny blended into the general scene, and he knew Spivey was too lackadaisical to notice him. After all, he thought, I've just followed the little toe-rag all the way from Market Melbourne to Scarborough, and he hasn't got a clue.

The traffic lights ahead turned to red and the queue of traffic slowed. The left hand indicator light on Spivey's car began to flick. Where the hell was he going now? This wasn't the way back to Market Melbourne. Benny drummed his fingers impatiently on the steering wheel as traffic from first one direction and then another flowed across the junction.

Eventually the lights changed to green and he pulled the BMW slowly forward, turning left behind Spivey and keeping a safe distance to avoid being seen. The car creaked in objection as he turned the steering wheel and Benny grimaced. Why the hell did Craig insist on driving this rust bucket? Because he bought it from Danny Mitchell with his pocket money? Still, he thought, it was just as well they'd swapped cars this afternoon. Spivey wasn't exactly bright, and although he might recognize Craig's car at a push, he wouldn't expect to see it in Scarborough.

Half a mile along the road Spivey pulled up in a roadside parking space. Benny cursed under his breath. He cruised past Spivey's car with his head turned away, as if looking for something on the other side of the road. Once past, he looked in his rear view mirror. Spivey was out of the car, and walking across the pavement into an off licence. Benny swung the car down the next side street. He'd have to go round the block and park up somewhere farther back down the main road, ready to follow Spivey when he came out of the shop.

Parked up a safe distance away, Benny turned off the engine and contemplated his afternoon. He didn't like the idea of Spivey working for Henry Campling, didn't like it enough to feel the need to follow him to see what he was up to. He'd watched him go into the Bellevue flats with interest. Henry had insisted these flats would be a good investment, but he was glad he'd passed on the opportunity. He didn't like the location, or the smell, and he didn't want to carry the guilty feeling that would go with taking money from some youngster who couldn't afford anything better. Of course, Henry Campling didn't possess anything resembling a conscience, and what he couldn't sell he would rent out to some otherwise homeless kid. One or two of the flats looked to be occupied now, and Benny guessed that Spivey was collecting rent from some muppet who'd taken on a tenancy, and maybe checking that the empty flats were OK while he was here.

He sighed, and shifted in his seat. The car was old, and the driver's seat was uncomfortable, and it contributed to his bad mood. He knew a bad mood was no basis for making business decisions, but today he didn't really care. Spivey was becoming an overhead, and he didn't need the hassle. Maybe it was time to cut him loose.

'Of course I'm going to send you the full report, Clive. By email, later this evening. But I thought at the very least you would want to know the salient points.' Rose opened her spiral notebook and spread it out on Lu's dining table. 'And you'll be pleased to know I'm back at the cottage, so our discussion can be as frank as necessary without the risk of being overheard.'

At the other end of the line, Clive cleared his throat. 'I suppose this conversation is necessary, then. I hope you're bringing me good news, Rose. I want to lay this to rest, so that there can be no suggestion of it overlapping the Pandora Mitchell investigation.'

Rose smiled to herself. He wouldn't be sounding quite so smug in a few minutes. She placed a finger on the top of the left hand page. 'I'll rattle through this as quickly as I can. To begin with, the remit you set me was to investigate mistakes in account opening made at the Market

Melbourne branch, to determine whether or not there was any risk of staff collusion or fraud. I've reviewed the account opening process with three members of staff, particularly with respect to the checking of personal ID documents. Hazel Grant and Tommy Fletcher are both process-perfect. Marge Baker, on the other hand, made significant errors in the assessment of customer identification documents, errors that were out of proportion with her experience and years of service at the bank. As a result of this, I requested a further review with Janis Porter. That request was refused.'

'Refused?' Clive barked the word down the phone. 'She refused your request? Why didn't you tell me?'

'I'm telling you now. She made it pretty clear that she would still refuse if you got involved, even if it meant disciplinary procedure. Anyway, that refusal is material to my report. I consider it inappropriate in the circumstances, given that she is the branch manager.'

She heard him snort at the other end of the phone. 'Shall I go through my recommendations?' She didn't wait for a response. 'Under normal circumstances I would have said that the errors at the branch were due to carelessness in process by one member of staff, and recommended re-training for Marge Baker. However, due to Janis's refusal to submit to a process review, and due to there being evidence to suggest that Janis Porter and Pandora Mitchell had a professional disagreement regarding the opening of a potentially fraudulent account, I am strongly recommending that a full investigation be carried out into account opening at the branch over the last three months. Further, as any accounts opened by Pandora Mitchell were not validated correctly at the time of opening, I recommend that they be monitored on a daily basis for at least three months to check for evidence of fraudulent activity. Finally, I think you should appraise the appropriate law enforcement agencies of the situation at the earliest opportunity.'

She paused for breath. Clive was still silent at the other of the line. 'Shall I go through the risks?' Again no answer. 'OK ... well, there is a risk that the Bank may be in breach of its regulatory obligations, because it failed to "know its customer" at the time of account opening. This may incur a fine from the Regulator. Also, I believe there has been a breach of regulation in failing to report suspicious activity to the appropriate authorities when it became apparent that an attempt was being made to open a fraudulent bank account.'

There was still no response from the other end of the line. Rose sighed. 'Clive, are you still there? Have you nothing to say to any of this?'

He cleared his throat. 'So Janis is in the clear.' There was no inflection in the phrase. It was a statement of fact, not a question.

'I beg your pardon?' Rose thought she had misheard him, and there was incredulity in her tone.

'Janis. Her only failure, apart from refusing to submit to your review, was not to submit a report when Pandora Mitchell suspected a fraudulent account was being opened. And that in itself may not have been a failure, because Pandora may have been mistaken.'

Rose leaned back in her chair and closed her eyes. Who said there was no deceiver like a self-deceiver? She puffed out a heavy sigh. 'Clive, the official remit you set me was to check out whether the branch was following process, and whether there was any risk of fraudulent activity. We both know that what you really wanted to know wasn't just whether fraudulent activity was taking place, but whether or not your ex-wife was aware of it, or even worse involved in it. You were hoping that I was going to report back that a few silly mistakes had been made, and that there was nothing that could rebound on you.'

'I resent that remark.'

'You can resent it all you like, but it's evident in the way you're trying to twist my words. Janis is the manager of that branch. She's responsible for what goes on there. She's failed to ensure that her staff open accounts correctly, and she's refused to acknowledge a serious problem when a member of staff tried to bring it to her attention. I'm not accusing her of doing anything deliberately fraudulent. But I'm as sure as I can be that she has turned a blind eye to bad practices in that branch in order to achieve her sales targets.' She gave him a moment to think about it, and then asked 'would you like me to clearly state that in my report?'

'No, that won't be necessary. I have taken your comments on board, Rose.'

'Fine. Then I'll mail the full report over to you this evening, and consider myself off the case.' She thought for a moment, and then asked 'what about Mr. Mulligan?'

'Mulligan?' Clive sounded puzzled. 'What about him?'

'You asked me to work with him, to be his eyes and ears at the branch. Has that assignment ended too?'

Clive's response was sharp. 'I can't see that you have discovered anything relevant to Pandora Mitchell's disappearance. I'll call DI Mulligan now and let him know that your work is finished, and that as far as the Bank are concerned, Pandora's disappearance is a purely personal affair.' He cleared his throat again, and his tone softened a little. 'Thank you for your assistance again, Rose. You know that I appreciate your willingness to occasionally - what shall I say? - blur the boundaries?'

She closed her eyes and smiled. 'Clive, you're the bane of my life. But I take my hat off to anyone who could have spent six years married to Janis. I don't envy you having to sort out the mess she's in. I'm just glad that I'm not going to be around to see it.'

The phone clicked as Clive hung up. Rose closed the spiral notebook, and laid her mobile phone down on top of it. There were so many other things she could have discussed with him. The changes of address on the fraudulent accounts, the evidence of money laundering, the possibility that Janis could be involved in Pandora's disappearance, it was pointless discussing these with Clive. He already knew all about them. He just wanted assurance from Rose that no-one else did.

And Rose was happy to give him that assurance. Best to let him think she didn't know what was going on, beyond a bit of deliberate carelessness and self-interest on Janis's part. No, it was better she discussed the real issues with someone other than Clive. Someone who was interested in these facts coming to light, not someone who wanted to see them covered up. She picked up her mobile phone again, and began searching for DI Mulligan's number.

21

'I've come to talk to you about that thing that was dug in your garden, that grave or whatever it was.' Benny perched uncomfortably on the edge of Lu's sofa, and tried to look penitent. He put out a hand and waggled his fingers at Mac, who was lying under the coffee table close to his feet. 'I had a visit from your niece this afternoon. She made it pretty clear that she thinks it were down to me.' Mac sniffed at his fingers and gave them a cursory lick, then looked round at Lu in case he'd misjudged the situation.

Lu smiled indulgently at the terrier and settled back in her armchair. 'I know she does. But for what it's worth, I don't. I might not agree with some of your business methods, but I don't think you'd stoop to frightening people out of their homes.'

Benny's face showed his surprise. 'Well, I appreciate that, Lucinda. Thank you.' He sniffed apologetically. 'I don't think she has too good an impression of me.'

'I wouldn't let that worry you. Rose always thinks the worst of people until she sees otherwise, and even then she'll think twice about it. She's popped out for a couple of hours, but when she gets back I'll tell her that you've been round to make your peace.'

He nodded his appreciation. 'Thing is, I didn't have anythin' to do with it, but in a roundabout way I think I might have been responsible. And so I wanted to come here and set things straight with you. If you'll hear me out?'

'Go ahead.'

'I have a bloke workin' for me as a kind of gofer. He minds the shop now and again when me and Craig aren't around, runs errands, that sort of thing. His name's Michael Spivey.'

Lu frowned. 'Never heard of him.'

'No, well, I didn't think you would have. I couldn't see the two of you movin' in the same social circles, if you know what I mean.' He chuckled at the thought. 'Thing is, he's started doin' a few odd jobs for Henry on the side.'

'Campling?'

Benny nodded. 'Now I ain't got no proof, but I think Michael dug that grave. And bein' as he has no axe to grind with you or Rose, I can only guess that Henry asked him to do it. Henry's been talkin' about findin' other ways of persuadin' you to move on from here, and Michael's dumb enough to do as he's told if there's money in it for him. Now, you'd be within your rights to tell the police about this, and press charges if they think that's appropriate. But I'd be obliged if you don't. Henry's got no conscience, he'd deny havin' anythin' to do with it, and Michael ... well, he's a bit of a lame dog, and that's a fact. There ain't no pleasure in kickin' a lame dog, is there?' He looked down at Mac, who eyed him with resentment at the suggestion. 'If it would help you make a decision, I could oil the wheels. Nothin' criminal. A donation to your favourite charity, maybe, and we could call it quits?'

'I don't know.' Lu was thoughtful. 'I appreciate you coming to talk to me about this, Benny, but if you weren't involved then the crime wasn't yours to apologise for. Calling a truce with you doesn't necessarily mean that Henry will leave me alone.'

'I'll have a word. With Michael, and with Henry. I'll tell him I've squared it with you. For what it's worth, I'm goin' to tell Henry I'm pullin' out of our plans for your cottages. He says everybody has a price, but I don't think you do, and I respect you for that.' He looked round the room sheepishly. It was comfortable, tasteful, lived in. 'To be honest, if I lived here I wouldn't let a couple of two-bit property developers heave me out onto the street.'

'Why Mr. Bradman, don't tell me you're developing a conscience?' Lu's tone was teasing.

'Not so much developin' one, as remembering I had one in the first place.' He looked wistful. 'Can I say somethin' out of turn? Your niece Rose, she reminds me of my late wife. She had red hair and a willful nature as well.' He laughed, and checked himself. 'That's all, mind. There was no-one to match my Catriona, and there never will be. But bein' reminded of her, well it reminded me that she was my conscience, and now she's gone I need to develop a better one for myself.' He put down a hand and ruffled Mac's ears. 'As a matter of fact, it's all Catriona's fault that I'm draggin' Michael along with me. He was her last case, before she died. She got him off a false larceny charge, but he lost his job anyway. She asked me to find him somethin' in the business, so I did.'

'And he came with you when you moved up here?' Lu asked.

'He had no family or friends, and no chance I could see of gettin' another job. I suppose I did what Trina would have wanted me to do.' He laughed. 'And see where it got me? Sittin' in your livin' room havin' to apologise for his behaviour.'

'Well, he's very lucky to have you watching out for him.'

Benny shook his head. 'I can't watch out for him if he's goin' to go off and harass decent folk like yourself, Lucinda. I think I'm goin' to have to let him go. He's gettin' quite thick with Henry now, he's been doin' some errands for him up in Scarborough today. Henry owns flats up there, nothin' to do with me. Thing is, I actually followed him to Scarborough. I was worried enough about what he was gettin' up to with Henry to waste my afternoon drivin' to Scarborough and back on a wild goose chase. And I ain't got time for that sort of caper on a regular basis.' He paused thoughtfully. He'd said more than he meant to, and all this soul-baring was making him uncomfortable. He put his hands purposefully on his knees. 'And talkin' of time, I think I've taken up enough of yours this afternoon. Do we have a deal, then? I'll do somethin' for you, and you'll look the other way this one time and give Michael a chance? Maybe we can call it the last thing we'll both do for him?'

Lu smiled. 'Tell you what. Why don't you come for dinner, and bring Craig with you? I like a bit of male company around the place now and again. You do that for me, and I'll square things with Dave Gilling about the grave. I'll tell him it was a practical joke that back-fired.'

'Well that's very kind of you Lucinda. We'll take you up on that.' He took in a breath. 'And you'll square it with Rose?'

'Steady on, I said I'd sort it out with the police. I didn't say I could work miracles.'

'I'm off the case officially once this report goes in, and Clive's made it clear that my remit to assist the police ends at the same time. At least as far as the ENB is concerned.' Rose pulled a copy of the draft report from her briefcase and pushed it across the table to George Mulligan. 'I'll be completing the detailed version this evening, and emailing it over to him some time before midnight.'

Mulligan frowned and pulled the document towards him. He licked a finger and leafed through it. It was only three or four pages long. 'How long will the full thing be?'

'About ten pages. But what I've given you here should be enough to put you in the picture.' She waited until he met her gaze again. 'I'd be grateful if you didn't reveal to Clive that I gave you this. Strictly speaking it is confidential to the bank, but I think it will help you to formulate some questions for Clive that might help you in the search for Pandora.'

Mulligan's face crumpled into a wry smile. 'Any chance of a few hints while you're here then, or am I going to have to work it all out for myself?'

She smiled back. 'That's why I came in to the station to speak to you. I thought a conversation would be useful.' She folded her arms and leaned on the table. 'We know that Janis and Pandora argued because Pandora refused to open an account with what she believed to be stolen ID documents.'

He nodded. 'And we know that later Pandora tried to tell Janis that she thought other fraudulent accounts had been authorised by Marge Baker.'

'Correct. I've managed to track down details of those accounts. The eight accounts authorised by Marge were opened with addresses matching the ID documents, then within days a request was made for each account to have the correspondence address changed to an address in Scarborough. The addresses were all in the same block of flats, Bellevue Mansions.'

'Do we know if these accounts have been used for anything?'

'Mm. They're being used for laundering. Large sums of money are being transacted through, and siphoned off to receiving accounts, some of them offshore. And whoever is using these accounts appears to have inside information. The ENB monitors transactions over a certain threshold, and that threshold hasn't been crossed.'

'So Marge or Pandora could have provided that information?'

'No, it's management information. Only Janis would have known the actual threshold, although admittedly she could have unwittingly shared that information with someone else at the branch.'

'You think Janis is involved?'

Rose frowned. 'I think she's up to her neck in something, but I don't know what. I thought that she was just turning a blind eye to the regulations to make sure that she made her bonus, but this all looks too organized.' She tapped on the report to emphasize the point. 'These accounts follow a formula. They've been opened to plan. I don't know if Janis realizes that or not.'

Mulligan considered the idea for a moment, and then asked 'so what about names and addresses for the accounts? Will these be in your report?'

'No. I don't report at that level of detail. I've recommended to Clive that he appraise the appropriate authorities as soon as possible, and I've no reason to believe he won't follow my advice. They'll ask for all the detail you'd need, and more besides. But Clive's pretty desperate to disassociate the ENB from Pandora's disappearance, and my guess is that he won't voluntarily include you in the discussions. I would suggest that you ask him directly for full details of any accounts Pandora opened, and any transactions put through them.'

Mulligan nodded thoughtfully. 'And what about the ninth account, the one that started the argument? Is that also connected to the address in Scarborough?'

Rose leaned a little further over the table. 'Yes, but there wasn't an address change requested this time. The applicant asked for the account to be opened with the Bellevue address, and he presented a rent book with that address on it. He also presented a driving licence for an address in Kirkby Park, claiming that he'd just moved to Scarborough and hadn't had chance to get his licence changed. From what I've heard, he didn't look the Kirkby Park type, and Pandora was pretty quick to recognize it as a fraudulent application.'

'So we have an additional suspect, then.' Mulligan's face folded into a frown. 'The unknown applicant who almost had his application refused.' He leaned back in his chair. 'I don't suppose you can tell me the actual names and addresses?'

'I can't break the bank's confidentiality to that extent. If you get that request in to Clive for the account details, it shouldn't take him more than twenty four hours to turn that around, even at the weekend.' She gave an impish smile. 'And after all, you live in Kirkby don't you? I wouldn't have thought it would be too far out of your way to pass Bellevue Mansions on your way home.' She let him think about it before adding 'I've heard the view from the second floor is worth a look.'

22

Mac gave a low growl, and lifted his head from Rose's lap. She ruffled his ears. 'It's only Lu in the kitchen. Go back to sleep.' The dog wasn't convinced. He twisted his small body upright and jumped off the sofa, then up onto the back of the armchair at the window. He poked his snout between the closed curtains and sniffed at the window. Outside a car door slammed, and Rose heard the click of a door lock, then footsteps on the path to the front door of the cottage.

Mac barked as the doorbell rang, and Rose hushed him. Who the hell was calling at this time of night? She unfolded her legs from under her and was about to stand when the lounge door opened, and Lu's voice announced 'someone for you, Rose.'

Janis stepped into the room and turned to speak to Lu, but the door was already closing behind her. She turned back to Rose and forced a smile. 'Sorry to disturb you so late. I … I needed to speak to you.'

'At this time of night?'

'It couldn't wait.' She stepped forward towards an armchair. 'Is it OK if I sit down.'

'Of course.' Mac, trapped in the room with them, sensed the tension and looked around for a safe harbour. He slithered under the sofa behind Rose's feet and rested his nose on his paws. 'If it's about breaking the regulations, I'm afraid you're too late. I submitted my report to Clive half an hour ago. I'm off the case.'

Janis gave a quiet laugh. 'I wish that's all there was to it.

The fact is, you were right. Everything you said to me this morning was true. I've got myself into a real mess, and I don't know how to get out of it.' She sighed. 'They say confession is good for the soul, so here I am.' She took in a breath to steady herself, and then said 'I've allowed the branch to be used for opening fraudulent accounts.'

The existence of fraudulent accounts wasn't news to Rose, but Janis's voluntary admission was unexpected. Rose heard the words but it took a moment for them to register. 'Fraudulent accounts? Who for?'

'I can't tell you. I'm sorry, I wish I could.'

Rose studied Janis's face. She still looked strained, tired, but there was an air of resignation about her now. 'I take it we're talking about the accounts opened by Pandora?'

Janis nodded. 'I suppose you found out about them during the review?'

'You must have known I would.'

'Yes, of course.' She gave another quiet laugh. 'I thought we had all bases covered, but I hadn't bargained for you turning up.'

Rose got up from the sofa and crossed to the sideboard. She took two glasses from the shelf and poured two generous measures of whisky, handing one of the glasses to Janis without asking whether or not she wanted it. Janis took the drink from her and sipped on it gratefully.

Rose went back to the sofa and perched on its edge, wrapping her hands around her glass. 'I know that eight accounts have been opened by Pandora, and that Marge authorised them. I know that the ID documents were invalid, and the accounts shouldn't have been opened. I also know those accounts are being used for laundering.' She watched as Janis turned her head away, and saw that she still had the grace to blush. 'I also know there was a ninth account that Pandora refused to open, and which you authorised yourself. I know the address on that account was in line with the others.' She paused. 'I know what, and I know how, and where, and when, but what I don't know is why.'

Janis shrugged. 'Because I needed the money.'

It was Rose's turn to laugh. 'You don't get rich on the commission from a handful of current accounts. I can't believe you'd risk your job for that.'

'I didn't. I was paid to do it.'

'To open the accounts?'

'To ensure that they were opened. And to make sure that the correspondence addresses were changed shortly after opening.' She sighed again. 'And to provide assurance that the money laundered through them wouldn't be picked up in any monitoring.'

'So how much did you make, Janis? What's your integrity worth these days?'

Janis's voice became a hoarse whisper. 'Two grand per account. There were meant to be ten accounts, so I stood to make twenty grand in total.'

The time for sipping was over, and Rose took a deep swig from her glass. 'Still not enough to risk losing a manager's job.'

'It is if you're in over your head.' Janis nestled back into the arm chair, and wrapped her arms over her body, resting the whisky glass close to her face. 'We're in a mess Rose, and I couldn't see a way out.'

'Over-extended?'

'Up to our eyeballs. Mortgage we can't afford, car loans we shouldn't have taken out, credit card debts for holidays we shouldn't have had.'

'So why not restructure? You and Jimmy both have good jobs, you have child maintenance from Clive, you have collateral in the house, you're a good risk. You could have remortgaged.'

Janis lowered her eyes and stared into her glass. 'We couldn't restructure. And I can't tell you why.'

'Is it something to do with Jimmy?'

'Let's just say his credit rating isn't as good as mine.'

Janis looked away, and Rose thought she saw the

beginning of tears starting to show. 'So Jimmy's got a debt problem?' She thought about the way Benny Bradman had bundled Jimmy into his car, and his refusal to talk about his relationship with Jimmy. Benny had dropped enough hints, only she hadn't realised it until now. She sighed, and swilled the remaining whisky around in her glass. It wasn't just a debt problem. 'I take it Benny Bradman isn't his only creditor?'

Janis smiled at the mention of Benny's name. 'What Jimmy owes Benny is just the tip of the iceberg. Most of it is on credit cards. He's been gambling on the internet. Of course, that stopped when he maxed out all his cards. Lenders had been increasing his credit limit for months, but once he stopped making payments ... well, you know enough about banking to know what happened next.'

Indeed she did. A gentle reminder for the first missed payment. A stronger reminder for the second. Then the phone calls start, cajoling at first, then tougher, and tougher, and tougher again. Then the recoveries people get involved, they talk about helping, but all they want is their money back. Letters fall through the letter box talking about credit files, and default notices, and veiled threats of court action. You ignore them, but they won't go away. And then the statements start to get really scary. No payments to reduce the balance, but the late payment charges start kicking in, and more interest is applied, and then interest on the interest, and then interest on the interest on the interest.

'Has Benny been putting pressure on Jimmy to pay him back, then? Is that why he threw him out of the shop?'

Janis shook her head. 'Far from it. Benny's been an angel. Jimmy started gambling at the shop when his credit lines for the internet ran out. Benny extended him some credit but realised pretty quickly that there was a problem. He barred him straight away.' She forced a smile. 'He's been great. He's been trying to help him, talking to him about it, even tried to square things with another bookie that Jimmy got involved with.'

'But I saw him push Jimmy into his car and drive off with him. Jimmy looked terrified.'

Janis nodded. 'Benny gets a bit exasperated with him some times. When you saw him Jimmy needed a fix and Benny thought the best thing to do was bring him home. He waited at the house with him until I got in, to make sure he didn't try to get a bet somewhere else.'

'Janis, was it Benny who asked you to open the fraudulent accounts?'

'No, of course not. He doesn't know anything about it. Neither does Jimmy.' She stared down into her glass. 'I told him over supper that we'd argued about work, and that I wanted to put things straight with you. He thinks that's why I'm here now.'

Rose was still puzzled. 'I still don't see why you had to commit a crime. You could have looked for help. Benny's been helping you, you could have gone to one of the gambling charities, spoken to a debt charity, there are plenty of things you can do to sort these things out without breaking the law.'

Colour suddenly flared into Janis's cheeks. 'Is this where I get the lecture, then, Rose? You shouldn't have done that, Janis. Naughty Janis, letting the side down.' She banged her glass down on the table beside the arm chair and Mac whimpered quietly, and backed a little further under the sofa. 'Of course, if it had happened to you, you would have handled it all perfectly.'

'I wouldn't have resorted to crime.'

'Well bloody good for you.' Janis's tone hardened. 'And just how would you have got out of it all?'

'Janis, you're a bank manager. You know how it works. You talk to the creditors. You apologise for the mess, tell them you're going to turn it round, and get a repayment plan in place. If you're up front about it, they'll be reasonable. It's when they don't know what's going on that they play hard ball. The more you stick your head in the sand, the more insistent they're going to be.'

Janis was less composed now, clearly struggling to keep her emotions under control. 'I know I'm a bloody bank manager, Rose. That's the problem.' She spat the words out. 'Do you think they'd let me keep my job if it got out that I'm married to a chronic gambler, and we're up to our eyeballs in bad debt?'

'You mean any more than they'd let you keep it when they find out you've turned criminal just to pay your credit cards off? Does Clive have any idea of the mess you're in?'

'Of course not. The equity in the house came from my divorce settlement, and Jimmy is on the mortgage. If any of his creditors force a sale to recover their money, we'll lose the house, and Clive's money with it. And do you think he would accept the boys living with us if he knew what a mess we were in?'

'Maybe you should let them go and live with him for a while, until it's all sorted out.'

'I can't afford to. He'd stop the child maintenance payments.' The words were out of her mouth before she could check herself. Shame flooded into her face, but it was too late.

Rose closed her eyes and pictured again the photographs in Janis's dining room. On the top shelf were photographs of Janis and Jimmy, looking tanned and happy in holiday locations they couldn't afford to visit. On the next shelf down, the large professional portrait of the angelic Millie was just another pointless extravagance on the credit card. And below that, the humourless faces of Joey and Jake, old beyond their years. Rose thought about the bottom shelf, and couldn't help thinking that those solemn young faces deserved something better.

Michael Spivey took the two white envelopes from his document folder and laid them on his lap. The long slim one was bound to contain a cheque book, it couldn't really be anything else. He put it to one side on the coffee table, a foregone conclusion not worthy of his attention.

The large envelope was infinitely more interesting. He ran a grubby fingernail under the flap and teased it open, then pulled out the flimsy cardboard folder it contained. The folder was slightly creased, and he straightened out the damage with grubby fingers. A letter was attached to the front of the folder with a paperclip, and he glanced down it, muttering to himself. 'Dear Mr. Thomas, Welcome to the ENB, thank you for choosing us as your bank.' What a load of bollocks. He opened the folder and pulled out the contents, a set of glossy three-fold leaflets and a small white booklet.

He examined each in turn, mumbling as he went. 'Car insurance, don't need that.' He flung the leaflet onto the coffee table. 'House insurance, nope, card protection, nope, savings accounts, nope, credit card application …mm, might be worth keeping that one.' He tossed the first three leaflets onto the coffee table, and placed the one of interest next to him on the sofa. 'What's this? Bank account terms and conditions?' He flicked through the small white booklet. 'Ain't wasting me time reading that.' He ran his eyes down the front page of the last leaflet and gave a hearty chuckle. 'Identification and Fraud – Your Responsibilities as a Customer. Bit late for that, mate.' He threw the leaflet on top of the others on the coffee table.

There was nothing else in the folder. He picked it up again and poked his fingers into the middle. Nope, nothing else in there. He picked up the outer envelope and turned it upside down. Nothing in there either.

A mild panic began to rise in his stomach. Where the bloody hell was the card? The card should have been in the welcome pack shouldn't it? It wouldn't be with the cheque book. He remembered that. It wasn't safe to send the cheque book and the card together. Was that right? Or was he wrong?

He reached out for the long slim envelope and ripped it open. He pulled out the cheque book, and flicked its pages like a fan. Nothing inside it, and nothing inside the envelope.

He closed his eyes and rubbed his brow with a nicotine-stained finger. What happened the last time he opened a bank account? Bloody hell, it was years ago. He knew a replacement cheque card turned up every few years, but what happened at the beginning?

He couldn't remember. Bollocks, he couldn't remember. Calm down, Mikey boy. Think it through. There must be another envelope to come. Yes, he remembered now. The post he collected from 2b today. There was one for Hills, and two for Smith. The two for Smith had looked like the ones he had here. The one for Hills had been long and slim, like the cheque book envelope, but not as bulky. That must have been the card. And it came later than the first two envelopes. Those envelopes for Hills came last week.

He snatched up the welcome letter and scanned it again. Oh bollocks, there it was in black and white. 'Your new debit card will arrive within ten days.' For a moment he fell calm, and then he remembered the keys. He'd given the keys back to Henry. But he'd have to go back to the flat next week to pick up the card. Shit, what if Henry didn't ask him to go? What if Henry decided to go himself? He'd see the envelope.

Henry would see the envelope addressed to Thomas, and he'd *know*.

23

'Of course I knew it wasn't right.' A timely appearance by Lu with a tray of hot drinks had broken the tension, and Janis had composed herself again. She wrapped her fingers around a mug of hot chocolate and sat forward in the chair, her eyes fixed firmly in the distance, avoiding Rose's gaze. 'It's easy for you to be rational about it. It's not happening to you. But I thought it was a lifeline. I thought it would give me enough money to pay off the arrears and get things back on an even keel.'

'And this person who paid you, was it someone you already knew?'

Janis gave a wry smile. 'No comment.' She sipped on the hot chocolate. 'He knew about Jimmy's gambling, said he'd heard about it on the grapevine, and that he could see how embarrassing it would be for me if word got out. He said he could put some additional business my way, help me to make some extra cash to deal with any debts. I didn't know what to say at first. I thought he just meant ordinary accounts. A few extra accounts wouldn't make much difference to my bonus, but I said it would be appreciated. I suppose at the time I was more upset that someone knew about Jimmy's gambling, and I didn't know how much he knew.'

'Did he say where the business was coming from?'

'He said at first that he had contacts who needed current accounts, people who would probably fail the normal account opening process. That these people just need bank accounts, like anybody else, to bank their salary cheques and pay their bills.'

Rose nodded. 'So he made out they were bad credit risks?'

'He said they had poor customer profiles. Some had bad credit files, some were seasonal workers, outside the mainstream, that sort of thing. Some moved home a lot, weren't on the electoral role. I suggested they could apply for basic bank accounts but he said that wouldn't work. Some of them might struggle for acceptable ID, even for a basic account.'

'And he said you'd be paid two grand for each one?'

Lu, nestled in the corner armchair with Mac on her lap, gave a low whistle. She'd missed the first part of the conversation, but she was catching up fast. 'So if these were low earners, who was going to cough up the two grand?'

Janis turned to look at her. 'If I'd asked that question at the time, I might not have been so quick to get involved. He told me that the applicants were going to borrow authentic ID from friends or relatives prepared to help them out. Once the accounts were open, they would ask for a change of address to match their own address. It seemed fairly straightforward, and fairly low risk if they were going to use authentic documents rather than something they'd bought over the internet, so I agreed to do it. But I told him that I couldn't open the accounts myself, because it's not something I do normally. It might raise suspicion if I suddenly opened a set of accounts. He said he wasn't interested in how I did it, so long as the accounts were opened.'

'So when did you realize there was more to it, and you weren't just being asked to be charitable to a few benefit-scroungers?' Lu made no attempt to hide her skepticism.

'After the first few accounts had been opened. We did the address changes, and I thought that was the end of it. Then he came to see me again. He said if I didn't tell him how to safely launder money through the accounts, he would call Clive and tell him about Jimmy's gambling and the mess we were in. I couldn't take that risk.'

'Did Marge know about this?'

Janis didn't answer. She looked away, avoiding both their gazes.

It was Rose's turn to question. 'So how did you persuade Marge to play along?'

'To be honest, it wasn't as difficult as I thought. I thought that if Pandora opened the accounts she wouldn't notice the kind of inconsistencies that might show up in the documents, because she hadn't been trained. And if Marge authorised them, people would assume that she'd been careless. No-one would expect an employee with her long service record to carry out deliberate fraud.'

'And neither would I.' Lu's face showed her dismay. 'How could you, Janis? How could you drag an innocent person into your mess?'

Janis's face remained impassive. 'I told her that we had money problems. Serious problems, bad enough for me to lose my job. I told her that I had the chance to make some money to straighten things out, by turning a blind eye on some new accounts. I asked her what she would do, if she was in my place.'

'And she said she'd do it?' Lu's tone was incredulous.

'She said if someone offered her two grand for each account she'd bite their hand off. She said that paying for Jean to be in The Larches was eating into her savings, and she was worried about her nest egg for retirement.'

'And so you asked her to help?'

'No Lu, I offered her money to help.' She paused while the idea sank in. 'And she took it. I gave her £500 of the pay-off for each account.'

Rose saw Lu flinch, and knew she was thinking of Jean. She looked back at Janis. 'So you and Marge were in it together, and Pandora was just a pawn?'

Janis paled. 'You know, don't you, that she was on to us? After she got her training?'

Rose leaned forward. 'Where is she, Janis?' Her voice was low, her tone deliberate. 'Where's Pandora?'

'I don't know.'

'I don't believe you.'

Janis's weary face crumpled. 'I don't know, Rose, truly I don't.'

'Who asked you to open the accounts?'

'I can't tell you. I can't. I'm so scared that something's happened to Pandora because of these accounts. And I'm scared that something might happen to me or Marge if this all comes out.' Tears began to roll down her face. 'You have to help me, Rose. I don't know how to get out of it. Please, you have to help me work out what to do.'

'Well I think you're mad to even think of helping her.' Lu pursed her lips and cast a critical glance at Rose. 'She's broken the law, betrayed her employer, lied to her husband and kids, dragged poor Marge into her scheme, and possibly even endangered Pandora's life, and all she could do was sit there and snivel "what if something happens to me?" I hope they put her away. She deserves everything she gets.'

Lu paused for breath, and Rose knew her aunt was waiting for her to disagree. She sighed and closed her eyes. There were never any grey areas in Lu's opinions, only ever black or white. Rose didn't see it quite the same way. 'It can't have been easy finding out about Jimmy's gambling. Forget the clichés about living with a gambler, at the end of the day money has been draining out of their household behind her back and she's been trying to keep everything together.'

Lu's reaction was much as Rose expected. She narrowed her eyes and leaned forward in her seat. 'No, Rose. She's not an innocent victim. She's been taking illegal money to fund her lifestyle. Yes, living with a gambler must be tough, but you don't have to commit a crime to deal with it. Plenty of people accept it and deal with it. They could give up the fancy cars for a start. They could change their habits, take the boys out of public school, move to a smaller house. None of these things are the end of the world. It's a shame for Jimmy, he probably can't help his addiction, but no-one held a gun to Janis's head and forced her to commit the crime. There's always a way, Rose. Always a decent, legal, honest way to deal with things. But not for Janis. No, Janis will always put herself first. She didn't think about the fall-out for anybody else when she took that money. Not Jimmy, not the bank, not even her kids. And don't you dare tell me that she was thinking about the kids when she did it.'

Rose began to smile. She had learned over the years that the best way to deal with Lu's outbursts was to roll with them. 'Have you finished venting? Can I have my say now?' Lu muttered under her breath, and Rose interpreted the mutterings as consent. 'I'm not helping her so that she can get away with anything. I'm helping her so that the right people can be told in the right way, and at the right time, to get the best result for everybody.'

Lu snorted. 'In your opinion.'

'OK. In my opinion.' Rose nodded. 'There are other people involved in this than Janis. And in my *opinion*,' she stressed the word for Lu's benefit, 'Jimmy deserves to hear about this from his wife, not from the police or the press. And whatever I think of Clive personally, he deserves to hear about this from Janis as his ex-wife so that he can do what's best for his kids, as well as what's right for the bank. And Marge deserves to know that Janis is going to blow the whistle so that she can prepare herself for what's to come, and decide the best way to tell Jean about it before it becomes common knowledge. Surely you'd rather your friend heard about it from her daughter, than read about it in the papers?'

The mention of Jean touched a nerve, and Lu's manner calmed a little. 'Will Marge go to prison?'

'I honestly don't know. I don't know how seriously the police will view her involvement. She didn't initiate the crime, but she did collude. I suppose her involvement wasn't as significant. She didn't have anything to do with the transaction monitoring stuff.' Rose decided not to upset Lu by pointing out that Marge could have tried to stop Janis, or at least expose what she was doing, but chose not to.

'I don't know what I'm going to say to Jean when I see her. You wouldn't think that Marge was capable of such a thing, would you?'

Rose merely shook her head and smiled at Lu, too diplomatic to give an honest answer. After all, Lu hadn't witnessed at first hand just how convincingly Marge had portrayed herself as incompetent during her review.

Lu sighed. 'So what happens now?'

'If Janis does what we've agreed, she'll go home now and tell Jimmy what she's done. First thing in the morning she'll call Clive and admit to the collusion, and ask him to start the investigation. She'll do everything she can to help. She'll tell Marge that she's blown the whistle, and that they have to prepare for what's to come. Then Marge will be able to tell Jean in her own way. By then, I guess the police will be on their way to see her.' Rose paused and thought about the fall-out. 'I'm going into the branch myself at nine to speak to Janis and make sure that she's done everything we agreed. If she hasn't, I call Mr. Mulligan.' She laughed under her breath. 'Actually, if it makes you feel any better, I plan to call Mulligan anyway. He needs to know.'

'Isn't there a danger that she'll tip off whoever asked her to do this?'

'There is, but I think she's too scared. And what would it achieve? The accounts will be investigated now anyway. If whoever is behind this takes steps to stop the laundering and close the accounts, it will only give the police fresh evidence and speed up the investigation.' Rose paused, and then said 'Poor Janis. She must have thought she'd died and gone to hell when I turned up at the branch asking about the account opening process.'

Curled up in her armchair, Lu was deep in thought. Neither of them spoke for a few moments, then Lu said quietly 'Do you think Janis is involved in Pandora's disappearance?'

It was a question that Rose had been trying to avoid. 'She might have let slip that Pandora was on to them. Even if she only expressed concern, she may have put Pandora at risk.' Rose sighed. 'And yet again, it might have been absolutely nothing to do with Pandora's disappearance. Pandora might have been attacked or abducted by some unknown person while she was out running. That's for Mulligan to find out.'

And please, God, let that be how it is, Rose thought. The fall-out from Janis's crime was bad enough to contemplate, without thinking about what had happened to Pandora. How would Janis and Marge feel if their crime had led to Pandora being hurt? How would they live with themselves?

24

George Mulligan leaned back in his chair and yawned, a great cavernous expulsion of air that reflected his disturbed and sleepless night. If there was one thing guaranteed to leave him restless, it was the nagging sense of failure that resulted from a head full of ideas and the inability to piece them all together into a coherent whole.

He'd driven home via Bellevue Mansions yesterday evening, as Rose suggested, but it had been a fruitless trip. From the outside there wasn't much to see in the dark, and the door to the block operated on a master key so he couldn't get in to take a look at the second floor. He'd hung around for a while in the car park at the rear of the building, hoping for a chance to tailgate into the block behind a returning resident, but no-one came. He'd given it half an hour before giving up and driving home to a lengthy reprimand from Mrs. Mulligan about being late for supper … again. At least the supper he'd been late for involved fish. That had saved him from a further scolding. He chuckled to himself. There would have been hell to pay if he'd been called to account for the delicate aroma of herring in the Mulligan bedroom.

The door of the interview room opened, and Bob Shepherd lumbered into the room with a mug of coffee and a greasy paper bag containing a bacon sandwich. 'Where do you want them?' He looked meaningfully down at the table. Every inch was covered with papers and photographs and newspaper cuttings.

'Anywhere you like, Bob.'

Shepherd hovered, reluctant to choose between official police reports and the grainy image of Pandora Mitchell. Mulligan huffed at his indecision and prodded the top of Gilling's initial report with his finger. 'Bloody hell, just put them down there.' He watched as Shepherd followed his instructions then said 'Sorry Bob, didn't mean to bite your head off.'

Shepherd gave a sheepish smile. 'It's not going too well then?'

Mulligan shook his head. 'She's been missing for over three days, and we haven't had a sniff apart from the sightings of her running. It's going off the boil.' He pointed to a pile of newspapers at the corner of the table. 'The press have lost interest because there's been no new information. The public aren't interested in hearing that we're searching places we've already searched, and questioning people we've already questioned. The only real leads we have are related to her work at the bank, and they could just be coincidence.' He scratched at his temple. 'We'll know about that soon enough.' He looked up at the wall clock. 'I thought Dave was due in at eight this morning?'

'He was, but we had a call late last night. About Pandora.' Shepherd grinned. 'He wanted to tell you himself, but I suppose I've blown it now. We've had another sighting.'

Mulligan sat to attention. 'Why the bloody hell didn't you tell me?'

'It might be nothing. Dave didn't want to get your hopes up. It was the bloke who was driving the black people carrier. He rang the station late last night. He's been in Scotland on business since early Wednesday morning, so he's been off the radar. He read about it in last night's evening paper. Dave's gone to see him on his way in this morning.'

'Well I hope he turns something up, otherwise she's likely to be yesterday's news.' He tried to sound buoyant for Shepherd's sake, but he didn't share his optimism. The black people carrier had been just ahead of Lu Aylesbury on the way up Market Melbourne hill. The best he could hope for was confirmation of her statement. He looked up and smiled. 'Fingers crossed, eh?'

Shepherd sensed his pessimism and gave a sympathetic nod, backing away from the table. 'I'll leave you to it, then.' The door closed behind him before Mulligan had time to answer.

Left alone with his thoughts, Mulligan helped himself to the bacon sandwich and pulled the coffee closer to him. If Dave Gilling was going to be late, he may as well start to put a plan together for the day. He flipped over Gilling's initial report and started to scribble on the back of it.

No sightings since Tuesday evening. No hard and fast evidence to support the Tommy Fletcher theory. Craig Bradman has an alibi. Her silver chain has turned up, but there's no evidence to suggest she was even wearing it when she went missing. Danny Mitchell was still at work when she left the house, and her mother didn't notice whether she was wearing it or not. He was fairly certain the chain had been planted, but no idea by who, when, or for what reason, other than to make them think Pandora had been in that lay-by.

His eyes narrowed in thought. That chain had been dropped deliberately by someone who was playing with them. Tampering with the case. Distorting the evidence. And it had to be someone who had access to the chain. Which could be ... who? Her family? Her boyfriend? Possibly her work colleagues? Pandora herself? Her killer?

Her killer. There, he'd said it. Well, thought it, anyway. *Her killer.* Was it going to have to be a murder enquiry after all? He'd waited three days, hoping for a lead, praying for a sighting or a call, some new piece of evidence that would really start the ball rolling. But nothing had come. Nothing concrete, anyway.

He swallowed down the last piece of bacon sandwich and sucked the grease off his fingers, then traced the word "bank" in large letters on the paper. He underlined it, twice, three times, and then drew a curly cloud around it. That bloody bank. It was clouding everything, he was sure of it.

Rose had confirmed that Janis Porter had been opening fraudulent accounts and getting her fingers burned with money laundering. He knew that by now Clive Barden would be liaising with the authorities, and that an official investigation would be kicked off today. Did that matter? Was it relevant? He frowned. If Janis Porter was taken in for questioning about the fraud she might be off-limits to him for a while. Did he need to speak to her again? Probably. He couldn't see her as a killer, but what about the people behind the laundering? Had she tipped them off that Pandora was a threat? Were they responsible for her disappearance?

Janis had refused to tell Rose who they were. He laughed to himself. She wouldn't be keeping that little nugget to herself once the Fraud boys started to question her. But why had she refused to tell Rose? They must be local, must be known to her. If they were using these addresses at Bellevue Mansions, they must have access to the properties. He needed to get confirmation of the exact addresses from Clive Barden, so they could trace the owners and get access, search for evidence of Pandora. He frowned to himself. But would that tip them off, and get in the way of the fraud investigation? Oh bugger it, this was all getting too complicated. Maybe instead of tackling Clive officially he should have another go at trying to get access to the building, ask a few questions of the people who lived there.

Yes, that would probably be best. An unofficial poke around the second floor at Bellevue Mansions, and see what it turned up. He thought a moment and then sniffed subconsciously at his shirt sleeve, and decided that it would be a job for Dave Gilling.

'And just what is so important that it couldn't wait until Monday? You know I don't like my weekends being interrupted.' Henry Campling rested his elbows on the arms of his chair and steepled his fingers, holding Benny Bradman's gaze with a forceful stare.

From the other side of the desk, Benny observed him with interest. He knew that Campling's Saturdays at the golf course were sacrosanct, but there was a brittleness about the man this morning that indicated more than mere displeasure at missing a round of golf. Benny folded his arms and stretched his legs out under the desk. 'Indeed I do, Henry. I'm sorry if I've made you miss your round this mornin', but when we've done I reckon you'll be glad we've had this little chat sooner rather than later.' He picked up the phone and jabbed at the keypad. 'Sal? Has Spivey gone yet? Good. Can you make sure I'm not disturbed until Henry leaves?' He replaced the handset on its cradle. 'Let's have a little chat about Michael first, shall we?'

Campling frowned. 'Spivey? Why would we need to discuss *him*?'

'I had an interestin' chat with Michael this mornin'. He's admitted to diggin' that grave in Lucinda Aylesbury's garden.'

Campling's brow creased further, and he tutted his disapproval. 'What on earth would make him do a thing like that?'

Benny grinned at him. 'You're a card, Henry. You really are.' He leaned across the desk. 'Because you asked him to, of course.'

'Me? Why ever would you think that?'

Benny leaned a little closer and lowered his voice. 'Because Michael told me.' He drew back and watched Campling's face contort into an angry scowl. 'Go on, then,

Henry. Your turn next.'

Campling's tone was guarded. 'I have no idea why he would say such a thing.'

'Probably because I was leanin' on him at the time.' Benny grinned. It don't really matter why he said it, does it? Fact is, he dug that grave because you asked him to. Because you wanted to ... what was it you said? Find another way to persuade her to move on?'

'You are making a totally unfounded accusation against me, Bradman. And I would advise you to be cautious.'

'Oh, I'm bein' cautious Henry.' He paused and studied Campling's face. 'In fact, it's because I'm bein' cautious that I've decided to let him concentrate on his work for you.'

Campling frowned, and when he spoke his displeasure was evident in his voice. 'You mean you're letting him go? I thought he was your pet project?'

'He was. But he's runnin' a lot of errands for you now, and I ain't got use for a bloke with split loyalties. Nah,' Benny shook his head, 'I think it's best he just works for you now. You can have him. I'll tell him when he comes back to the shop. Now, about the second thing I want to discuss with you. That involves Lucinda Aylesbury as well.'

'In what respect?'

'I'm backin' out of the plans for her cottages. I'm leavin' the field open for you, Henry. You can have the whole development to yourself.'

Campling's eyes narrowed to slits, and when he spoke it was with slow deliberation. 'Just what exactly are you playing at?'

'Me? I'm not playin' at anythin', Henry. Unlike you.' He sniffed. 'You can deny any involvement in that grave until the cows come home, but I know you was behind it. And that ain't how I do business. No,' he shook his head, 'I've been to see her, and I've told her I'm backin' out. And that's an end of it.'

Campling paused and thought for a moment. 'It seems

rather foolish to throw away such a strong business opportunity on the word of a … shall we say, such an unreliable person as Michael Spivey? However, if that is your intention I have no choice but to accept it.'

'Well that's very sportin' of you, Henry.' Benny leaned back in his chair. 'And there was me thinkin' you'd cut up rough about the idea of us goin' our separate ways.'

'Perhaps on reflection we have become a little too … involved.' Campling licked his lips and forced a smile. 'I take it that you are only suggesting that we cease our partnership with regards to property development? I would be sorry to sever all our professional connections.'

It was Benny's turn to frown. 'All our connections? How many have we got, then?'

'I'm your solicitor, Bradman, as well as your business partner. Is this severing of professional connections going to extend as far as the legal representation I provide for your businesses?'

Benny considered the question. 'No, I weren't sackin' you as my solicitor, if that's what you're askin'. I just thought the extent of our dealin's could do with a bit of … what would you call it? Judicious prunin'?' He chuckled at his own joke.

'And so you also wish me to continue representing Craig? In the matter of Pandora Mitchell's disappearance, I mean.'

Benny's face darkened. 'Craig don't need no representin'. He's off the hook. I know that from DI Mulligan.'

'Oh come now, Bradman, surely you don't really believe that. One day that young woman will re-appear, and if she re-appears as a corpse, your son will need all the help he can get. And so will you.'

'Me?'

Campling's smile twisted. 'You claim to have been with Craig at the approximate time of Pandora Mitchell's disappearance. You claim to have dropped him off at The

Feathers just before eight o'clock. I hope that you are able to substantiate those claims. It would be very unfortunate if you couldn't, for yourself as well as for Craig.'

'I hope you ain't suggestin' that my lad had anythin' to do with it.'

'Of course not. But then you weren't too fond of Miss Mitchell yourself, were you? It's lucky that Craig can also give you an alibi.'

'Are you sayin' I gave him a false alibi?'

'I'm not saying anything of the sort. Where were you after eight o'clock?'

'Me? What the hell's that got to do with anythin'?'

'Do you have an alibi?'

'I don't need an alibi.'

'You had a motive for wanting Pandora Mitchell out of the way. You disapproved of her relationship with your son.'

Benny put a hand up to his face and rubbed at his forehead. What the hell was happening here? How did the conversation move onto Pandora Mitchell? Was he imagining it, or was Henry Campling threatening him? He looked squarely into Campling's oily face. Was Henry Campling threatening to set him up? Campling was watching him intently, and his face bore a sneer of assumed superiority.

Benny took in a breath and leaned forward. 'You know what, Henry? If I ain't got use for a gofer with split loyalties, I certainly ain't got use for a solicitor who thinks he can dangle me on the end of a string. On reflection, maybe you're right. Maybe goin' our separate ways on everythin' wouldn't be such a bad idea after all.'

25

Elizabeth greeted Rose with a cold efficiency. 'I'm afraid Janis is unavailable at the moment. Can I help?'

Rose smiled amiably. 'No, it was Janis I particularly needed to see. I'll wait, if that's OK.' Her tone of voice suggested that Elizabeth's opinion on the matter was irrelevant, and that she would wait as long as it took. She began to move towards the door leading up to the staff room and Elizabeth stepped into her path, holding out a hand towards a small public waiting area in the corner of the branch. Rose took the hint with a good humour. Elizabeth could hardly be blamed for doing her job and following Clive's instructions. She settled into a faux-leather armchair and folded her arms across her lap.

The atmosphere in the branch was distinctly subdued. Behind the counter, Hazel and Marge were working their way quietly through a small queue of customers. Marge looked tired. Her face had lost its rosy plumpness, and her cheeks sagged dully underneath puffy eyes. Beside her, Hazel's pixie face looked sombre, but her eyes were still alert. Rose knew those eyes had seen her come into the branch, seen her talk to Elizabeth and seen her take a seat in the corner. It would only be a matter of time before Hazel looked over and acknowledged her.

Out of the corner of her eye she saw the door to the right of the counter open, and Tommy stepped out into the banking hall. He walked past Rose towards the main door of the branch. Rose leaned forward and spoke to him. 'Tommy? Is everything alright?'

He turned an anxious face towards her and started to speak, then caught sight of Elizabeth. She was watching him intently. He forced a smile. 'Alright Rose? Just on my way out to get some milk. You know we can't get through a day without our coffees.' He spoke loudly, so that Elizabeth could hear him.

Rose smiled back, and spoke so quietly he had to lean forward to listen to her. 'Let me know if there's anything I can do to help. Hazel has my mobile number.'

He nodded gratefully. 'Will do.'

'Well, go on, then. I shall expect a coffee when you get back.' She spoke loudly now, for Elizabeth's benefit, and flicked her hands at him to shoo him out of the door. When he'd gone she turned and smiled at Elizabeth, who simply turned her head and looked away.

Hazel was serving the last customer in the queue now. Their conversation appeared heated, and Hazel glanced over at Elizabeth. She gestured towards the woman with her hand, the man nodded, and suddenly Elizabeth was on the receiving end of his complaint. Hazel slipped off her stool, opened the door at the end of the counter, and trotted briskly over to Rose.

'Am I glad to see you.' She crouched down on her haunches beside Rose's chair. 'I think it's all going to kick off today.'

'What's happened?'

Hazel glanced behind her. 'I'll have to keep it quick. Elizabeth's watching us all like a hawk this morning, and his complaint won't take long.' She turned back to Rose. 'Janis came in late this morning, looking like shit. Elizabeth's in charge now. Two official-looking blokes turned up at half past nine, and have been in with Janis ever since.' She paused for breath. 'They looked like police to me.' She cast another furtive glance at Elizabeth. 'I asked Marge what was going on, and she said something about Jimmy and Janis having a falling out. But I don't believe her.' She looked straight into Rose's eyes. 'Marge is in a right state, too. And I bet you know what it's all about, and can't tell me.'

Rose bit her lip, and tried to look apologetic. 'Sorry Hazel, I can't. I'm off the case officially now. You know how it is.'

Hazel nodded. 'I thought so.' She sniffed her disappointment. 'I suppose it's to do with Pandora?'

'It's to do with the accounts Pandora opened. That's all I can say.'

'Did you know they were going to put *her* in charge?' Hazel jerked her head in Elizabeth's direction. 'She's acting manager today. And a complete bloody pain in the arse she is, too.' She turned back to Rose, and suddenly her face became serious again. 'Did Janis have something to do with Pandora's disappearance?'

'I don't know Hazel, and that's the truth.' She put a hand on the woman's arm to reassure her. 'I think you'd better go back to the counter before Elizabeth gets rid of that customer. I'm not going anywhere until I've seen Janis, so let's try and speak later.'

Hazel nodded, and trotted back to her place beside Marge. She put a hand on Marge's arm and spoke into her ear, but Marge's attention was fixed elsewhere. It was fixed on Rose. And suddenly Rose felt Marge's eyes burn into her with a loathing that she could barely comprehend.

'It's odd, isn't it? It's all so calm. I don't know what I expected, but it's like slow motion, waiting for the axe to fall.' Janis looked composed today, still tired and pale, but the heightened anxiety of yesterday appeared to have dissipated overnight. 'I'm sorry I can't offer you a coffee. We've run out of milk.' She glanced at her watch. 'I sent Tommy out twenty minutes ago, he should have been back by now.'

Rose nodded. 'I know, I saw him go. He's probably staying out of Elizabeth's way.'

'I know how he feels. At least I still have the sanctity of my office.' Janis forced a smile. 'Elizabeth might be acting manager, but we're supposed to make it look like I'm still running the branch.' She sighed. 'I suppose you've come to check up on me, make sure that I've done all the things I promised last night?'

'I wanted to know that everything was OK.'

Janis sat back in her chair. 'Well, I suppose that depends on your definition of "OK". Let's see … I went home and told Jimmy what I'd done, as you suggested. He shouted a lot, told me I was a stupid bitch, and walked out, taking the kids with him.'

Rose's heart sank. 'Janis, I'm so sorry …'

'Well, don't be. Now that it's done, now that it's out in the open, I can see that it was right to tell him. Like a boil that had to be lanced.' She looked away. 'He says that what he did was stupid, losing all that money gambling, but it wasn't criminal. He didn't commit a crime. And he doesn't want to be married to a criminal.'

'It's been a shock to him. Give him time.'

Janis put up a hand. 'Please don't say any more about it, Rose. It's done. Like I said, a boil that needed lancing. It hurts to lance a boil, but it can't heal otherwise. Now, what else? Oh yes, Clive. I called Clive very early this morning, and told him about the accounts. Of course, he knew about them anyway, and as you would expect he's furious with me. Apparently I've ruined the bank's reputation, ruined my own reputation, and ruined things for the boys.' She paused for breath. 'He called the police immediately, and two lovely officers have been here since eight o'clock this morning questioning me. But I'm not to be arrested. Not yet, at any rate. I'm to stay "in role", as they put it. Like I said, Elizabeth is running the branch, but as far as the world outside is concerned, I am still the manager here, and nothing untoward has happened.'

Rose nodded. 'Business as usual, eh? Avoid tipping off your contacts that the game is up?'

'Something like that.' Janis leaned her elbows on the desk and rested her chin on her hands. 'The worst part is not knowing how long we have to play the game for.'

'Have you told the police who paid you to open the accounts?'

'Yes, I have. They didn't leave me much choice. I believe now it's a case of gathering evidence, and once they have enough evidence to bring charges they'll make their move. God knows how long that could take.' She sighed. 'Have you seen Marge?'

Rose gave a gentle laugh. 'Yes, I've seen Marge. I can't say she looked too pleased to see me.'

Janis shrugged. 'She blames you, of course. She's distraught about the effect it will have on her mother.'

Rose bit her lip, and resisted the temptation to point out that Marge should have thought about that before dabbling in the crime. 'Has she spoken to Jean yet?'

'No. She can't bring herself to do it. Actually, she thinks you should do it for her. You or Lu.'

'Me? Surely it's better if …'

'No, Rose, I don't think it is. I think it's the least you can do. Marge is only involved in this mess because of me, and she's only having to face the consequences of her actions because of you. If you won't do it for her, do it because I'm asking you to. I've done what you asked, I've faced up to my own mess and talked to Jimmy and to Clive. Now please, I'm asking you to do this one thing for me in return. Make it a little easier for Marge, and ask Lu to tell Jean what she's done. Marge can't do it, and it will be better for Jean if it comes from a friend.'

Rose and Janis were still discussing the pros and cons of Janis's suggestion when Tommy returned to the branch. He flew through the front door into the banking hall, collided with a departing customer, mumbled an apology, and made straight for Hazel. His hands clutched a pair of paper milk cartons, and he balanced them on the customer side of the counter, peering through the glass at her. 'Haze, I've seen him. I've seen *him*.'

'Seen who? The milkman?' She raised her eyes skyward. 'Elizabeth's on the war path. You've been gone for nearly three quarters of an hour. Where the hell have you been all this time?'

'I've been following him. That's what I'm trying to tell you. I saw the man who opened the account. The one that Pandora and Janis argued about.'

Hazel's smile faded. 'The one with the stolen ID? You've seen him? You're absolutely sure about that?'

'Yes.' He nodded violently. 'I was on my way back with the milk, and I saw him walk into the newsagents.' He looked around furtively and lowered his voice. 'I followed him, Hazel. He paid a paper bill at the newsagents, and then he went down to the Co-op and bought biscuits and tea bags, cool as you like. And then he went all the way back down the high street, and went into Bradman's betting shop.'

'Did you follow him in there?'

Tommy flushed pink. 'No. I didn't like to. Craig might have been in there.'

She rolled her eyes in despair. 'You mean you lost him?'

He shook his head and beamed at her. 'No. He works there. He *works* there, Hazel. I watched him through the window. He went into the shop, and he spoke to Henry Campling.'

'Campling? What was he doing there?'

Tommy shrugged. 'I dunno. Maybe he was putting a bet on.' He knew it was unlikely, but he had no other explanation. 'Anyway, he spoke to Henry Campling, and then he went behind the counter and spoke to one of the girls. And then he went into the back of the shop. And nobody challenged him.' He looked at her expectantly. 'What do we do now?'

At the other side of the counter Hazel smiled and

leaned closer to the glass. 'I'll tell you what we do now, Tommy,' she whispered. 'We tell Rose Bennett.'

George Mulligan pulled his car up onto the grass verge and turned off the engine. Out of the car he leaned on the open door and took in a deep breath of fresh air. The landscape beneath him was bathed in a yellow haze, the cornfields lit up by the intense August sunlight, and here and there the light glinted off the wing mirrors of an army of harvesting tractors.

He slammed the door shut and ambled along the verge to Dave Gilling's car. Gilling turned off the radio as he climbed into the passenger seat, and turned to look at him.

Mulligan shook his head. 'You're looking far too pleased with yourself for my liking. Why wouldn't you tell me on the phone?'

Gilling beamed. 'I thought you'd enjoy it better in context.' He chuckled to himself. 'Like I told you on the phone, the driver of the black people carrier backs up Lu Aylesbury's story. He saw Pandora running up the hill at about ten to seven. He turned right at the roundabout at the top of the hill, and drove down here to his mother's house. She lives on the left hand side, just past The Larches care home. He was dropping his kids off with her. She was babysitting for him while he and the wife went to the pictures.'

Mulligan grunted. 'Alright. So he drove down Larch Road. What does that tell us?'

'He dropped his kids off and chatted with his mother for a few minutes, and then he drove back up Larch Road to the roundabout to go back home and pick up his wife.'

'So?'

Gilling could hardly contain his excitement. 'He saw her again, George. He saw Pandora here, on Larch Road.'

Mulligan's eyes widened. 'A positive sighting? Is he sure?'

'Absolutely certain. He said he saw the same girl around about there,' he pointed down the road to a gentle bend, 'outside the house with the iron gates.'

'Running down the hill?'

'Oh, better than that, George. She was talking to somebody.'

Mulligan's stomach did a somersault. 'Bloody hell Dave, you've had a result.' He closed his eyes and took in a deep breath. 'Please tell me there's a description.'

Gilling hesitated. 'Well, there's a description of sorts. The car was a green hatchback. He thinks it was a Ford, possibly a Fiesta. He didn't see the driver properly. He thinks it might have been a man but he may have been mistaken. He didn't have any reason to be that interested in the driver. But he was interested in Pandora. He remembers how she was standing. She was leaning on the top of the car, and bending forward to talk to the driver. He said it looked like she was comfortable, talking to someone she knew, not a stranger.' Gilling blushed. 'He said you couldn't help but notice, a pretty blonde like that bending over in those little shorts.'

'Spare me the details, Dave.' Mulligan was trying to concentrate. 'Did he give you a time?'

'Not exactly, but he thinks roughly ten past seven. Definitely no later than quarter past, because he was back home by twenty five past and it takes him ten minutes to drive.'

'And his wife confirms the timing?'

'Yes. She was with us while I questioned him. They seem a nice couple, George. I couldn't see him in the role of suspect, with her as a dodgy alibi, if that's what you're worried about.'

'You know what this means, don't you? That bloody chain *was* planted to throw us off the scent. Someone wanted us to think she ran straight across at the roundabout.' Mulligan stared out of the window, and then turned back to Gilling. 'Right, I've got a couple of things for you to follow up on now. Get yourself over to the Mitchell's and see if they know anyone with a green hatchback. It doesn't matter whether it's a Fiesta, or even a Ford. And then check with Craig Bradman. I want to know if anyone known to Pandora had a car matching that description. And then give me a call when you've finished. I've got another errand for you to do over in Kirkby.'

'What about her colleagues? We know Tommy Fletcher drives a blue Golf. What about the others?'

'I'm going over to the branch later to see Janis Porter. I'll ask while I'm there.' He opened the car door to get out, and then turned back to Gilling with a warm smile. 'Well done, Dave. I think this is the turning point.'

26

Bradman's shop was busier today, and Rose felt more comfortable entering for a second time. A handful of middle-aged men clutching folded newspapers chatted in the corner, and a couple of punters queued at the counter. Michael Spivey was taking a bet for a jovial-looking man who fancied Kirkby Town's chances against Chelmsford that afternoon. Spivey looked at ease, joking with the man about the outcome of the match, and then he caught sight of Rose. His face fell and he looked away quickly, back to the customer. He passed the betting slip hastily over the counter, forced a cheery smile for the man, and melted away into the back of the shop.

Rose walked up to the counter and hovered at the side of the queue. Sal, in mid-transaction, looked up at her questioningly. Rose smiled. 'Sorry to bother you. Is Benny around?' Sal nodded. 'Could I have a word with him?'

'He's upstairs, in his office.' Sal nodded towards the staircase.

'Thanks.' At the top of the stairs Rose tapped briskly on the door. Through its edges she heard Benny's voice say 'Thanks Sal', and the sound of a telephone receiver being clicked back onto its cradle.

'Come in Rose, it's not locked.' He shouted to her through the door, and she smiled to herself. At least he was direct.

He grinned at her as she opened the door. 'Two visits to my shop in a week? I hope you're not developin' a habit.'

'Well if I am, I'm sure you'll be able to help me with it. I hear you're something of an expert in dealing with problem punters.' She closed the door and walked over to the desk, and rested her hands on the back of the visitor's chair.

He shrugged, but his face registered understanding. 'Jimmy told you, then?'

'Janis, actually. She's very grateful for what you've done to help him.'

Benny scratched at his forehead. 'I ain't done much, Rose. Not enough to save him, anyway. That's somethin' he'll have to do for himself.' He straightened in his seat, and tried to look business-like. 'Anyway, it ain't good for business, havin' a sick punter around the place.' He pointed to the chair. 'Have a seat, tell me what you've come about. I take it you ain't just come here to chat about Jimmy Porter?'

'No, I haven't.' She sat down and leaned forward, resting her elbows on his desk, a casual gesture designed to put him at ease. 'Although I know I should thank you for what you've done for Jimmy. And for trying to hint to me that he had a problem.'

'Me? Did I?' Benny feigned bewilderment. 'Maybe I did. Anyway, if it's all out in the open now, it's done, ain't it? No more to be said.'

It was something he clearly didn't want to discuss further, and Rose took the hint and used it to her advantage. 'OK then, let's talk about Michael Spivey.'

Benny let out a sigh of irritation. 'Please don't tell me you've come here to bend my ear about that ruddy grave again. Ain't Lu told you I've apologized about all that?'

'Yes, of course she has. And I suppose that's a second thing I've got to thank you for today. How about we go for the hat-trick? I'd like to have a chat with Michael Spivey, and I'd like you to arrange that for me. Now. And it's not about the grave.'

Benny folded his arms and turned away from her. He

leaned back in his chair and pursed his lips. 'What's he supposed to have done now?'

'Well, if you get him in here and hang around as a witness to the conversation, you'll find out, won't you?' She was trying to sound teasing, but she wasn't convinced it was working. Benny didn't look too pleased at the idea of her questioning Spivey, and she couldn't decide if he was just exasperated with the man, or whether he himself had something to hide.

He thought about her request for a moment, and then picked up the phone. 'Sal, send Spivey up will you?' He cast a glance at a photograph on his desk, and then spoke again to Rose. 'I told Lu yesterday, I've just about had enough of pickin' up the pieces behind this one.' He jerked his head towards the door, and Spivey opened it on cue and slithered into the room.

'What can I do for you, Boss?' He closed the door behind him and stood in front of it, nervously shuffling his feet.

'Pull up another chair and come and sit over here. Rose wants to have a word with you about somethin'.'

Fear crossed Spivey's face. 'Me? I don't know …'

Benny waved a hand at him. 'Never mind what you don't know. Pull up a bloody chair and sit down. You ain't goin' to have to apologise for the grave, I've already done that for you. Ain't that right, Rose?'

Rose nodded and smiled at Spivey. 'That's all forgotten now. Water under the bridge.'

Spivey looked unconvinced. He reluctantly dragged a chair over to the desk and placed it beside Benny's. He sat down and rested his hands on his knees, and regarded Rose with a nervous but expectant stare. It was the first time she'd really seen him, and she felt an unbidden pang of sympathy. He was younger than she had thought, a seedy-looking creature with bad skin and thinning greasy hair. He was wearing the cream shirt and brown suit that Tommy had described to her. Both were cheap and ill-fitting, and his collar was flecked with dandruff, and Rose suspected that there was no-one in his life who cared that he was so badly turned out.

No-one who cared, apart from Benny. Benny's concern for Spivey didn't seem to extend to his appearance, but where did it end? Did he really look after this creature because the late Mrs. Bradman would have wanted it? Or was there another reason?

She looked away for a moment, and then turned her eyes directly on Michael Spivey. What does the name "Richard Thomas" mean to you, Michael?'

What little colour there was in Spivey's face drained away. His eyes darted to Benny's face, and then down to the desk. 'I don't know what you mean. I don't know a Richard Thomas.'

'You might not know him, but that's the name you used when you opened the bank account, isn't it?'

Benny raised himself up in his seat and turned to Spivey. 'What bloody bank account? What the hell have you done now?'

'I don't know what she's talking about, Boss. Honest, I don't. I ain't never heard of any Richard Thomas.' Spivey looked back at Rose. 'You're nuts. Why would I open a bank account in somebody else's name?'

Rose feigned surprise. 'What, you don't know why you did it? Well, let's see now …' She pulled a hand up to her face and started to count on her fingers, tapping each one in turn. 'You could … write fraudulent cheques to pay for goods you can't afford, use the debit card to buy stuff on the internet, give the account details to support a fraudulent credit card application.' She paused and added 'use the account for laundering cash that wasn't yours?'

Beads of perspiration broke out on Spivey's forehead, and his face crumpled. For a moment she thought he was going to cry, and then he jolted forward and thrust his greasy face into hers. 'You're off your head. Why would I do any of that stuff? You ain't got nothing on me.' He thrust a hand out behind him and pointed at Benny. 'You tell him you're lying. I ain't done nothing.'

Benny put out a hand and grabbed the back of Spivey's jacket, pulling him back into his seat. 'Shut up and sit down.' He turned back to Rose. 'Mind tellin' me just what this is all about, Rose? I mean, fair dos and all that, but it ain't very nice to come in here and start accusin' one of my employees without a bit of evidence.'

She nodded. 'OK. Michael has been positively identified by a member of staff at the ENB as the man who opened a fraudulent bank account at the branch the day Pandora disappeared. That man gave his name as Richard Thomas, and presented authentic ID documents in that name to support the application.'

Spivey shrank a little further into his chair and waited for Benny to vent his anger, but his fear appeared unfounded. Benny's face softened a little, and he turned to Spivey with a look of fascinated amusement. 'You crafty little toe-rag. I didn't know you were up to that sort of caper. Where did you nick that ID from, then?'

Spivey relaxed a little, softened by the hint of camaraderie, and fell straight into the snare. 'Can't tell you that, Benny. Wouldn't be fair, would it?'

Benny shook his head and laughed. 'You never fail to surprise me, Michael.' He looked at Rose and shook his head again. 'You wouldn't credit it, would you?' He leaned back and folded his arms. 'You *muppet*.' He spat the word out, and all the good humour of the last sixty seconds dissipated in its wake. 'You complete fuckin' muppet. What the bloody hell did you think you were playin' at?'

'Benny …'

'Don't you fuckin' "Benny" me. You just admitted you nicked somebody's ID.' He frowned and looked at Rose. 'Here, if it was somebody else's ID, how could he get hold of the cheque book and card? It wouldn't be sent to his address."

Rose shook her head. 'He claimed to have just moved

house, and he gave a rent book as ID for the new address. Some place called Bellevue Mansions, in Scar …'

'Scarborough.' Benny finished the sentence for her. He turned back to Spivey. 'Does Henry know?'

Spivey flinched at the mention of Campling's name, and that was really the only answer Benny needed.

Dicky took hold of Jean Baker's hand and gently squeezed her fingers. 'I think you're being very brave. It's not easy, giving up your home.'

Jean blinked. She wanted to cry, but not in front of Dicky. She cleared her throat. 'It's all arranged. I've shaken hands on it with Matron this morning. And I'm going to ask Lu to take me to the bungalow this afternoon to collect some more of my things. Marge will be at work, so she needn't know anything about it.' She frowned. 'I'm afraid it means I won't be able to come out for afternoon tea today.'

'There'll be lots of days to have afternoon tea when you're living here properly. The important thing is to get you safely out of the bungalow, and into The Larches.' Dicky pulled her hand a little closer to him. 'Are you sure you don't want me to come with you this afternoon?'

'No, I'd rather you didn't, if you don't mind. Lu's a good friend, she'll know what needs to be done. It will be enough if you can speak to Henry Campling for me, and put him in the picture.'

'And you're absolutely certain that you don't want to speak to Marge first?'

She gave a violent shake of the head. 'There's no talking to her, Dicky. I realized that last night. I thought Lu was teasing me about Marge wanting to move to the Lake District, but she wasn't. Marge is adamant that we're selling up and moving to Kendal. She told me last night. She's going to resign from the Bank and take early retirement. I don't know what she thinks we'd live on.'

Tears welled up in her eyes. 'She's got a day off on Monday, and she's planning to drive up there tomorrow and stay overnight. She's going to start house-hunting.' A tear escaped and trickled down her cheek. 'There was no talking to her, Dicky. She didn't want to know about what I felt or wanted.'

Dicky stroked her hand. 'It wasn't very thoughtful of her to argue with you in front of the other residents.' He chuckled, hoping to break the tension. 'Mind you, one or two of them told me this morning that they enjoyed the cabaret.'

Jean forced a smile. If only it had been a just a show, nothing more than a brief power struggle between mother and daughter, a few meaningless angry words born of frustration, soon healed and soon forgotten. But it wasn't. It was worse than that. She couldn't tell Dicky, kind friend though he was, because he wouldn't understand. But she knew with a mother's certainty that there was something behind Marge's outburst.

This wasn't just about moving to the Lake District. Jean had seen more than temper in Marge's eyes last night. She'd seen fear. This wasn't about a change of scene and a cosy retirement.

Marge was running away from something.

'I had an appointment with somebody called Baker. I don't know why the gel was opening my account.' Spivey could barely hide his misery.

Benny prodded him with a finger. 'She might have recognized you. Ain't you got any nous at all?'

'Course I have. I've seen her about, with Craig and that, but I've never spoken to the gel. Why the hell would she notice somebody like me?' He directed the question at Rose, as if a woman would better understand it. 'And why would she know my name? Even if she did recognize me, how would she know my name wasn't Thomas? I've never met her. She'd just recognize me as some bloke who worked in the bookies.'

Rose cut in. 'That might be true, Michael. But I think she might have worked out that you'd never lived in Kirkby Park.' She leaned an elbow on the table and rested her chin on her hand. When she spoke again her voice was more kindly. 'Just what *did* you think you were going to do with this account?'

He shrugged. 'I dunno. I've heard people talking about having spare bank accounts, how they're handy and that.'

'Handy for what?'

He looked unsure. 'Well, like you said. Paying for stuff, but not having to come up with the money.'

'And you didn't think about what would happen if you tried to use the account to pay for something? You didn't think about what would happen when the Bank refused the payment, and the seller tried to recover the goods?' He stared at her blankly. 'It didn't occur to you that the Bank might refuse payment?'

'There was an overdraft on the account, a thousand pounds.'

'OK, when the overdraft was done, then. What happens then?'

He shrugged. 'I throw the card and cheque book away, and be glad I got a grand's worth of gear for nothing.'

'And when the Bank come looking for their money back?'

'Well, I don't live in Bellevue Mansions, do I?' His face didn't betray the fact that he wished he did, and had just realized that that particular fantasy could never have become reality, thanks to his own stupidity.

'Did someone ask you to open this account for them?'

His face became wary. 'Like who?'

'I don't know. Someone who wanted the account for themselves. Henry Campling, for example?'

Benny shifted in his seat. He'd been staring out of the window while Rose questioned Spivey, considering various options for Spivey's future, but Campling's name rekindled his interest in the conversation. 'You think that because Henry owns those flats, he's involved in what Michael's done?'

'Not necessarily. But if he isn't, then Michael's taken a hell of a risk to use one of his flats for the scam.'

'He'll have to be told, then, will he?'

Panic flared in Spivey's face. 'No, please. Don't tell Henry.' He looked from Benny to Rose, and back again. 'He'll kill me.'

Rose put a hand on his arm. 'Michael, he'll have to know. You used the address of a property he owns to open a fraudulent bank account. It'll all come out in the investigation anyway.'

'Investigation? You're going to shop me for this?' He drew his arm back away from her touch. 'You can't do that. I've got a record. They'll put me away again.' He turned to Benny. 'Tell her she can't do that. I'll close the account. I ain't used it. Nobody has to know about it, do they? I've said I'm sorry.' He started to whimper. 'I ain't even got the bank card yet.'

Dave Gilling retreated to the safety of his patrol car to make his call to DI Mulligan. 'George, it's Dave. I've just spoken to the Mitchells about the green car.'

'Any luck?'

'Nothing useful. Neither of them knows anybody with a green Ford Fiesta. I've taken a list from them of the cars driven by all family members and friends, so we can eliminate them from enquiries. Danny Mitchell says he sells second hand Fords at the garage, but he doesn't think he's had a green one on the forecourt recently. He's going to check paperwork at the garage today.'

'What about the Bradman side of things?'

'I've tried to get hold of Craig on his mobile number, but I just keep getting the answering service. I'm going to go over to Scarborough now, to take a look at those flats. After that if I haven't managed to get hold of Craig by phone I'll pop into Bradman's and ask the staff about their cars.'

'Thanks Dave. How are the Mitchells?'

Gilling winced. 'Not good. They've had a few days of grief and misery, and they're moving onto the next stage now.'

'Meaning?'

'They're angry. I've just had a right earful from Selina Mitchell about how incompetent we are, and Danny's threatening to kick up a stink about us not doing enough to find his daughter.'

'Can't say I blame them, Dave. It's the grief kicking in. Is Mitchell planning to make an official complaint?'

'Worse than that. If we don't have some news for him by the end of the day, he's going to the press.'

27

It was almost midday when Lu pulled the Volvo up outside The Larches. She turned to her passenger. 'Come on, then. Let's get it over with.'

Rose had been silent during the drive, cogitating on the morning's events, and wondering whether she'd been right to trust Benny Bradman to take Spivey to the police station. She hoped that a voluntary confession from Spivey might reduce the punishment that would eventually be meted out to him, and she knew also that it would give DI Mulligan evidence that the Bellevue flats belonged to Henry Campling. The mist was lifting, but it hadn't lifted far enough yet to see the full landscape. She knew she should have gone to the station with them, but time was moving on and she knew that Marge would soon be questioned about her part in the fraud. They had to break the news to Jean before someone else did.

She got out of the car and followed Lu into the building without a word. She'd never visited The Larches before, and didn't know what to expect. Lu led her down a wide hallway lined with antique bookcases full of classic novels and reproduction oil paintings showing chocolate-box scenes of rural life. A galleried staircase wrapped itself around the inner part of the hall, rising two floors above them. Rose looked up to see more bookcases and more pictures, and landings punctuated with console tables bearing vases of fresh flowers. It was definitely more hotel than hospital, and she could understand why it might suit Jean to stay here.

They were almost at the end of the hall when a cheerful young woman in a tailored green overall came out of a doorway to their right and smiled at them. 'Looking for someone?'

Lu answered her. 'Yes, we've popped in to see Jean Baker. I thought we might find her in the residents lounge.'

'She was in there with Dicky earlier this morning. If she's not there now, pop back and find me. She may be upstairs. She's swapping over to her new room today.' The young woman's smile broadened. 'She's a sweetie. We're all delighted that she's going to be staying on with us now.'

The young woman fluttered away through another door. Rose moved closer to Lu and lowered her voice. 'It sounds like things have moved on since you visited yesterday. We'd better find out what's going on before we say anything about Marge.'

Lu nodded and gently pushed the lounge door open. Jean was alone in the corner, cocooned in a large armchair and scribbling furiously on a notepad. She looked up as they approached and her face brightened at the sight of them, especially at Rose. 'Why Rose, how lovely to see you. Lu said that you might try to pop in.'

'Well it's lovely to see you too, after all these years.' There was a small sofa to Jean's left, and Rose sank into it, twisting her body sideways to look at Jean as she spoke to her. 'How are you feeling now? All the broken bones mended?'

'Yes thank you, dear.' Jean smiled. 'D'you know, I've become so settled here that I've almost forgotten why I came in the first place.'

At Jean's other side, Lu had settled into armchair and was regarding her friend with some concern. 'You look peaky this morning. What's been going on?'

Jean pursed her lips. 'A visit from my daughter, that's what's been going on.' She shook her head. 'You were right about the Lake District. She came here last night, all guns blazing, and announced that we're moving to Kendal, and there's to be no argument.' Jean snorted. 'No argument, indeed. She made a terrible scene here last night, in front of all my friends. And I won't do it, Lu. I won't be ordered around. I'm staying here. I've spoken to Matron, and I'm moving into my permanent room today.'

Lu put out a hand and stroked her friend's arm. 'Calm down. You're getting agitated again, and it doesn't do your blood pressure any good.' She cast a concerned glance at Rose. 'How are you going to pay for this room, if Marge won't agree to you staying here?'

Jean took in a deep breath to steady herself, and spoke more calmly. 'The bungalow will have to be sold. I've asked Dicky to arrange for Henry Campling to come here on Monday and discuss it with me. If he still wants to buy it, he can have it. If he doesn't, he can deal with the sale on my behalf.' Her face took on a wistful look. 'Dicky has been wonderful. He's going to lend me the fees to stay here until the bungalow is sold, and then I'll pay him back out of the proceeds.' She was still clutching her pen and notebook, and she tapped one against the other. 'I've been making a list of things to collect from the house, clothes and books and so on. I wondered ...' She looked from Lu to Rose, and back again. 'Well, I wondered if you would mind taking me home this afternoon to collect my things. While Marge is out of the way at work.'

Lu frowned. 'Behind Marge's back, you mean?'

'I asked her to take me herself, Lu, and she flatly refused. What else am I to do?'

Lu took hold of her hand. 'It's difficult, isn't it?' She looked across at Rose, who gave a nod of agreement. 'Well, I can't say I'm comfortable with the idea of going behind her back, but I can see there aren't many options, and you seem to have made up your mind.' She gave Jean's hand a gentle shake. 'Alright then, I'll take you.'

Jean's gratitude was evident in her smile. 'Thank you, dear. You know it's very important to me.' She turned to

Rose. 'Rose, I'm so sorry. It *is* lovely to see you, but I'm afraid you've found me in a bit of a quandary. But now that I've had my say to Lu, I shall organise some tea for us, and then you can tell me all about what you've been up to.' She got to her feet and headed for the door.

Behind her back Lu arched an eyebrow at Rose, a silent gesture that said 'maybe now wouldn't be such a good idea to tell her quite everything that you've been up to'.

'George, it's Dave. I'm at Bellevue now. Just parked up in the car park.' Dave Gilling turned off the engine. 'How do I get into the building?'

Mulligan's voice crackled at the other end of the line. 'You'll need to use the door at the front of the building. There's an intercom system. You'll have to pick a flat at random, and use the intercom to ask someone to let you in.'

'On what pretext?'

'You don't need a bloody pretext, you're a police officer.' Mulligan clicked his teeth. 'Alright, I'll give you a pretext. I've just found out that those flats were redeveloped by Henry Campling. The ones I want you to look at on the second floor are still supposed to be empty. Find some willing resident to let you in, and tell them that Henry Campling's concerned about vandalism, and you've been asked to take a look around. That way you can fish for information about people coming and going at the block. And don't forget to ask about green cars, and blonde girls.'

'Blonde girls? You think Pandora might have been here?'

'It's a possibility. Look Dave, I can't go into it all on the phone, but it turns out that those addresses are being used for money laundering. Keep that under your hat, for God's sake, or Fraud will have my hide for compromising their case. I'm trying to flush out whether that laundering has anything to do with Pandora's disappearance. I need you to scout around in the block, and look for anything suspicious. Give the residents the vandalism story, and ask them about strangers coming into the block. Ask them if anyone has a green Ford hatchback. And have a good poke around the front doors of those flats. Look through the letterbox if you can.'

Gilling screwed up his face. 'Through the letterbox? What the hell am I looking for?'

'Post. Particularly anything in white envelopes that looks like it might have come from a bank. And signs of life. Any evidence that anyone is living there, or being held there.'

'Wouldn't it be easier just to get a warrant?'

'We can't. We'd risk tipping off if these flats are definitely being used for laundering.' Mulligan sighed. 'Look Dave, just do your best. I'm trying to get Campling in to the station for a face to face. If you turn anything up give me a call straight away, and if it's necessary I'll try to get him down there with the keys.'

The call disconnected, Gilling opened the glove compartment and pulled out a small torch and a compact digital camera, and tucked both into his jacket pocket. He opened the car door and got out, stretching out his arms in the sunshine, yawning to clear his lungs of the car's stale air, and was instantly enveloped by the overpowering stench of freshly-gutted herring.

Lu placed her cup and saucer down on the coffee table. 'That's settled then. We'll come back for you at two o'clock, and we'll use Rose's car because it's got a bigger boot.'

Jean turned and smiled at Rose. 'It really is very kind of you to help, dear. It shouldn't take very long.'

Rose smiled back at her. 'I don't mind helping at all, Jean. Just make sure you're ready to roll at two o'clock.

These things always take longer than you think, and we don't want to get caught in the act, do we?' She tried to sound whimsical, as much for her own sake as for Jean's. The thought of being confronted by Marge before they'd had time to break the news of her crime to her mother didn't bear thinking about.

Jean understood what she was trying to say. 'I wouldn't want there to be any unpleasantness. Marge has quite a temper on her at the moment, and it's not fair to expose you or Lu to that.' She got to her feet. 'Shall I see you both out, then?'

They were almost at the lounge door when it opened, and a distinguished if frail-looking man entered the room. Jean beamed at him. 'Dicky. Right on cue. Come and say hello to Rose.' She took hold of Rose's arm and led her forward. 'This is little Rosy Bennett, that I've told you all about.'

He smiled and held out a gnarled hand in greeting. 'Lovely to meet you at last, Rose. I've quite enjoyed hearing about you from Jean. I'm Dicky Thomas.'

Dicky Thomas. Rose took his hand, and blinked at him. 'Dicky Thomas? As in ... Richard Thomas?'

He blinked back at her. 'Yes, of course. But no-one calls me Richard nowadays. All my friends call me Dicky.' She looked distracted, and he wondered what was troubling her. 'Is there something wrong, Rose?'

'No, not at all.' She shook herself, and returned his smile. 'I know it's an odd question to ask a stranger, but before you moved into The Larches, I don't suppose by any chance you lived in Kirkby Park?'

28

'I'm sorry to insist on you coming down here at such short notice, but when I explain what it's about you'll understand the importance.' In fact George Mulligan wasn't in the least bit sorry, but he knew that platitudes were expected when dealing with someone like Henry Campling.

The solicitor pursed his lips. 'I hope for your sake that it *is* important, Inspector Mulligan. I had just started a round of golf with a very influential client, and I can't see that being hauled off the green by some provincial policeman with no respect for the game or its players will have enhanced his opinion of me.'

Despite his thoughts, the policeman's face remained impassive. Bob Shepherd's pithy description of the event had been far more accurate. 'It was no big deal. He was only playing that mardy little git from the council.'

Mulligan sat down opposite Campling and tugged up his shirt sleeves, resting his arms on the table. He stared straight into the man's oily face. He didn't like lawyers as a rule, and he particularly didn't like this one. He'd encountered him once or twice before, and had been quick to recognize him as the sort who used their proficiency in the law to find ways round it, rather than uphold it. 'Can I ask you if the name "Richard Thomas" means anything to you?'

Campling thought for a moment. 'Yes, it does. May I ask why you are asking the question?'

Mulligan smiled. 'I'll answer that in a moment, sir. In

what way is the name familiar to you?'

'I have a client named Richard Thomas.'

'Has he been a client for long?'

'About six months.'

Mulligan regarded him expectantly. He had no intention of dragging the information out of him piece by piece. 'Perhaps you could tell me the details of your relationship with him, and then I can explain to you why I'm asking.'

Campling clicked his teeth. 'I cannot break client confidentiality.' He paused and considered the question. 'However, I'm sure neither of us wish to draw out this conversation any longer than we have to. Richard Thomas procured my services as his legal representative six months ago, when he sold his home in Kirkby and moved into The Larches residential home in Market Melbourne. I am entrusted with management of his financial affairs, pension, investments, and so forth.'

'Does that management include the safe-keeping of his personal documents?'

The lawyer's expression took on a guarded look. 'Mr. Thomas entrusts a number of documents to my safe-keeping, mostly those relating to his financial affairs.'

'Do you have possession of his driving licence?'

Campling's brow furrowed. 'I may have. I would have to check. The documents are in the safe at my business premises.'

Mulligan nodded. 'I believe you own some properties in Scarborough, in a block called "Bellevue Mansions"?'

'I do, yes.' Campling leaned back in his chair, putting distance between himself and Mulligan. 'I really must insist, Inspector Mulligan, that you tell me what this is all about. I understood this to be an informal chat, but your line of questioning is, if I may say so, obtuse and rather threatening.'

'Very kind of you to say so, sir.' Mulligan smiled. 'Alright, I'll tell you what it's about. About an hour ago,

Benny Bradman brought one of his employees into the station, a chap called Michael Spivey.' He watched Campling's face as he spoke, and wasn't surprised to see his expression change at the mention of Spivey's name. 'In a very commendable display of remorse, Mr. Spivey had come to confess that he'd stolen some documents in the name of Richard Thomas. He admits to stealing those documents from your office, when your back was turned, along with a number of blank rent books which he has used to his own advantage.'

All the advantage was on Mulligan's side now. Henry Campling was listening intently to his words, and unless Mulligan was mistaken those words had shocked him. 'He's openly admitted to this?'

'To this, and to a further misdemeanour relating to those documents. He claims to have forged one of the rent books, using the address of Flat 2d Bellevue Mansions, and then used that rent book, along with other documents in the name of Richard Thomas, to open a fraudulent bank account at the Market Melbourne branch of the ENB.'

Campling's astonishment was obvious. 'Michael Spivey did that? On his own?' He shook his head. 'Frankly, Inspector, I'm surprised he managed to devise such a scam. He's not exactly …'

'… bright. No, sir, we came to the same conclusion. There is, of course, the possibility that he was working under someone else's instructions, and is frightened to tell us.'

'You say Benny Bradman brought him in to confess?'

'That's right.'

'Have you considered that Bradman might be behind it? He is Spivey's employer, after all'

Mulligan displayed no surprise at the suggestion, despite its disloyalty to a client. He didn't think Campling was the loyal type. 'We have. We're still considering that possibility.' He watched Campling's mouth twitch into an unpleasant smile. 'And we are also considering the other possibilities. You, for example, own the property that was used as the fraudulent address. And you gave Michael Spivey access to that property.'

The unpleasant smile on Campling's face evaporated. 'I admit that I was foolish enough to engage Michael Spivey to run some errands for me and yes, foolish enough to entrust him with the keys to some of my properties in Scarborough. But I can hardly be to blame for his stealing documents and opening a fraudulent bank account.'

The policeman shrugged. 'Perhaps not. Anyway, it's not really my bag, bank fraud. I'll be passing this over to my colleagues at Kirkby. I just happened to be here when Bradman brought him in.' He smiled again at Campling. 'As the documents were stolen from you, I thought you should be told as soon as possible. There is a possibility that Spivey may have taken other documents from your office. It might be wise to check that today.' He scraped his chair back from the table and got to his feet. 'Well, I won't keep you any longer. You'll be hearing from us again as part of the investigation. Meantime, if you think anything else has been taken I trust you'll let us know.'

Mulligan waited expectantly, but Campling seemed disinclined to follow his lead. He remained seated, and looked up at the policeman with a contemplative expression. 'Before we finish, Inspector, may I ask how things are proceeding in the Pandora Mitchell case? Is there any news?'

Mulligan stayed on his feet. 'We have several lines of enquiry open at the moment, but I'm afraid there's still no news of her.'

'I take it that you've questioned Michael Spivey on the matter?'

It was Mulligan's turn to be surprised. 'Spivey?' He paused and thought for a moment. Pandora Mitchell refused to open the account for Spivey, but surely he wouldn't have harmed her because of that?

Campling was insistent. 'I believe Spivey was quite

taken with the young lady. I must admit to harbouring a concern myself that his interest bordered a little on the obsessive. Of course, he would deny it if asked. It would hardly do to admit that he carried a torch for Craig Bradman's girlfriend.' He licked his lips. 'No, indeed, I don't think Craig or even Benny would have been too impressed by that notion. But as you presently have him here at the station, and in such a communicative mood, you may want to take the opportunity to discuss it with him?'

In the staff room at the ENB Hazel's lunch break was coming to an end. She wrapped her hands around her coffee mug and pulled it up to her lips. Even on a warm day there was something comforting about the way it felt, and if ever she'd needed to feel comforted it was today.

Marge could be so infuriating. Hazel had tried and tried again to get her to talk about what was happening at the branch, but she just wouldn't be drawn. She knew the police had been to see Janis, Rose had hinted enough to confirm that suspicion, but she still didn't really know what it was about, and if Marge knew anything she wasn't in any hurry to share it with her.

Except ... it had to be about Pandora. What else could it be? When asked, Marge had shrugged and said she didn't know what was going on. It was a lie, of course, and not just because Marge would always defend Janis to the hilt. No, it was a lie because when Hazel pressed the point, Marge had lost her temper. Matronly Marge, Marge the Placid, Marge who always calmed everybody down in moments of tension had completely lost her rag. She had banged the counter with her fist, and demanded 'who the hell cares what's happened to the silly little tart?'

She'd checked herself immediately, of course, and apologized in that docile motherly tone they were all used to. 'You know I didn't mean that the way it came out. But

I'm so very worried about Janis.'

And she wasn't the only one. Hazel was worried about Janis too, and she wondered if she and Marge were worrying about the same thing. She wished now she'd never shared the knowledge with Marge, never told her that she'd been outside the staff room when Pandora called Craig, never told her that she'd heard Pandora telling Craig that she was thinking of blowing the whistle on Janis.

Marge had wanted to tell Janis straight away, but Hazel disagreed and made Marge promise that she would keep it to herself. It wasn't their place to interfere, and it would only make things worse.

And now things *were* worse. Much worse. And Hazel couldn't help thinking that maybe Marge hadn't kept her promise.

'He said *what?*' Benny ran a hand through his hair and scratched at the back of his head. 'Just what the hell does he hope to achieve by suggestin' that?'

George Mulligan wasn't surprised by Benny's exasperation. He didn't trust Henry Campling either, although he wasn't going to come right out and admit that to Benny. 'I'm not sure what he's trying to achieve. I'm not taking it too seriously, but I'm afraid I'll have to talk to Spivey about it before I can let him go.'

'Well blimey, George, I'm still tryin' to get my ahead around the fact that he had the nous to open a dodgy bank account. I can't see him bein' darin' enough to abduct Pandora as well.'

'Did you ever see him show an interest in her?'

'Nah. She's too much of a prissy miss for him. He's got his eye on that barmaid at The Feathers.'

'Not the one with the tattoos?'

Benny grinned. 'Lovely girl. Just his type.' He leaned across the table. 'Confidentially, she's playin' hard to get, but he's hangin' in there.'

Mulligan shared his amusement, but there was a serious point there too. 'He tells you about his personal life, then? Would you have known if he'd had a thing for Pandora?'

'Course I would. That's part of Michael's trouble. He can't keep a secret. His face gives him away.'

'Not all the time. He managed to keep that fraudulent account a secret. Unless you're bluffing, and you already knew about it.'

Benny took the suggestion with good humour. 'Gettin' paranoid, George?   D'you really think I would have brought him here to cough it up if I was behind it all?'

Mulligan shrugged. 'You might have done, if you were planning to lay the blame at his door. How do I know you haven't paid him off to take the blame?'

Benny looked slightly hurt. 'I brought him in because Rose Bennett asked me to. I've already told you, she flushed him out all on her own. It was her idea to get him to confess. I'm just runnin' the errand because she had somethin' more important to do.' He rolled his eyes. 'I must be gettin' soft in me old age.'

'Aren't we all.' For Mulligan it was a statement of fact, not a question. He leaned back in his seat and regarded Benny with curiosity. 'Is Henry Campling a good lawyer?'

'Depends what you mean by good. He talks posh, knows a lot of dodges, has some useful people in his pocket, plays hard ball when he needs to. But he has one weak point.'

'Being?'

'He ain't trustworthy. Not even for his clients. I don't trust him as far as I could throw him.'

'Does he cross the line?'

Benny smirked. 'What is this, Twenty Questions?'

Mulligan was insistent. 'Does he?'

'Yeah, he crosses the line, George. I promised I wouldn't say anythin', but he was responsible for that grave in Lu Aylesbury's garden. I'd call that crossin' the line, wouldn't you?'

The policeman whistled. 'You're not telling me he dug that thing himself?'

'Nah. He got Michael to do it for him.'

Mulligan nodded in understanding. 'Could you see him being behind that fraudulent bank account?'

Benny took a moment to consider the question. 'Only if he were sure of not bein' found out.'

Mulligan nodded again. 'And if he was found out, what then? Would he be vengeful?'

'I think he holds grudges, if that's what you mean.'

'Enough to kill?'

'Blimey George, I don't know about that. Are you worried he might do somethin' unpleasant to Michael because of this bank account business?'

'No. I'm worried he might have already done something unpleasant to Pandora Mitchell.'

29

Rose took a circuitous route to Jean Baker's bungalow. She headed out of town up Larch Road to the top of the hill and then turned left down towards the bypass, skirting round the clusters of new housing that had sprung up to fill the bare land between town centre and trunk road, and turning back towards the High Street from the south of the town. The direct route, a full five minutes shorter, would have taken them down the High Street and past the ENB, running the risk of being spotted by Marge.

And the last thing any of them wanted was to be spotted by Marge.

With the car pulled up safely on the drive, Rose helped Lu to carry an assortment of bags and boxes upstairs to Jean's bedroom. Dropping the last bag on the landing, she spoke quietly to Lu. 'Do you think we were right not to tell her yet about the fraud?'

'Of course.' Lu craned her neck around to glance into the bedroom where her friend was pulling clothing from a mahogany chest of drawers. 'Jean might look strong-willed at the moment, but this is going to be distressing for her. This has been her home for so long, packing up her stuff is going to bring back a lot of memories.' She grimaced. 'We can tell her about the fraud when we've got her safely back to The Larches. At least Dicky will be there to help her come to terms with it.'

Rose glanced at her watch. 'I need to make a quick phone call. Can I leave you to help Jean?'

Lu nodded. 'Yes, but can you make us some tea when

you've finished your call, and then come and help me get some of the bags into the car?'

'Sure.'

As Lu made her way into the bedroom to help Jean, Rose wandered downstairs and into the lounge. It was a large sunny room, traditionally furnished in a twee cottage style which was out of keeping with the bungalow's boxy outer appearance, but perfectly in keeping with an aging mother and daughter household. She could imagine them cosied up here in the evening, garbed in dressing gowns and sipping from mugs of hot chocolate while they watched TV together. But not any more. The thought made her shiver. She perched on the edge of a chintz armchair and made her call.

DI Mulligan answered his mobile phone immediately. 'Rose? I'm glad you've called. Thanks for persuading Bradman to bring Spivey in. I think we've had a result.'

She felt an inward sense of relief. Trusting Bradman had been a leap of faith, but it looked like he'd kept his word. 'So you know now that those flats belong to Campling?'

'Better than that. I've had Campling in here this morning. Richard Thomas is one of his clients.'

'I know. I met him this morning.'

'You *met* him?'

'Yes, at The Larches. Marge Baker's mother is a resident there.' She raised her eyes up to the ceiling, conscious of Jean's presence, and lowered her voice accordingly. 'I'll have to speak quietly. I'm at Jean Baker's house now, and I don't want her to overhear. I've been asking a few casual questions of Dicky and Jean, and I think I've found something else that might help you.'

'Such as?'

'There are at least four other residents that Dicky knows of who use Campling as their solicitor and financial adviser. Their names all sounded familiar to me, so I checked the report. There are some subtle variations – Jim instead of James, for example – but basically all four names match against four of the eight accounts that Janis opened for money laundering.'

'Bingo!' Mulligan's tone was jubilant. 'That shyster Campling's a nasty piece of work. He's at the bottom of all this, Rose. I know he is. I've just got to get Janis Porter to admit it.'

'I think you'll find she's already done that, just not to us.' Rose's own tone was more cautious. 'She had a visit this morning from your Fraud colleagues. She's already admitted to them who set her up to arrange the laundering. She's under orders not to reveal it to anyone else, and they've left both her and Marge in the branch like a pair of tethered goats until they've gathered more evidence.'

'Evidence be buggered, I'm not interested in who's been washing their dirty tenners in the ENB machine. That girl's caught up in this mess, Rose, and I think Janis Porter knows what's happened to her.'

'Bloody hell, Dave, is the wind blowing from the west this afternoon?' Bob Shepherd sniffed the air as Dave Gilling took off his jacket.

'Cheeky bugger. You'd whiff if you'd been where George Mulligan sent me this afternoon. Those bloody flats in Scarborough stink.' He pushed a hand into the inside pocket of his jacket and pulled out his notebook, then hung the jacket on the back of his chair and looked around him. 'Where's George? In the interview room?'

Shepherd shook his head. 'You've just missed him. He's gone to see Janis Porter.'

'Damn, I need to speak to him. I think I've got a lead on the green car.' He sat down at his desk, and opened the notebook. 'What's he gone to see Janis about?'

'Oh, it's all been going off here this morning, mate.' Shepherd leaned on his desk. 'Some low-life who works for Benny Bradman has admitted to nicking ID documents from Campling's office, and opening a bank account using the documents and the address of one of those flats you've been to see. And Rose Bennett's come up with information that ties Henry Campling to a bunch of old biddies at The Larches, whose identities might have been nicked to open other accounts. Mulligan's convinced that Campling's behind Pandora Mitchell's disappearance, and he's gone to the ENB to put pressure on Janis Porter. He wants to question her about Pandora before Fraud take her in.' He scratched his ear. 'I'm fair worn out with it all. I'll be glad when it's done and dusted and we can get back to normality.' He pushed his chair back from the desk. 'Fancy a brew?'

Gilling nodded. He turned the pages of his notebook until he found what he was looking for, leaned back, pulled his mobile phone from his outer jacket pocket, and called Mulligan's number. The call diverted straight to voice mail. 'George, it's Dave. Can you call me when you get this message? I managed to speak to one of the residents on the third floor. He's seen a green Vauxhall Astra in the car park at Bellevue on a number of occasions. The last sighting was yesterday afternoon, sometime between four and five. The driver visits Campling's flats on the second floor, but the witness doesn't know what he does there.' He paused, and then said 'He hasn't seen a blonde girl there at any time, and all the flats listed seem to be empty. I looked through the letterboxes. There was post on the mat in all three, but I couldn't make out what it was. I'll tell you the rest when you call me.' He disconnected the call.

He was still staring blankly at the notebook pages when Shepherd returned with the tea. Shepherd placed Gilling's mug on his desk before sitting back down at his own. He pushed his chair back and stretched out his legs. 'Want to talk about it?'

Gilling looked across at him. 'There's been a sighting of a green hatchback at the Bellevue flats, but the witness reckons the driver doesn't look too desirable. A bit scruffy, he reckons, sometimes unshaven. Sleazy, that was the word he used. The bloke looks sleazy.'

'So?'

'Well, Pandora was supposedly seen chatting to the driver of the green car as if she knew him. How likely is it that a girl like Pandora Mitchell would have a friendly chat with somebody sleazy?'

Shepherd shrugged. 'You can't tell with girls these days. Some are always up for a bit of rough. Isn't it trendy these days? I thought they called it grunge?'

Gilling laughed. 'I know all about grunge, mate, I've got two teenage daughters, remember? Apparently grubby and unshaven is alright if the bloke looks fit underneath it, but this punter …' He stabbed at the notebook with his finger. 'This punter is skinny, greasy-looking, hair going thin …'

'Sounds like the bloke Benny Bradman brought in today. About the money laundering. He's been running errands to those flats for Campling.'

'That would make sense. The witness sees him visiting the flats for Campling. Doing what? Picking up the post? George asked me to look through the letterboxes for any post. There was mail in all the flats, but I couldn't make out what it was.'

Shepherd sipped on his tea and sighed. 'I'm not sure where you're going with this, mate.'

Neither was Gilling. He put a hand up to his face and rubbed his chin. 'Just because she was seen talking to someone in a green hatchback, doesn't mean she got into the car. She could have talked to the driver of the green car, and then carried on running, and got into another car further down the road.'

Across the desk, Shepherd was now equally thoughtful. 'Larch Road. That's where The Larches residential home is. Henry Campling's got clients there. I suppose that means he must visit the place?'

Gilling's face brightened at the suggestion, then fell again. 'Campling drives a grey Saab. I've seen him in it.' He ran a finger round the edge of his mug. 'Tommy Fletcher drives a blue Golf. The Mitchells don't know anyone with a green hatchback. Bradman drives a black Merc, and his lad has an old blue BMW.' He sighed. 'There's something missing.'

'Maybe the green car has nothing to do with it. Like you said, maybe it was someone she knew and she stopped to chat, and then the car drove on and she was picked up by somebody else.'

Gilling was peeved. 'In which case I've just been to Scarborough on a bloody wild goose chase.'

Shepherd grinned. 'Better than that, mate.' He sniffed the air theatrically. 'You've been chasing a red herring.'

Henry Campling slipped the key into the lock of Flat 2d and turned it briskly. The door clicked open and Campling looked furtively around him before stepping inside and closing it behind him.

He flicked on the light switch and glanced around to get his bearings, and then looked down at the letterbox. On the floor directly underneath lay a slim white envelope. He picked it up and turned it over. It was addressed to Richard Thomas.

He stepped into the kitchen and threw the envelope onto the counter with the three envelopes he had already retrieved from the other flats. His face took on a disdainful look, and he sniffed at the stale air in the kitchen. Damn that idiot Spivey. Couldn't he have mentioned how bad the smell was getting before it permeated the carpets? Couldn't he have showed some initiative and set up some air fresheners? The flats would have to be cleaned now before they were remarketed, and that meant expense. Unnecessary expense.

He clenched his teeth, irritated by the situation. Damn

Spivey. Even Bradman was getting tired of him. The man was becoming an overhead, not an asset. And Campling didn't have much time for overheads.

He stepped back to the counter and picked up the envelope addressed to Thomas. He could feel through the paper that it contained a bank card. He ripped it open and pulled out the insert, a bank debit card glued to a covering letter. The card was embossed with the name "R Thomas". Campling's brow furrowed and his eyes narrowed to slits. More waste. More damned waste. Dicky Thomas's identity was good for a lot more than a paltry current account and now, thanks to Spivey, it was useless.

He leaned against the counter and folded his arms, the debit card still clutched between his fingers. Just how much damage had been done? The police knew this account was fraudulent. They knew the ID had been stolen from his office. What else did they know? Did they know about the other accounts? Had Spivey's little independent venture into bank crime made them suspicious? Had it alerted them to the other accounts that had been opened at the branch?

Perhaps he needed to take some mitigating action, advise the account holders that the accounts needed to be emptied temporarily, perhaps stop transactions for a week or so until he'd been able to ensure that the set up was still safe.

He thought back to his conversation with DI Mulligan. How had Spivey's crime come to light? He'd admitted it. *He'd admitted it.* Why on earth would he do that? Mulligan said that Benny Bradman took him to the station to admit to it. So Bradman knew about it.

How? Spivey was hardly likely to drop it casually into the conversation. Oh by the way, Benny, I've turned my hand to bank fraud. He gave a derisive snort. No, someone had found out. Someone had found out that Spivey had opened that account, and persuaded him to admit it to the police, but who, and why?

He looked again at the debit card. If Spivey didn't have the card yet, then he couldn't have used the account. So, he reasoned, if there was no logical reason for Spivey to admit to opening the account before he'd even used it, then the only plausible explanation was that someone at the Bank had found out about it, and confronted him. Someone who worked there, someone who had access to the details of new accounts, someone ...   The penny dropped. Someone who'd been looking at the account opening processes.

Rose Bennett. He hissed the name through his teeth, and slammed the debit card down on the counter. Janis Porter had warned him that Rose Bennett was there to look at the account opening process. He'd have to go back to Market Melbourne, speak to Janis Porter now, make sure that everything was alright. He glanced at his watch. The branch closed early on a Saturday, but he might just make it, if the traffic wasn't too bad.

And if he didn't ... well, perhaps he'd just have to visit Janis Porter at home.

30

'I've already told you everything I can, Inspector Mulligan. I really don't see the point of any further discussion.' Janis folded her arms across her chest and looked away into the distance. The shutters were well and truly down.

From the other side of the desk Mulligan sized up her stubborn expression and defensive body language, and concluded only that she definitely had something to hide. 'Look, Janis,' he tried to sound coaxing, 'I can't imagine how you might be feeling right now. I know all about the money-laundering, and I know about your part in it. And I know that Fraud have left you here like a tethered kid to give the impression that the accounts haven't been spotted.' He waited for her to respond, but she continued to stare away from him. 'I know they're going to take you in pretty soon for formal questioning, that's why they've given me permission to speak to you now.' Still no response.

He tried a different tack. 'Don't you care what's happened to Pandora?'

She turned her head back to look at him with expressionless eyes. 'Are you any closer to finding her?'

'Yes, I believe I am.'

Janis nodded. 'You think she's dead.' It was a statement, not a question.

'Yes, I'm afraid I do.' He answered her quietly. 'I think she's dead, and I think her disappearance and her likely death are directly related to her involvement in opening those fraudulent accounts.'

Janis's face remained impassive. 'Can you prove that?'

'Not yet. But I will. I can promise you that.'

She seemed more interested now. 'How can you be so certain, if you don't have any proof? How do you know she wasn't just abducted while she was out running, taken by some pervert with a fetish for young blondes?'

He gave a quiet laugh. 'How do I know she wasn't abducted by young Tommy because she wouldn't go out with him? How do I know she wasn't abducted by Craig Bradman because she had decided to dump him?' She nodded expectantly. 'Well, I don't know for certain. But I do know that those theories are just based on speculation and hearsay.' He leaned across the desk. 'You, on the other hand, had a very definite motive. She was going to blow the whistle on your fraud.'

'Me?' Janis was clearly shocked by the suggestion. 'You think I got rid of Pandora? You think I'm capable of that?'

'I know you're capable of breaking the law. Of colluding with criminals. I know …'

'Inspector Mulligan.' She held up her hand to interrupt him. 'I didn't abduct or murder Pandora Mitchell.'

'But you may have led someone else to do so.' He watched her face. 'I'm not suggesting that you did it intentionally, but if you believe you said too much, if you believe that you led someone else to get Pandora out of the way because she was a threat, now is the time to cough it up.' She looked away again, avoiding his gaze. 'If you're up front about it now, it will help your case.'

She looked up at the ceiling, still avoiding eye contact with him. 'I've already told you I don't know what happened to Pandora. It's because I don't know what happened to her that I confessed about the fraud to Rose. Because,' she turned her gaze full on to him, 'I'm frightened that whatever happened to Pandora might also happen to me.'

'I know those accounts lead back to Henry Campling.'

Across the table from him Janis blinked sharply at the name, but her face remained impassive. 'You don't owe him anything, Janis. If you believe he's responsible for Pandora's disappearance, it would be better if you said so now. Did you tell him she was going to file a report about the laundering accounts?'

'No comment.'

Mulligan sighed. He leaned back in his chair and observed her closely, her pursed lips, her arms still folded tight across her chest. He didn't believe for one minute that her confession to Rose had anything to do with Pandora. She didn't look frightened. Her body language screamed of self-defense, of self-preservation. She gave herself up because Rose was on to her and there was no way out. Maybe she thought that throwing herself at the mercy of an old friend would offer her some sort of escape route.

Or maybe she thought that confessing to the collusion would disassociate her from Pandora's disappearance, diverting suspicion away from herself to others. He still couldn't understand her determination to be unhelpful, her refusal to help him find the girl. Did her hatred of Danny Mitchell run so deep that she got a kick out of watching his misery? Did it run so very deep that she would dispose of Pandora herself, thus removing the risk of exposure and extracting revenge on Danny at the same time?

He sighed again. He hated defeat, but it was pointless going round in circles. 'Well, if you have no comment then I guess we're done here. I'm sorry you haven't been able to help me.' He was half way to his feet when his mobile phone bleeped, heralding the arrival of a text message. He pulled the phone from his pocket and glanced at it, then shoved it back again. 'Before I go, can I just ask you what sort of car you drive?'

Janis frowned. 'Car? A BMW coupe. I don't see the relevance …'

He ignored the query. 'Colour?'

'Silver.'

'And your husband?'

'A silver Mondeo.'

'And the other staff here at the branch? Would you be able to tell me what make and colour of vehicle each of them drives?'

Janis looked bewildered. 'Yes, of course. If you think it's really necessary.'

'She's finished packing up the stuff she wants to take back to The Larches. This is the last bag.' Lu dropped the carpet bag onto the kitchen floor. 'I think it's full of shoes.'

'Well I hope it's not too heavy because you'll have to sit with it on your lap.' Rose leaned against the counter. 'The boot's packed to capacity, and I've filled as much of the back seat as I can, given that Jean is going to be sitting in there on the way back. Where is she now?'

'She's gone out to the garage to finish the inventory. They keep the freezer and the tumble drier out there, and all the gardening stuff.' Lu glanced at her watch. 'She's completely drained, but at least it's done. I'm going to make a quick cuppa to keep her going, and then we can be on our way.' She set about filling the kettle.

Rose turned and looked out of the window towards the garage. The right hand door was open and pinned back, and Jean was just about to disappear inside. She looked across at the window and waved to Rose. Rose put her head out of the kitchen door. 'Everything OK, Jean?'

'I can't get in properly, Rose. Do you think you could move the car out on to the drive? Marge always leaves the keys on a hook in the kitchen. Next to the boiler.'

The keys were easy to find, and it barely took a minute for Rose to pull the car forward and give Jean enough clearance to get into the garage. 'Do you want me to stay and help?' Out of the car, Rose surveyed the domestic detritus on the garage shelves. 'I don't want to hurry you, but we don't have a lot of time.'

Jean smiled. She looked tired but determined. 'It won't take long. Perhaps if you could lift those boxes down off the freezer? I don't know what's in them.' She looked around. 'I'll just make a list of the important things.'

The boxes were heavy, full of old magazines and other junk. Rose lifted them onto the garage floor. At the back of the garage Jean was fluttering around with her pen and notepad. Rose called to her. 'Lu's making some more tea, Jean. Why don't I bring yours out here?' Jean, lost in her own thoughts, was mumbling about the amount of junk and where it all came from.

Rose backed quietly out of the garage and edged past Marge's hatchback, and back into the kitchen to speak to Lu. 'I've left the keys in the ignition, so I can move the car back when she's finished.' She shivered. 'You might want to take that tea out to her yourself. That garage is full of rubbish, she might need persuading to just come away and leave it.'

'Before I go, I'd like a quick word with Marge Baker.' DI Mulligan, passing through the banking hall on his way out, addressed his request to Hazel. 'Do you know where I can find her?'

Hazel's pixie face creased into a frown. 'She went up to the staff room. I didn't see her come down.' She thought for a moment. 'I suppose she must be still up there. Would you like me to take you?'

Mulligan nodded his agreement, and followed Hazel back through the door that led to the staff offices. They ascended the narrow staircase without a word, and he followed her into the small staff room. There was no sign of Marge.

He placed a hand on Hazel's arm. 'She hasn't been back into the banking hall?'

'No. She must be up here.' Back on the landing, Hazel

opened the door of the small kitchen and peered in. 'Not in here either.' She gave an awkward smile. 'Well she must be around somewhere. Someone of Marge's size is a bit difficult to hide. I suppose she could be in the loo.'

Mulligan hovered discretely on the landing while she checked the cloakroom. It was the only other place she could be. Unless, of course ... He glanced back down the staircase. At the bottom, the door on the left led back to the banking hall, and to Janis Porter's office. And the door on the right?

Hazel re-appeared on the landing. 'She's not in there, I've checked.' There was anxious curiosity in her face now. 'Is Marge in some sort of trouble?'

Mulligan was non-committal. 'What sort of trouble?'

'I don't know. It's just ... well, I checked her locker. And it's empty.' She looked confused. 'Her jacket's gone, and her handbag. We don't close for another hour, but if I didn't know better, I'd say Marge had gone home.'

'I told her she had five minutes, and then we'd have to go.' Lu dropped Jean's mug into the washing up water and swilled it round. 'She's all in, Rose. Let's give her a couple of minutes, and then shut up the house and coax her into the car.' She put the mug on the draining board and reached for a tea towel.

Rose, still leaning against the kitchen counter, was growing restless. It was almost two thirty, and as she'd predicted time was running out. 'We can't afford to be here when Marge gets back. Jean's been through enough already this afternoon.'

'Rose, I meant to ask you ... why hasn't Marge been arrested?'

'For her part in the fraud, you mean?' Rose shrugged. 'It's all part of the tipping off thing, I suppose. Janis has admitted the crime, and she'll have admitted drawing Marge into the scam. Marge has probably been questioned today, but it will all be very low key. Arresting them would flag up that the accounts have been discovered. The police won't want that to happen until they've gathered enough evidence to build a case. It might take several days to do that.'

'And they just carry on at the branch as if nothing's happened?' Lu set about drying the dishes. 'Isn't there a risk that Janis and Marge will tip off whoever paid them anyway?'

'There is, but what would it gain them? The police already have enough to charge Janis and Marge, tipping somebody off wouldn't get them off the hook. And Janis has agreed to co-operate. I'm sure Marge will have done the same. I mean, it's not as if either of them is a danger to anyone. They've committed bank fraud, not murder. The police wouldn't leave them at the branch unless they thought it was OK.' She turned and glanced out of the window. Jean was still hidden in the depths of the garage. 'I wish she'd get a move on.'

Lu hung the dried mugs back on their rack and scooped up the teaspoons from the draining board. She gave them a cursory rub with the tea towel and opened a drawer to put them away. She tutted. 'I always get the wrong drawer.' She opened the next drawer along, and slid the spoons into the cutlery tray. She hung the tea towel back on its hook, and then half-turned back towards Rose. 'That was odd.' She put out a hand and re-opened the first drawer. 'Look at this.'

Rose crossed the kitchen and peered into the drawer. It contained kitchen utensils, graters, carving knives, meat skewers, and serving spoons, all the ephemera that belonged in a kitchen but never seemed to fit in the cutlery drawer. And something else. Tucked towards the back of the drawer was a small, pink iPod, its headphones still attached, their wires wound tightly round its compact body.

She pulled it out of the drawer and examined it. 'It

looks like Marge is a bit trendier than we gave her credit for.'

'You think it belongs to Marge, then?'

Rose unwound the headphones and pressed one to her ear, switching the player on with her other hand. 'Unless Jean has developed a taste for hip hop.'

Lu grinned. 'Unlikely.' Her grin faded. 'Marge? Hip hop? Are you sure?' She looked puzzled. 'And why put it in a cutlery drawer?'

Rose opened her mouth to speak, but the noise they both heard didn't come from her lips.

Jean's scream was deafening, terrifying in its intensity. Lu started, and then grabbed at the kitchen door and hurled herself out onto the drive. 'Jean? What is it? What's the matter?' She grabbed at the half open garage door and lurched inside.

Rose was only a moment behind her. Jean was on her hands and knees on the garage floor, retching, vomiting, her body convulsed with intermittent sobs. Lu fell to the floor beside her and wrapped her arms around her. 'Dear God, Jean, what is it? What's happened?' She held the woman's frail body as it shook violently, looking back at Rose in complete bewilderment. Jean raised her head and tried to speak, and Lu placed her hand on her forehead, stroking it, trying to calm her. 'Jean, you're frightening me. What is it? What's happened?'

The older woman struggled to get off the floor, pushing herself back out of Lu's embrace. She straightened her back and, turning a terrified face to Rose, tapped with a frail finger on the white metal box beside her.

Rose walked over to the freezer cabinet and stared down into Jean's face. Her eyes were wide, overflowing with tears, pleading for Rose to ... what? Open the freezer? Rose put her right hand on the lid, and suddenly remembered what she was holding in her left. She looked down at the pink iPod, her eyes glazing momentarily, and then she turned back to the freezer and with a deep and fearful breath she slowly lifted the lid.

31

Pandora Mitchell lay in the bottom of the freezer cabinet. She was on her side, her legs folded up to her chest, her arms arranged neatly in the cavity between chin and knees, a curled up, frozen foetus. Her long blonde hair lay in an icy sheath over her shoulder and her brows and lashes were white with flecks of frost.

For a moment she looked like a snow-covered princess, and Rose felt tears sting the back of her eyes, and then reality began to kick in. Beneath that sheath of hair Pandora's face was swollen and blue, and her frozen eyes bulged out from behind the frosted lashes. A wave of nausea flooded Rose's stomach and she swallowed it back, dropping the lid of the freezer, clamping her hands on the top as if afraid that any moment the frozen remains might try to escape. She fought to keep the sickness down, and then turned to Lu and Jean and whispered 'it's Pandora'.

Lu turned back to look at Jean and cupped the woman's face in her hands. 'Jean, I'm so sorry. I'm so very sorry.'

Jean stared back at her, the horror of the discovery still written on her face. 'Sorry? Why? Don't be sorry. It's not your fault that I found her.' The horror melted a little. 'That poor girl. Oh my God, Jean, how did she get there? What happened to her?' She began to cry. 'Thank God we found her. Could you imagine? What if it had been Marge? What if poor Marge had found her, and there was no-one here to help her?'

Rose took in a sharp breath, the unmistakable hiss of

disbelief. Beneath Lu's hands, Jean began to shrink away. 'No.' A simple word of denial. 'No, not that.' Jean pulled back and freed herself from Lu's embrace. Her voice became a whisper. 'How dare you.' She looked across at Rose, and her voice became louder. 'How dare you. You can't mean …'

A solitary tear trickled down Rose's face. How could she answer that question? Did she mean that? Did she mean that Marge had killed Pandora? Of course she didn't. She couldn't possibly. It was ludicrous, utterly ludicrous.

'Go on, Rose. Tell her.' The instruction came from the doorway behind them, and all three turned to look. Marge's ample figure was framed in the garage doorway, her hand on the edge of the door. 'Just tell her, and then we can get it over with.' She walked towards them, into the garage, gently closing the door behind her.

Rose didn't have to say anything. Jean struggled to her feet and leaned on the freezer top for support. She was regarding her daughter with utter incredulity. 'If you did it, tell me why.'

'Because of the fraud, of course.' She saw the puzzlement on her mother's face, and turned to Lu. 'You did tell her, didn't you?' She turned back to Jean. 'I asked for Lu to tell you about it.'

Lu was on her feet too, now, and she stepped towards Jean. 'I was going to tell you, Jean, but we wanted to get you back to The Larches first. I didn't want you to be any more upset than you already are.' She turned to Marge. 'How could you, Marge? How could you do this to your mother?'

Marge shook her head. 'I didn't do anything to my mother. I did it *for* my mother.' She smiled affectionately at Jean, and then sighed. 'I suppose I might as well tell you myself now. You see, Janis and I have been taking money to open fraudulent bank accounts.'

The incredulity in Jean's face grew. 'You? You

couldn't. You haven't got the … the …'

'Bottle?' Marge finished her mother's sentence. She nodded to herself. 'That's what I hoped you'd think. That's what I hoped everyone would think.' She leaned on the garage door frame. 'It would hardly have been sensible to let everyone realize how clever I was, would it?'

'Clever? You think what you've done is clever?' Lu spat the words out. 'You've broken your mother's heart for a few measly grand? What's clever about that?'

Marge shook her head again. 'It was never my intention to break Mum's heart. And certainly not for a few measly grand, as you put it. How do you think I was planning to pay for the alternations to the bungalow? And when Mum changed her mind about wanting to come back here, how do you think I was going to pay for the move to the Lakes? You think I could do that on an ENB pension?'

'You told me you had savings, tens of thousands, money you'd saved over the years.' Jean was still trying to make sense of it all. Her voice became a whisper. 'And I didn't believe you.'

Her daughter smiled. 'Well, it is savings in a way, isn't it? I haven't spent the money I earned. It's all still in the bank.'

'The money you earned?' Lu's tone was scornful. 'I wouldn't call it earning. And Janis was only giving you a few hundred for each account. You couldn't retire on that.'

Marge regarded Lu with interest. 'Janis told you what she paid me? I didn't know that.' She gave a gentle laugh. 'Poor Janis, what a mess she's in. Tell me, does she still think she did me a favour?' She watched the bewilderment on their faces, and nodded. 'She's very naïve, you know. She has no idea I set her up.'

'You set *her* up?' Lu was disbelieving.

'Oh yes. Henry Campling told me how bad Jimmy's gambling had got, and I knew how weak Janis was, the lengths she'd go to protect her lifestyle and her image. You can't work closely with someone day in and day out, and not know what makes them tick.' She nodded to herself. 'Henry needed a number of bank accounts, and I knew Janis would take the money if it was offered to her.'

'But you took money from her. Five hundred for each account.'

'I had to make it look realistic, didn't I? Henry paid me a lot more than that, five thousand for each account.'

'Five *thousand*?'

Marge's smiled was self-satisfied. 'Oh yes. Henry's customers pay very well for laundering accounts. We agreed that Janis's two thousand would come out of my five for each account, so really Janis was just giving me back five hundred of my own money.' She laughed. 'Poor Janis actually thought I needed the money.' Her face straightened. 'We needed her, of course. We needed to know the transaction monitoring levels, and however hard I tried I couldn't get her to share that with me. She passed that information directly to Henry. And I suppose I thought it gave me a bit more protection, having Janis tied up in the fraud with me. As the senior member of staff she would always be first in the firing line.'

Rose had been silent until now, still resting on the freezer cabinet next to Jean, taking in everything Marge had to say. She licked her lips and quietly asked 'so where did Pandora fit into all this?'

Marge paused and turned to look at her, her face etched with loathing just as it had been that morning in the branch. 'I thought you'd already worked that out, Rose. Pandora was a smokescreen. She wasn't authorised to check customer ID, you know that. It was just an extra layer of insurance, to get her to open the account, so that all I had to do was sign off the documents.'

'But when she'd had her training …'

'It was all going beautifully and then that idiot had to ruin everything.' Marge's face folded into an angry scowl and she spat out the name. 'Spivey.' She pursed her lips. 'I told Henry he was a risk, but he didn't agree with me. Of course I recognized him when he came into the branch. Henry told me to expect two more applicants before the end of the week, so I thought he'd come on Henry's behalf. His appointment was with me, but Pandora asked if she could deal with it because she wanted the practice. We didn't know what to do, but Janis thought it would keep things consistent if she opened the account, like all the others. There was a risk that she might spot something with the documents, because she'd had her training, but it was a fairly small risk. We agreed that Pandora should check the documents, but if she had any concerns she would bring them to me, and I would disagree with her and tell her the account could be opened.'

'But you weren't prepared, were you, for her to question your decision?'

Marge scowled again. 'Arrogant little mare. Who did she think she was, to disagree with me? Off she went to Janis, and of course Janis agreed with me. And Pandora dug in her heels and argued the toss with Janis as well.' She sighed now. 'We had to open that account. We could hardly report it as a suspicious activity in case it led the audit people to look at the other accounts that had been opened.'

'And so that's why you killed her. To cover your tracks.' Rose's words were a simple statement of fact.

Marge shrugged. 'Hazel told me that she'd overheard Pandora making a phone call in the staff room. That Pandora was going to report the account as suspicious activity, and report Janis for not taking her suspicions seriously. Hazel told me, but she asked me not to tell Janis. She didn't want to make things worse for Pandora.' She snorted a laugh. 'She had no idea that I was as much at risk as Janis was.'

'But how did she end up in our freezer?' Jean's question was almost a wail of despair. 'How could you do that to her?'

For the first time, Marge looked uncomfortable. She

looked down at the floor, avoiding her mother's gaze. 'I didn't plan to kill her. It just … happened.' She blinked back an unbidden tear. 'I was driving down Larch Road to come and see you, and she was running down the hill in front of me. I stopped the car, and called to her. I told her that I was on my way to see you, but that I needed to speak to her about Janis. I told her that Hazel had overheard her conversation, and that I agreed with her, and that Janis needed to be reported for what she'd done.' Marge's face twisted at the memory. 'I said we wouldn't be able to talk about it at work, so she'd better come back to the bungalow and talk it through with me. She said she didn't have time because she was planning to meet Craig, so I said I'd drive her back home once we'd agreed a plan for the next day.' She cleared her throat. 'Once we'd got here, I told her I'd lied. I told her that Janis was in trouble, and desperately needed to keep her job. I tried to persuade her to forget about what had happened, to turn a blind eye, to think about Janis and her kids and what it would mean if Janis lost her job.' Her eyes narrowed. 'She wouldn't have any of it. She told me that it wasn't just about that one account. That she knew I'd authorised invalid ID on the other accounts, and that she intended to report me too.'

'And so when you told me that you were late because you had to go home again to get the batteries for my hearing aid, you were here, killing Pandora.' Another simple statement of fact, but this time from Jean. 'You killed that poor girl because she was going to show you up for what you were. A lying, dishonest, deceitful …'

'No.' Marge banged her fist against the garage door. 'I killed her because she was an arrogant, spoiled, self-righteous little prig. Who the hell was she to talk down to me? Who the hell was she to ruin my chances of a better life? To ruin *our* chances of a better life?'

Jean shook her head. 'Don't you dare say you did this for me. None of this was for me. You're just trying to avoid the blame. You always try to avoid the blame. Nothing is ever your fault, is it, Marge? Nothing is ever your responsibility. Is that why you wanted to retire, to move to Kendal? Running away again? Better to run away than to face up to what you've done? I suppose next you'll be telling me that it's Pandora's fault that she got herself killed?'

'I was trying to protect you.'

'Protect me? Protect me from what? The truth? So that I'd never find out that my own daughter is a fraudster? You think it's better to find out that you're a killer?'

Shame flooded into Marge's plump face. 'You would never have found out if Spivey hadn't been so stupid. And if she hadn't turned up.' She flicked a hand at Rose. 'Your precious little Rosy Bennett. If she hadn't come poking her nose in I would have got away with it all.'

Dave Gilling pulled his patrol car across the end of the driveway and switched off the engine. George Mulligan's car was already parked up against the kerb, nose to nose with Rose's saloon. Mulligan himself was still sitting in the driver's seat, his head turned towards the bungalow, his face clouded with some unpleasant thought.

Gilling got out of his car and walked over to join him. He bent down and spoke through the open window. 'Are you sure about this, George?'

Mulligan turned and looked at him. 'As sure as I can be, now that I've seen that.' He nodded towards the driveway.

Gilling followed his gaze to a green Ford Focus parked outside the garage, and remembered the words of the witness statement. 'It looked like she was talking to someone she knew.' He puffed out a sigh. 'Could she have planted the chain?'

Mulligan screwed up his face. 'I don't know. It would make sense. To draw our attention away from Larch Road.

Her mother's in The Larches, you know.'

'We questioned the residents. Nobody saw anything.'

'I know. I checked the paperwork before I came out. Jean Baker said her daughter was late that day. Had to come back home to collect something she'd forgotten.'

'Or maybe deal with something she'd just collected on Larch Road? Like Pandora?' He turned back to Mulligan. 'What happens now?'

Mulligan opened the car door and got out. 'That depends on who's in there. I think Rose is there with Lu Aylesbury, and Jean Baker. I don't know whether Marge has come back here or not. She's certainly done a bunk from work.' He slammed the door shut behind him. 'Jesus, Dave, I bloody hate this part of my job.'

32

'I hope you don't mind me stoppin' by, Lu. I just wanted to make sure you and Rose were alright.' Benny hovered in the doorway of the cottage. 'I brought you these, I thought they might cheer you up.' He held out a generous bouquet of oriental lilies. 'Not that a bunch of flowers makes up for what you two have been through this afternoon.'

Lu took the flowers from him and cradled them in the crook of her arm. 'That's very thoughtful of you, Benny. They're lovely.' She stepped back from the door. 'Come in and have a drink with us?'

'Nah, I'll be gettin' on my way, if that's alright with you. I don't want to intrude.'

'It's no intrusion.' She lowered her voice. 'Rose has taken it very badly. I think it would do her good to see a friendly face. Take her mind off it.'

Benny, uncertain, glanced back down the path towards his car. 'Well, I suppose I could leave the car there and walk home.' He turned back to her and smiled. 'I don't suppose a quick one would do any harm.'

He followed her into the cottage. She gestured down the hall towards a partly open door. 'You go through and make yourself comfy while I deal with the flowers, and I'll be through in a minute to pour us a drink.'

As she walked away he pushed gently on the lounge door and peered into the room. Rose was curled up in an armchair, with Mac on her lap as a comforter. The television was on, but she didn't seem to be watching it. Caught off guard, she looked pale and unhappy, and he thought she'd been crying.

The visit suddenly felt like a mistake, the intrusion he'd feared it would be, but before he had chance to back out of the door and make his escape she turned and looked at him, and her face brightened. 'Just passing?'

He grinned. 'There's a Sunday meetin' on at Beverley tomorrow. I thought as you're developin' a habit you might appreciate a tip. There's a cert runnin' in the three forty.'

'That was kind of you.' She laughed and flicked off the television with the remote control, and then her face straightened and some of the gloom returned. 'How's Craig?'

Benny perched on the edge of the sofa. 'Not good. I'm only just beginnin' to realize how much he cared for her.' He sighed. 'Still, at least there'll be no more wonderin' now that we know what's happened to her.' He shook his head. 'The girl had more guts than I gave her credit for. I wish I'd tried a bit harder to get to know her, and that's a fact.'

'If it's any consolation, I wish I'd never got involved at all.' She sighed and rubbed at Mac's fur. 'All those lives turned upside down.'

'Blimey Rose, I never had you down as the sort for wallowin' in self-pity. You found Pandora. Everybody's very grateful to you for that.'

She wrinkled her nose and shook her head. 'I doubt it.' She lifted her left hand from her lap and started to count through her fingers, staring at them as she counted. 'Marge is going to prison, and Janis won't be far behind her. Jean's in bits because Marge is going to prison. Jimmy's lost his wife, and his kids have lost their mum. Your pal Michael could be going back to prison. And knowing how the legal system works, Henry Campling will probably get off the hook on a technicality.' She swallowed back an unwanted emotion, and then said 'Danny and Selina have lost their daughter, and your son has lost his girlfriend.' She looked back at Benny. 'Where is he?'

Benny shrugged. 'Round at Danny and Selina's.' He tried not to look too hurt. 'But he's grateful, Rose. At least he knows now. It might be hard for him for a bit, but he'll mend in time. They all will.' Rose didn't look convinced, and he wasn't sure what else he could say to make her feel better. Worse than that, he wasn't even sure why he wanted to make her feel better. Except that this was a situation he was used to, a role he'd played before. There had been times when Trina had won a case and the satisfaction of victory had been tainted by misplaced guilt. It was an unwritten law that whenever there's a winner there has to be a loser, and that losers have families and loved ones who also lose out through no fault of their own, but he knew that didn't make things any easier.

The conversation was in danger of getting a bit deep for him now, and there was no sign of Lu to break the ice. He glanced around and found what he was looking for on the sideboard. 'Mind if I help myself to drink, Rose? Lu said she'd be through in a minute but she's takin' her time, and I ain't used to doin' so much serious talkin'.'

If he'd expected Rose to spring to her feet and apologise for not being more hospitable he was mistaken. She just smiled and nodded, and went on stroking the dog. He got up and walked over to the sideboard, and pulled two glasses from the shelf. 'Want one?'

'Thanks. I'll have a whisky.'

Just like that. All the formality gone, just pour yourself a drink Benny, and get me one while you're at it. He poured the drinks and returned to the sofa, handing her a glass as he passed by the armchair. He lifted his own glass in a toast. 'Your good health, Rose. Here's to a better outcome than you're expectin'.' He took a sip and grinned at her. 'Blimey, I thought my Trina ...' He checked himself. 'I thought my late wife could be a mardy cow, but you're makin' her look like an amateur.'

She raised her eyebrows at the insult. 'Am I indeed? And you don't think I have cause to be miserable?'

'Nah, not yet. The case ain't finished yet. You've still got the pleasure of givin' evidence against Henry.' He sniffed. 'If he ever turns up.'

'Turns up?' She looked interested now. She shifted in the chair, straightening her back and her legs, and unsettling Mac in the process. He lifted his head and eyed her with disdain, then wriggled his body until he found a comfortable position across her lap. 'Where's he gone?'

'Done a bunk, accordin' to George Mulligan.' Benny sniffed again. 'Blimey Rose, I was nearly in trouble there. Good job you dug up all this launderin' business. If he's been developin' properties and usin' the addresses for money launderin', well he could have done that with properties I'd bought into, couldn't he? So you've done me a favour good and proper.' He shook his head. 'He might even have used this place, if Lu had seen her way to sell it to us.' He paused while she thought about it, and then said 'I reckon he might get away with it.'

The idea was ludicrous, but the suggestion of it won him her full attention. 'You *what?*'

'Yep.' He sniffed, and sipped on his drink. 'I reckon Henry's been very careful with the way he's done things. He's a slippery customer alright. If he's half the chancer I think he is there'll be nothin' leadin' back to him.'

'But he owns the flats.'

'True. But he could claim that the addresses had been stolen. He didn't apply for the bank accounts himself, did he?'

'Michael Spivey could testify that he asked for them to be opened.'

'Ah, no. See, Michael only opened one account, and he was doin' a bit of creative accountin' for himself there. Henry didn't ask him to open that account. And Michael's admitted to stealin' those documents, so Henry can't be held responsible for that.'

Rose gave a dismissive shake of the head. 'That doesn't really matter, does it? Once Marge and Janis give their statements …'

'Well, that's just their word against Henry isn't it?'

'But he paid them.'

Benny shrugged. 'He'll have paid in cash. No audit trail there.' He watched her face. Some of the colour was beginning to return to her cheeks. Maybe this wasn't going to be as bad as he feared. 'I suppose George might find somethin' incriminatin' in Henry's office. They're goin' to be takin' it apart tomorrow.'

'George? You're on first name terms with Mr. Mulligan, then?'

'We've had the odd pint or two in the last week. He ain't bad for a copper.' He grinned again. 'Mind you, between you an' me he's a bit of a dinosaur. Do you know, he didn't even know why they used real people to open those accounts? He actually thought it would have been safer to apply on-line.' He sipped on his whisky. 'I had to tell him that was too risky.'

'Because?'

'Because of the audit trail, of course. Henry couldn't risk a trail back to a specific computer now, could he?'

Rose started to laugh. 'Are you winding me up?'

'I'm tryin', but it's bloody hard work.'

She blinked and nodded. 'I suppose I deserved being called a mardy cow. But I only came here to look at a few dodgy accounts. I didn't expect all this fall-out.'

'You opened a can of worms, that's all. And it ain't all bad. I stopped off to see Jimmy Porter on my way here tonight. The boys have gone back to their Dad, so Jimmy's moved back in with his Mum and she's helpin' to look after little Millie. And ain't it better that Jean Baker knows about her daughter now, rather than Pandora's body turnin' up after they've moved to the Lake District?' He looked thoughtful. 'Here, Henry was talkin' about us developin' their bungalow site instead of this cottage. They weren't plannin' to leave the contents, were they?' He rolled his eyes. 'See, that's another favour you've done me, it might have been me what found the body.'

She flinched at his irreverence. 'Benny, that's awful. Poor Pandora …'

'I know, I'm sorry. I got a bit carried away.' He had the grace to look shame-faced. 'Anyway, the point is, it ain't all doom and gloom. Even Michael's goin' to do alright out of this. Since he had the bottle to admit thievin' those documents and take his punishment, I've decided to give him one more chance.'

'That's very magnanimous of you.'

He shook his head. 'Not really. Our Craig'll be on his way to London soon, and I still need a dogsbody to keep an eye on things.'

Mac lifted his head from Rose's lap and turned his one good eye on Benny. Benny chuckled to himself and winked at the dog. 'Sorry mate, no offence.'

ABOUT THE AUTHOR

Mariah Kingdom was born in Hull and grew up in the East Riding of Yorkshire. After taking a degree in History at Edinburgh University, she wandered into a career in information technology and business change, and worked for almost thirty years as a consultant in the British retail and banking sectors.

She began writing crime fiction during the banking crisis of 2008, drawing on past experience to create Rose Bennett, a private investigator engaged by a fictional British bank.

Dead on Account is the first Rose Bennett Mystery.

www.mariahkingdom.co.uk

Printed in Great Britain
by Amazon